WHISTLE'S WAR

BOOK SIX
THE DEMON SQUAD MC SERIES

BY MONIQUE MOREAU

Cover Design by Cover Couture
www.bookcovercouture.com

Photo © Lindee Robinson Photography

MEET MONIQUE!

Join Monique's Newsletter
(and receive goodies and release information):
www.subscribepage.com/moniquemoreau

Join Monique's FB reader's group, she'd love to hear from
you: Possessive Alpha Reads
Like her Facebook Page:
facebook.com/monique.moreau.books
Follow her on Instagram:
instagram.com/monique.moreau.books
Follow her on Book Bub: bit.ly/3gNvrsU
Learn all about Monique's books: moniquemoreau.com

AUTHOR'S NOTE

You may be wondering what kind of book you just picked up. What's all this talk of the Bratva and mafia in the blurb? Didn't I pick up a bad boy biker romance novel? Well, yes, you did! This book has all the biker yumminess you're used to reading from me, but it's also a segue into a new Romanian mafia series I'm launching. For those who don't read in the Mafia Romance genre, there are a few things I thought might be helpful to fill in the gaps.

First, there's the Bratva, which is also known as the Russian or Red Mafia. It technically means "Brotherhood," but in a different way than what "brotherhood" means to bikers. It's the brotherhood of thieves, and their oath is centered on helping each other in the pursuit of criminal activities.

Second, the heroine, Tasa Lupu, is a princess of the Romanian mafia, or *mafie*, of which there isn't a plethora of information. I've done a bit of research, and not finding enough details, I've let my imagination run wild and taken liberties by inventing rules and societal norms that I have not found any proof of in the real world. I've also given certain Romanian words special meaning within this unique world. I've introduced the Lupu clan, the main Romanian *mafie* family, whose center of power is in Sunnyside, Queens, in New York City. The surname Lupu does in fact mean "wolf" in Romanian, but I created the Lupu tat, a wolf baring its teeth, that is required of all members of the Lupu *mafie* clan.

One more thing, I wrote the novella, Her Bicycle Valentine, at the same time as I was writing Whistle's War, so there's an overlap of their stories. They can, of course, be read as stand-alones, but I just thought to warn you.

And with that, I'll leave you to read on. I hope you enjoy Whistle and Tasa's story as much as I've enjoyed writing it.

MONIQUE

CHAPTER ONE

TASA CHECKED THE cell phone in her clenched hand for the hundredth time. Her excruciating audience with Alex in his upstairs office was over. *Finally.* Once again, her eldest brother had overreacted. Simply because he was the head of the family, he assumed he could rule over every single aspect of her life. *The nerve of him, giving me an order like I'm a child.*

Tasa fidgeted as she once again glanced out of the bay window of the Dacia Café, the center of her family's world. She couldn't wait for Nikki to pull up to the curb so she could get out of there before she stomped back up the stairs and wrung Alex's neck. Leaning forward, she spotted the ubiquitous black Mercedes pulling up on the quiet 43rd Street. Quiet in comparison to Queens Boulevard, the bustling commercial center of Sunnyside, Queens.

From behind, she heard a scuffling sound. Her mother moved forward, giving her a quick last hug from behind. Twisting around in her seat, Tasa returned her embrace and lifted her left cheek for a quick peck. "See you later, Mama."

A stern frown descended on her face as she gently chided her mother, "I'm not happy that you didn't stick up for

1

me once with Alex. He's such a brute."

Her mother caressed her hair. "Darling, you have to settle down. You're too energetic, and you'll be graduating in the spring. It'd be one thing if you wanted to pursue a career in opera, but we know that's not your desire. What better way to move on to the next phase of your life but with a husband? Because with a husband, soon comes children."

That last part was the crux of her mother's never-ending argument.

Tasa rolled her eyes. "Always with the children."

"Children give meaning to a woman's life," her mother crooned.

"Not every woman," she grumbled under her breath, but the Mercedes was pulling up to the curb, and really, she had zero energy to continue this endless discussion. It's not as if her mother ever budged an inch from her notions of femininity and womanhood, all of which circled around being a wife and mother. Rather, she cudgeled her only daughter with them. Sure, that had worked out fine for her mother. She'd married the love of her life. Growing up in a small village in the valley of the Carpathian Mountains, she'd been utterly fulfilled by her role, but that wasn't Tasa. Not that anyone in her family seemed to care. She could've escaped those expectations with the opera. While she was a decent alto, she wasn't any more interested in pursuing an intensive career in the opera than she was in shackling herself to a man at the age of twenty.

Hitching her Dolce & Gabbana handbag over her shoulder, Tasa slipped out of the café, leaving behind the clinking of porcelain coffee cups on small saucers, and took in a deep breath of brisk, cold winter air.

Yanking the Mercedes passenger door open, she slid onto the leather seat with a sigh of relief.

"Tasa, are you trying to get me in trouble?" griped Nikki, giving her a side-glance with a small scowl.

"Oh, hush, and just drive if you don't want him catching you," she replied. Her control freak of a brother believed a princess like her shouldn't be seen in the front seat, beside her chauffeur-slash-bodyguard. There was a certain level of decorum to maintain. For Nikki's sake, she usually took the back seat when she came home to visit, but she was holding on to her temper by the thinnest of threads as it was.

"*Dragă mea*—"

Oh, sweetheart. Nikki always resorted to his mother tongue when he was upset.

"Don't *dragă mea*," she snapped as she dragged the seat belt over her chest and clipped it in. She didn't need his pity, the primary sentiment coming off his endearment. "Hit the accelerator already so we can get out of this godforsaken neighborhood. Then he won't see you."

He squeezed her knee briefly. His hand didn't linger, but Tasa was well aware of Nikki's feelings. It was only natural he should crush on her. After all, they spent so much time together, and she'd finally grown into her figure.

But he'd never cross *the* line. He might be family, but she was a princess. A princess supposed to marry a prince. *Gag.* The thought of Cristo made her stomach turn. He was a good enough guy, if you were into the clean-cut bro type. Well, as close a version to that as a *mafie* prince could get. She'd known him since they were in diapers. Being only a few years older than her, they hung out in the same scene. The idea of kissing him was about as appealing as kissing her twin brother, Nicu. And Cristo was half in love with his little side piece, a cute girl named Una. There was no way she was marrying a guy who was already in love with another woman. She didn't expect him to give up on Una, and Tasa wasn't the sharing type. Of course, she couldn't divulge any of this to Alex. If he found out, Cristo would be in trouble with his old man. More importantly, she was afraid of her own reaction if her brother responded the way she predicted. *What, Tasa? You think men are loyal. You think Tata never cheated on Mama?*

Grrr.

Seriously, the less she knew about the way *mafie* men lived their lives, the better. A second family was probably out there somewhere, with kids who sported the same deep-brown eyes as she and her beloved father. She shook her head. Again, not something she wanted to know. With three overbearing brothers, she didn't need additional stepsiblings creeping out of the woodwork. She could barely breathe as it was, with the ones surrounding her.

Nicu was her other half in many ways, but he was far from perfect. And he got to live a normal life because he was a male and he was Alex's good little soldier boy. Luca, her middle brother, might be the black sheep, but he had all the liberties he could possibly want. Pressing her lips together, she focused her gaze outside the window at the passing brick townhouses. Her eyes began to burn. Luca. She sighed, as she often did when she thought of him. Such a tortured soul, with everything so bottled up inside.

That one, she was going to miss.

"What's wrong, babe?" Nikki asked. "What happened in there?"

She let out a weary sigh.

"What do you think happened?"

She'd gotten her marching orders.

"Be a good little girl and fall in line like everyone else. The Lupu family are a bunch of empty-headed dunces, all walking to the tune of their pied piper, Alexandru Lupu," she grumbled.

The *Lupul*, or the Wolf, as people called him, was the puppet master, pulling the strings of the mafia family from America to Paris, Milan, Bucharest, and beyond.

Blood was blood.

Duty was duty.

Orders were orders.

Blah, blah, blah. She felt like gagging after the number of times she'd heard that litany throughout her life.

"Sorry, babe. When he gets an idea into his head, he won't let it go."

"You can say that again," she conceded as she swiped at a rogue tear. "I'm impressed you even went that far." It was unusual for Nikki to say *any*thing against Alex. Suggesting stubbornness, while completely accurate, was borderline betrayal in a secret society where loyalty was the be-all and end-all. Another reason Nikki had never so much as tried to kiss her. It wasn't even the idea that he might be murdered for such an infraction. He'd simply never cross that line. Lupu allegiance was implacable.

He may not have been born a Lupu, but she knew there was some sort of ancient, secret blood ceremony that made him as good as blood. Fucking her would be the equivalent of incest, regardless of what the tenting in his pants told her. Considering she wasn't in love with Nikki any more than she was with Cristo, she didn't push it.

That, and she didn't want to get Nikki killed.

"He catches me at one club and comes down like a dictator," she grumbled.

"Babe … it was the kind of club. And the fact that you escaped from me. You could've gotten killed … or worse. What were you thinking?"

Nikki was talking about the sex club she's gone to with her best friend, Nina. So sue them; they were curious little virgins. Unfortunately, Alex had found the selfie Nina posted, sitting at the iconic bar. A selfie that included part of Tasa's shoulder, which bared her Lupu tat of a wolf. In the darkness and the strobe lights, Nina hadn't noticed and posted the pic. A pic Alex happened to view on her Instagram feed.

Oh, boy, did all hell break loose that night. And so began the lockdown. Other than attending her classes at Juilliard, she could go to the apartment she shared with Nina and home in Sunnyside. That was it. Now, she couldn't even shake Nikki off her tale.

But if everything went according to plan, things would be irrevocably changed in a few short days. She wasn't a Lupu for nothing, and as her *tata* had always said, "You have to fight for what you want in this life."

Damn straight.

He wasn't the only relentless person in her family. For instance, it took her for-ev-er to get any action between the sheets, but she'd managed in the end. It had taken seducing one of her vocal instructors to finally learn her way around the male body.

At the end of the day, she'd kept her virginity intact, something she was coming to regret. Her verdict, after her little adventure, was that sex was *way* overrated.

Which is why she'd ended up in Tribeca at the infamous sex club NSFW with Nina. Her curiosity had been piqued by the idea of something beyond vanilla. She'd already done every vanilla thing on her non-intercourse sex bucket list during her brief affair and had walked away with little enthusiasm. A few hours at the sex club, on the other hand, and she'd seen things that made her toes curl.

Nikki dropped her off at the lobby of the high-rise on 68th Street overlooking the Hudson and went to park the car in the underground parking. Entering the apartment she shared with Nina, she dropped her keys in the little crystal-cut bowl on the small Louis XVI wooden table in the vestibule. Part of the deal of getting the apartment near Juilliard, instead of commuting from Queens every day, was to have Nina come live with her and to have her mother decorate their apartment. Of course, she'd decorated it like a Prussian aristocrat from the mid-nineteenth century. Hence the old-people's furniture scattered around their apartment like at an auction house instead of posters of Degas dancers or Callas like in the Juilliard student dorms.

The apartment's best feature was the wall of windows overlooking an unimpeded view of the Hudson and the Jersey coast beyond. Throwing her coat over another atrociously overwrought sofa, Tasa kicked off her high heels and threw herself down beside Nina.

"How was it?" asked Nina without bothering with a greeting. A little furrow dug between her dark, fine winged brows.

"Jellie, are you?"

"Over Alex? Hardly," she scoffed. "I'd never be jealous of you."

"Mm-hmm," replied Tasa noncommittedly, tossing waves of her long brown hair over her shoulder. Nina was head-over-heels in love with Alex, although she felt the need to deny it in deference to their friendship. They'd been best friends since the day Nina tottered across the broken sidewalk from her house to Tasa as a toddler. While Tasa had the ability to get Nina out of her shell and Nina was her number-one partner in crime, her friend was really a gentle soul inside.

"He's like a brother to me," muttered Nina.

Double lie.

"Just because we joke that we must've been switched at birth in no way means there's a shred of sibling-like feelings between the two of you," Tasa fired back.

God knows both of them would've had easier child-hoods if they'd been brought up by the other's household. Nina's mother was a badass who prodded Nina to take life by the balls, while Tasa's mother continually bemoaned her daughter's lack of ladylike manners. At least Tasa had *Bunica*, her grandmother, to serve as a buffer between her and her mother and Alex.

"It was disastrous. I swear the man thinks he's my father, and he acts worse than a tyrant. Besides the boring lecture about my reputation, which I truly think he actually believed, he gave me an ultimatum. Either the opera or marriage … to Cristo."

While this was no huge surprise, Nina's eyes squeezed together in commiseration.

"No," she breathed out. Nina's loyalty was solidly behind Tasa, but she always believed the best in Alex, no matter how irrational he acted. Which was why Tasa had to keep every detail of her upcoming jailbreak from Nina. It hurt to lie, but realistically, the woman would crumble in under five minutes in Alex's presence.

The theoretical scene played out in her mind. Alex would wrap his arm around Nina's shoulder, bringing her in tight to his side to woo her into feeling safe with him. Nina, a softie to her core, would instantly melt against him. She'd look up at him, batting those absurdly long lashes of hers. He'd grace her with one of his beatific angel-slash-devilish smiles, and she'd turn into a puddle of goo. Game over. She'd gush like a bad oil spill in the Gulf of Mexico.

Tasa clenched her fists. *Pathetic.* Her oldest brother got everything he wanted, anytime he wanted.

But not this time.

If she had any hope of escaping her predicament, she had to play it smart. And Tasa could pride herself on that much at least. She may not be respectful or obedient, but she was nothing if not conniving. She'd been fantasizing about this for years and plotting its execution for months.

"You always expect him to act decently," she reprimanded Nina, laying her arm over the intricately carved, gilded wood curling up from the top of the couch. Her eyes drifted toward the windows, sunlight splashing through the panes and highlighting the jewel-like colors of the Persian rug across the floor. That was another thing about

Romanians. Rugs everywhere. Almost every inch of their apartment was covered in intricate silk rugs.

"He's a decent guy inside. Granted, you have to dig *deep* sometimes, but he disappoints me when he acts like this. I expect better from him."

Tasa let out a little snort. "Good luck with that. He's such a hypocrite. The bedroom in his apartment is a revolving door of women, but he expects me to remain chaste and turn my virginity and life over to my husband at his command. As if."

"Well, there's the other option."

"Yes, be part of the bastion of high culture. What about giving me a chance to figure out what *I* want to do? I'm only twenty years old. You'd think I'd be given a few years to *live*. To travel the world and explore. Who knows, maybe I want to be a fashion designer."

Nina tipped her head to the side, her lips pressed together to suppress a laugh. Nina wouldn't dare laugh in her face. She was too polite and kind for that. "Do you?"

"No." Tasa huffed. "What about an organic-apple farmer in Upstate New York? Does it matter? The point is that because he has the imagination of a flea, he's only come up with two options, and I'm forced to follow one of those. It's arbitrary and absurd and … and … insane! Like him!"

Another thing she'd never told Nina. That she'd changed her major to experimental dance. Her family would have conniptions if she turned away from a refined career singing opera to experimental performance art, or what they'd mockingly describe as twisting and flopping around like a dying fish on the floor.

"It's because he was so young when he was thrust into his position as head of your family and of that business empire," defended Nina. "It doesn't help that your brothers immediately knew they wanted to follow in his footsteps."

"It's not like we don't live in the twenty-first century," she threw out.

"You know he doesn't think that way. Your parents instilled in him the same idea every immigrant has. Come here and make something of yourself. You can't just have a random job. No, you have to be a doctor, a lawyer, or something crazy impressive like alto for the Metropolitan Opera."

Fiddling with the two tassels dangling from her silk blouse, Tasa muttered, "Whatever."

Nina peered into her face, watching her with a concerned expression. "So, what are you going to do?"

"I have no idea. I have one more semester at Juilliard. That gives me a little more time of freedom."

Liar.

Tasa knew exactly what she was going to do. She'd checked with the bursar's office, and after three weeks of school, she could get fifty percent of her $30,000 tuition refunded to her bank account if she withdrew. And that was exactly what she was going to do. Then she'd disappear and make her way to the source of cutting-edge experimental dance, Madame Pierrette's dance company in Montreal, Canada. Everyone who knew anything knew of the notoriously exclusive workshop she hosted every spring. A workshop Tasa got accepted to. It was close to a miracle and she wasn't going to pass up the opportunity of a lifetime. Alex be damned.

CHAPTER TWO

WHISTLE HEARD THE clang of the last set of the metal doors of Duchess County Jail rattle behind him. Squinting against the glare of the bright morning sun, he lifted his hand to shield his eyes and scanned the parking lot. His gaze halted on Hoodie at the far end of the lot. Leaning against his Harley, legs crossed at the ankles, he was smoking a spliff. It wasn't even ten in the morning.

Letting out a soft chuckle, Whistle shook his head. That brother was as dismissive of authority as he was. In a government parking lot right outside the jailhouse, and he was exhaling an extra-large puff of smoke to add to the cloud of sweet-smelling ganga already hanging over him. Beside him was Whistle's bike. Now that they'd been patched in for a couple of years, it was their turn to order prospects around. Knowing Hoodie, he got a prospect to ride Whistle's bike over, then handed him a couple of dollars and politely instructed him to fuck off and take the bus back to the clubhouse.

Glancing over his shoulder toward the jail, Whistle frowned. He didn't like leaving Puck in the slammer alone, but the Squad's sergeant at arms had given him his orders and told him to get out once his bail was paid.

"You did what you could for him," Hoodie answered Whistle's unspoken concern as he clasped his hand and moved in for a man hug.

Swinging a leg over his Roadster, Whistle opened his hand and wiggled his fingers for Hoodie to throw him his keys. A second later, the engine of his bike was purring beneath him. Damn, he'd missed that sound. "Doesn't make it any easier to leave him there. 'Course he told me to get the hell out of there and go the fuck on home. Called me a liability to his ass in jail."

"You *are* a pretty boy," drawled Hoodie as if it was obvious as fuck why he'd be a danger in jail.

"Fuck you, asshole. Whose side are you on, anyway?"

"Never yours, motherfucker," he grunted. A lie, of course. But that's how it was between them, and Whistle wouldn't have it any other way. If Cutter and Puck were like fathers to him, then Hoodie was the brother he wished he'd always had. Hoodie might be rough around the edges, but he had the soul of an artist, whereas Whistle's blood brothers imitated all things civilized but were animals to their depraved core.

Yeah, he was used to being called a pretty boy. Hell, he couldn't help the way he looked. The unusual turquoise tint of his eyes had women and men stumbling in their steps. God knows he'd wanted to ruin his looks and tat up his face like Post Malone, but Hoodie had stopped him every time. Said it wasn't his place to fuck up the face God had given him. Whistle looked at him askance whenever he said that; it wasn't like the fucker believed in any type of god. Hoodie always went on to add that if the club was ever hard up for cash, they could send him out on the streets to

13

make a living with his dick. *Hardy-har-har.* Fucking hilarious. Asshole.

Seriously, though, Hoodie was his other half. They couldn't have been brought up in more different circumstances. Hoodie had been tortured by his parents, as almost every inch of the skin on his chest and back could attest to. Whistle, on the other hand, had been coddled by a smothering mother, a near prisoner in a mansion in Brighton Beach, the Brooklyn neighborhood bastion of Russian immigrants and, more importantly, the Bratva.

"Any of the men try anything, you being so pretty and all?" Hoodie smirked.

"Ya know, the usual. Ended up in the hole for a week for fighting. It's good to be out, brother. That was the least enjoyable stint in the pen I've had to date, and fuck knows, I've been in there too many times to count."

Nodding, Hoodie clapped him on the shoulder. "Some of the bitches are waitin' at the clubhouse to celebrate your release."

"I gotta stop and get Loki's roll-up futon first. My orders are to move into the Squad Bar. Puck wants me there day and night to watch the place. Keep it above water until he gets out. Could be a while."

Unlike his father and two older brothers, who were members of the Bratva and saw him as yet another disposable human weapon, the Squad brothers treated him like family. And he was going to start reciprocating. Having grown up in a tight-knit, enclosed community, before he became a violin prodigy and was forced to be home-schooled, he appreciated the Squad for giving him back what he'd had for a few blissful years as a kid.

Hoodie's eyebrows lifted. "You seriously gonna sleep there?"

"Yup. There's an office in the back. Seems like there's a thief to catch."

"And Puck thinks your dumb ass is the one who's gonna catch him?" Hoodie sputtered before busting out a loud guffaw.

"You got any better ideas? You gonna go instead of me?"

"Hard pass, brother," replied Hoodie. "I slept enough nights on the hard pavement. Get ugly flashbacks if I sleep on anything other than a bed nowadays."

"Spoiled brat," Whistle teased. Hoodie had been found by Kingdom and a few brothers one night, living rough on the streets. Dressed only in a hoodie. Hence his road name. It was around the same time Whistle had showed up at the clubhouse. Both underage, both running from their own version of hell. They'd hung around, doing whatever the brothers asked of them, until Prez allowed them to officially prospect. Whistle had kinks to work out, which he did with drinkin' and fightin'. Hoodie reacted in the opposite manner. Kept to himself. When they'd first brought him in, he refused to leave the clubhouse property for months on end.

Now that Whistle had turned twenty-two years old, it was time to put the fucking around behind him. Puck's one-and-only lecture, while they were in the pen together, hit him square in the solar plexus. It was time to grow the fuck up and take on responsibilities. After a decade of grueling violin practice routines and touring, once he joined the Demon Squad MC, he'd had a lot of living to make up for. Now, Puck was in a difficult situation, and after years of messing around, it was time to man up.

Hoodie extinguished the blunt between his fingers and tucked it into the front pocket of his leather biker jacket. "Sage's a good egg. Got you out on your birthday. The big double two. Whatcha wanna do tonight?"

"What the fuck do you think?"

It was a rhetorical question. Hoodie knew. Drink and fuck. What else?

"Anyone in particular?" Hoodie asked.

"Yup, the first one. I'm *that* particular," Whistle joked. He always took the first woman to hit him up when he walked through the clubhouse door. That was his rule: first one on him had him for the night. Kept things simple and nipped any potential catfights in the bud. He didn't have problems getting laid, but he liked the club biker bitches the best. There was an understanding; no talking necessary. He liked to give them a little extra attention by letting them sleep in his bed for the night. When he first came around the clubhouse, he'd done it to get them used to him since he was such a goddamn mess. Years later, he was among their favorites.

After their errands, he and Hoodie parked along the row of bikes, sauntered past the fence, and entered the clubhouse property. The club owned the building situated on a residential street corner, with empty lots on either side. The empty lots had been the main selling point for the property, and so far, no one had built on them. Not that the neighborhood was known for new constructions. Eventually, the plan was to buy the two lots and expand. But for that to happen, their current businesses had to be in the black. The Box, their boxing and MMA gym, was doing well. Their online merchandising business was pumping. The Squad Bar, however, was sinking like a pile of concrete thrown over the Walkway in the Hudson River.

"Yo, Whistle. Good to see you, brother," sounded Brick, the prospect on duty, with an enthusiastic whoop. Unlike the other brothers, who routinely gave the prospects shit, Whistle too easily remembered his prospecting days to give them too hard a time. After sharing a bro hug, he followed Hoodie into the clubhouse.

Immediately upon entering, there was a loud ruckus of shouts as the brothers and bitches spotted him. Cassie and Jazz jumped off their stools and ran for him, wrapping their arms on either side of him. He noted that Jazz got to him first, which meant she'd won him for the night. He extricated himself from being smothered by the bitches. Planting his lips on Cassie's mouth, he released her and made it clear that Jazz was his partner by hooking an arm around her neck and pulling her close.

"I got to you first, Whistle," Cassie whined.

"Good try, but you so didn't, bitch," Jazz shot back.

"Hey," Whistle chided with a soft chuckle. As attractive as he was, the women rarely argued over the men. Must be the inmate thing that got them riled up. "Next time, babe. You know I don't like fighting, and I'm an hour out of jail."

Cassie dropped a last kiss on his mouth. "Aww, Whistle, we heard how you got arrested to keep Puck company." She batted her eyelashes. "Sure you don't wanna share?"

Dark eyes narrowed, Jazz cut in, "*I* don't want to share, so back off."

"Fine," Cassie conceded and, pivoting on her heel, stomped back to the bar.

Jazz and he were old friends. Old fuck buddies, too, since the day she showed up, young and new. Taking a stool, he patted his knee for her to sit on it and asked Whiskey, who was bartending, for a beer. Flicking her dreads over her shoulder, she settled on his lap. One thing was for sure, that the woman had the finest ass in the clubhouse. She was a shapely little thing with mocha skin and bright brown eyes.

"How was it in there, brah?" asked Cutter, his vice-president.

"It is what it was. We both ended up in the hole for fighting. 'Course, the fucker blamed it on me, but there was gonna be a throw down, what with it being his first time."

Cutter shifted his old lady, Greta, to his other knee and clapped Whistle on the shoulder. "Fucking finally, I can say with pride that you're an asset to the club."

Whistle grunted. Cutter hadn't always felt that way. Before he'd gotten a lockdown on Greta, Whistle used to flirt with her when he'd stop by the law office where she worked with Sage, the president's old lady. He had no idea Cutter was into her, and when she rebuffed Cutter's advances, he took his frustration out on Whistle. It was around the time Whistle had patched in, and he'd expected to be treated like an equal, not like a little bitch. Cutter eventually calmed his shit down once Greta became his old lady, but Whistle had moved his allegiance to Puck.

That's why he'd purposely got into a bar fight after Puck got arrested for beating up the ex-husband of one of the club bitches. There was a simple and easy way to see

Puck safe in the county jail. Unfortunately, it wasn't by normal means. Only took a few hours to get processed and shoved into a police van transporting him to the Duchess County Jail, where he could be by Puck's side.

Grabbing the neck of the bottle that landed in front of him, Whistle took a sip and nuzzled his face into Jazz's neck. Although he was glad to see his brothers, there'd be time enough to catch up later.

Prodding Jazz to stand, he ordered, "Come on."

They ascended to his room on the second floor. He shoved the door open and swept her inside. Her back slammed against the wall, and he followed her body, not breaking the suction of their mouths. Jazz was one of the few women he actually kissed. Good friends allowed for that without any misunderstandings.

He tossed her on his unmade bed. Landing on her back, she propped herself up on her elbows and tossed her head back with a throaty laugh.

Unbuckling his belt, he commanded her, "Play with your tits."

Yanking down her tube top, she let her perky breasts pop out. Her top shimmied down her torso, and she jiggled them at him. Whistle palmed his hardening cock beneath his jeans. "You want this? Let me see it."

She jerked her stretchy mini skirt out of the way, brought her knees up, and dropped them open. Not only was she not wearing panties, but she was showing off her newly shaved pussy, slit wet and dripping for him. Jazz was quick to get fired up, and he liked that about her.

He tsked. "Such a naughty, naughty girl." He unbuttoned his Levi's, and his cock sprang out, raring to go. After weeks of no fucking, he was hard as a rock. Dropping to the bed, he played with her pussy as he pumped his cock.

"Whistle, stop teasing me," she moaned.

"Grab a rubber," he ordered. She reached over to his nightstand, rattling the drawer in her impatience to get to his stash. Pulling out a string of condoms, she ripped the top one open with her teeth. Swaying it teasingly between her thumb and forefinger in front of him, she bent over and wrapped her lips around his cock.

Whistle groaned.

Fuck, that felt good.

Finally pulling her mouth off him, she rolled the condom down.

He took hold of the backs of her thighs, wrapped her legs around his waist, and thrust inside. Motherfucker, it'd been enough time. Occasionally, he went without sex for a couple of weeks, but it never felt as bad as it did when spent in the slammer. Caging her between his arms, he took the dark bead of her nipple into his mouth as he pounded into her. She grabbed at his hair as he went savage on her. They'd been together enough times that he knew what she needed to tip her over. His thumb pressed down on her clit while his other hand landed a few quick slaps on her ass.

Within minutes, she was screaming his name and her pussy was milking him. He squeezed her tits roughly to trigger aftershocks, and she bore down on him harder. His thrusts lost their steady pace, and the metal bed frame slammed against the wall as he came. Groaning, he rocked in and out haphazardly as he emptied himself into the condom.

A bead of sweat rolled down the midline of his chest,

and Jazz leaned forward to lick it off. Sweet gesture on her part but Whistle never felt anything the instant his balls were drained.

As bad as he might want to roll over and crash like the dead, he tried respecting the girls by not tossing them out of bed right after he was done. That was a play out of his brothers' or father's playbook, and he swore never to be like them. Pulling out, he disposed of the condom and began to shuck off his clothes.

"You're so damn beautiful, you know that?" Jazz commented. She hadn't moved from her position, but her eyes gazed down his long frame.

"Yeah, Jazz," he scoffed. "You say that every time."

"Every time I see you naked, it takes my breath away. Seriously, it's sick."

"For fuck's sake," he grumbled. "You stayin' or what?"

"Nah, it's barely afternoon and you look wrecked. I'll go back downstairs and let you rest." Her eyes clouded over. "Was it that bad in there?"

"It's never easy, that's for fucking sure. There's always noise, but not like here. When there's noise here, you know people are drinking and having fun. There, you don't know if someone's plotting to stick their dick up your ass or a shank down your throat. You never sleep in peace."

Swiping the back of his hand over his burning eyes, he prodded her over and crawled into bed. She stood up, rearranged her clothes, and gave him a peck on the lips. "I'll let you sleep."

"Thank Christ. Tomorrow I start staying overnights at the bar. I'd like to sleep in a fucking bed before I have to share with the rodents on the floor."

MONIQUE MOREAU

"Eww," she replied with a small shudder of her shoulders.

He plumped the pillow under his head and turned to face the wall. Sex took the edge off, but he wasn't left satiated, and despite his fatigue, his thoughts bounced around like balls in a pinball machine. This casual shit wasn't doing it for him anymore. What the hell that meant, he had no idea 'cause he sure as hell had no intention of taking an old lady. That was a ball and chain he refused to touch with a ten-foot pole. But there was no denying that changes were a-brewing. First, the urge to step up in the club. Now, a good fuck session didn't leave him any more relaxed than before.

Jazz pulled the curtains closed and clicked the light off, plunging him in semi-darkness. His eyes dropped closed as the door shut softly behind him, but it took more than the usual amount of time before his mind settled down and he finally nodded off to sleep.

CHAPTER THREE

$11,840

That was not a lot of money. Much less than Tasa had anticipated, for sure. She let out a frustrated sigh as she considered the cash in her Hermes backpack. She should be grateful she had that much. It would set her up in Canada, preferably somewhere high up near the tundra where no one could find her. Looking out the window of the Greyhound bus, dressed in the only pair of jeans she owned, she let herself breathe freely for the first time. It would be at least five or six hours before anyone noticed she was missing.

A stunning feeling of elation vibrated in her chest. She'd done it. She'd gotten away.

Her eyes skidded over the Hudson River, glistening in the mid-morning sun. The crests sparkled white over the ripples of marine-blue and slate-gray below the bridge the bus was crossing. An expanse of blue sky, as far as the eye could see, called to her.

She was free to do anything she wanted. *Any*thing. Imagine that.

The water and sky called to her, and as much as she wanted to be in another country by now, the truth of the matter was that she had already succeeded by escaping New York City. Out of the City and the Tri-State area, where her brother had his network, she was safe enough to indulge in the impulse. Once across that invisible boundary, her brother's influence waned significantly. On top of the fact that he had no idea where she was, she was free. Her adventure could begin at any moment she chose.

Her life was no longer on cruise control—classes, studying, practicing, going to the gym, being with the family. Nina, *Bunica*, Luca, and Nicu, she would miss. Even Alex and her mother, she'd eventually come to miss, although it'd take a hell of a lot longer. But there was a price to pay for freedom, and there was no going back. Her hope was that, sooner or later, Alex would give up the chase and accept her independence. Shaking off the brooding thoughts about those she'd left behind, she considered taking this moment to flex her newfound freedom. God knows, she'd waited long enough for it.

Get off at the next stop and take in the sights of the next town, wherever that may be. The thought popped into her mind, calling to her, and she always listened to her gut. That was one lesson her *bunica* had taught her. She was superstitious, like all country-born Romanian women. Her grandmother always counseled her to "Follow your spirit," and her spirit told her this was the place to start her newest adventure. She'd still make it to Montreal for Madame Pierrette's rigorous workshop in the spring.

The bus pulled into the bus stop, and Tasa stumbled off just as the driver called out, "Poughkeepsie, Poughkeepsie."

For the first time in her life, she didn't know what was

around the corner, and it was exhilarating. She didn't have to wear prim pencil skirts and nice tops with heels. Here she was, strutting out of the bus in skinny jeans and a top cropped above her navel. Even though it was covered with a sweater and puffy jacket, at least *she* knew it was there.

Grabbing a cab idling outside the depot, she told it to go to the coffee shop on Main Street. There was always a Main Street in these small cities. And, lo and behold, she'd been right, because the cabbie pulled up to a hipster coffee shop and stuck out his hand through the hole of the glass partition for his payment. She slapped down enough cash to cover the trip and tip, threw the cab door open, and got out.

Dragging her carry-on luggage to the coffee shop, she opened the wooden-framed glass door, passed a bulletin board with flyers and papers tacked on, and beelined for the first free seat she saw at the large bay window overlooking the street.

Plopping down in the seat, she took in the entire space. Her gaze drifted over one wall covered with old LP records from the eighties and nineties, the barista counter and cashier, and over the expanse of haphazard groupings of tables, chairs, and couches. Her eyes ended at the door with the bulletin she'd noticed as she walked. It had several layers of flyers and notices tacked on it. Maybe she could find a place to rent there. She could check for Airbnbs at a computer in a local library, but she fancied the notion of doing it the old-fashioned way through a community bulletin board.

It was strange to be free. Free of bodyguards. Free of enemies. No one knew who she was or where she was. She no longer had to look over her shoulder everywhere she went. Old habits died hard, so she did it anyway, but the edginess of living in New York sloughed off her shoulders with remarkable ease. She was free to do most anything, and that was a revelation.

Stashing her luggage beneath the small round table, Tasa shrugged off her coat and laid it over the back of the chair. Smoothing down her cashmere sweater, which covered her more risqué top, she hitched her backpack over one shoulder, and keeping an eye on her luggage, sauntered up to the coffee bar. After ordering an espresso, she went to the end of the bar to wait for her drink. The hiss of hot air gushed out of the steam wand as the barista cleaned it. Pushing the filter of ground coffee into place, she took a porcelain espresso cup and placed it below to catch the two tiny streams of dark liquid.

Eyeing the place, Tasa noticed there was only the one employee for the entire shop that had at least thirty seats. There was clattering coming from the kitchen in the back, but in the ten minutes she'd been there, this one woman took care of everything. Cashier, the coffee bar, and cleaning up.

"Hey, there," she started.

The woman's dark eyes lifted to hers over the espresso machine. "How are you doing today?"

"Good, good. Busy here. Don't you have someone else to help you?" she asked as she eyed the growing line of customers by the register.

She let out a sigh. "Normally, yes, but she called out this morning. Not reliable, to say the least. Can't exactly blame her for the amount she gets paid."

"You get paid differently?"

"I'm the manager."

"Are you looking to hire someone reliable and hard-working?"

The woman's eyes flicked up from the espresso machine she was watching and inspected Tasa. Raking her over with sharp, intelligent eyes, she asked, "Why does a girl with a Hermes bag need a job as a barista?"

"I didn't exactly pay for this with my own blood and sweat," replied Tasa, a tiny, sardonic smile tipping one side of her lips as she twisted around and nodded to her backpack.

"Was it daddy or a sugar daddy?" the barista teased lightly with a saucy wink.

Tasa huffed out a surprised laugh. The woman had sass, that was for sure. "Something like that."

"Ah, a woman with a touch of mystery," she said.

Espresso finished, she grabbed a small plate and carefully placed the cup on top. "You have any experience?"

Did she have experience? Pfft. After Tata died, she'd thrown herself into upgrading the café with the newest specialty drinks. Her mother and brother, glad to have her occupied as they worked to salvage Tata's empire, had given her free reign. Besides learning what there was to know about coffee, and its different preparations, she'd changed the menu and helped train the staff. Granted, it'd been mostly pointless since the majority of customers were Romanian, Greeks, or other Eastern Europeans that only drank Turkish coffee or espresso. At the time, she'd been grateful for the distraction of doing something with her hands and learning a skill that made people happy. Their café was the heartline of their small community.

"I was raised in a café. I can do anything behind the bar. Any drinks I don't already know how to make, I can learn quickly. Who knows, I might teach you a thing or two."

"That so?" the woman replied mildly. "What's your name?"

"Tasa."

"Tasha?"

"No, Tasa. A diminutive for Nataşa, but it's Tasa. All s's."

"I see. Well, Tasa, my name is Jazz."

If ever a woman looked like a Jazz, it was she. Glittering, bright, happy brown eyes with golden glints, a broad set of lips that had permanent creases on the corners from laughing too much, and a luxurious head of dreadlocks. Tasa didn't like to compare herself to other women. She was attractive in her own right, but Jazz was vivacious. Energetic and charming.

"Nice to meet you, Jazz."

"You from out of town?"

Tasa stiffened slightly and had to remind herself she wasn't in danger here. "Something like that."

"Hmm …"

Jazz went to ring up several orders from the line of customers and returned to fill orders. "I might have a place for you to crash if you're interested."

"Sure, I'm interested." This was better than she could imagine. A job *and* a place to stay? At the rate her luck was going, she wouldn't have to use a dime of her small savings for a good while.

"I have an apartment, and I rent out the spare bedroom when I'm low on cash. Besides, I don't stay there every night, so you'll have it all to yourself for more nights than not."

"How much are you looking for?"

"Four hundred a month."

"I can swing that, especially if you hire me."

"Bring your luggage to the back, put your shit in a locker, and grab an apron. Let's try you out."

She gave a little yelp of excitement. "Thanks, Jazz. You won't regret this," she promised over her shoulder as she rushed to get her luggage and coat from her table. Following Jazz's finger pointing toward the back, she waved to a couple of employees in the small kitchen and stuffed her belongings into an empty locker. Grabbing a clean apron from a row of hooks, she threw it on and joined Jazz behind the bar. Jazz quickly showed her how to use the cash register, and she was off and running, taking orders and fulfilling them under Jazz's watchful eye.

Tasa already felt more alive than she had in months—no, years—if she was to be honest. It was enjoyable to get back into the swing of doing something useful, and it brought back fond memories of home but with the novelty of being in a new place.

By the time four o'clock rolled around, Jazz laid a hand on her shoulder as she was steaming a small stainless-steel pitcher of milk and said, "It's time to get off the clock. Marie is coming to take over the evening shift. I'm not working at the bar tonight, so we can go straight home after you fill out the paperwork in the office."

Tasa bit her bottom lip. She had a fake driver's license,

but she didn't want to have to use it and leave any kind of paper trail, if possible. "Is there any way I can be paid … under the table?" she said in a hushed voice. There was no other way to get around asking what needed to be asked.

Jazz patted her dreads with her hands, her eyes doing that roving-inspection thing they did when she was trying to figure something out. Her jaw tightened a fraction, and she asked, "You running from someone, Tasa? You need to stay gone?"

Tasa's eyes skittered to the right and then back down to the pitcher she was holding, pulling it away before she scalded the milk. Grabbing a wet towel, she flipped the switch, and a loud hiss of steam flew out of the metal wand as she cleaned it down. She slowly poured the milk into a cup, wiggling the pitcher until it created a flower design. With a shrug, she grabbed the stainless-steel pick and added a few flares to the flower drawn in foam over the darker milky espresso.

"Something like that," she mumbled.

"That seems to be your answer to most of my questions." Jazz expelled a sigh of resignation. "Alright, keep your secrets. We can pay you in cash at the end of the week."

Tasa glanced up at her, hope in her heart. "Yeah? Oh, thanks so much."

"There's one thing I need to ask you, and I need a straight answer."

Nervousness constricted Tasa's throat, and she croaked out, "Shoot."

"Are you involved in anything dangerous?"

Tasa released a pent-up breath.

"Not dangerous for you," she replied with as much earnestness as she could put into her tone. Which was true. The Lupus were a secret underground *mafie* society, completely segregated from the civilian world, and one that did not like to bring attention to itself. Ever. Alex would come looking for her—of that, she had no doubt. Besides his unrelenting sense of obligation to protect her, he'd want her back, if not for Cristo, then for Cristo's father. But he wouldn't hurt an innocent along the way. Anyway, Tasa had no intention of him finding her in the first place.

"If hidden is what you want, I have an even better idea than a coffee shop in the middle of Poughkeepsie's center of town," Jazz revealed. Tasa's head whipped over her shoulder to keep her attention on her as she placed the completed drink on the counter and called out the customer's name.

Once the customer picked up her drink and walked away, Tasa turned toward Jazz. Propping her hip against the bar, she folded her arms over her chest. An eyebrow arched high. "Don't think I'm not grateful, because I am, but first, tell me why you're being so helpful."

Jazz grabbed a bottle of lotion and squirted a pea-sized amount in her palm. Smoothing it over her hands, she gave a light shrug. "I'm part of a biker club. The Demon Squad MC, here in Poughkeepsie, and the president's old lady—that's lingo for a wife for bikers—is a lawyer who works with survivors of domestic violence. We've all helped out, at one time or another, with her clients. There are telltale signs of a woman who's been abused. You have a few. The main one is that you're running away from someone, and that someone is a powerful man." She quirked an eyebrow.

"Aren't all men?"

Tasa's head jerked slightly.

"Oh," squeaked out of her parted lips.

Her fingers flew to her mouth as her eyes bounced around the room. She hadn't expected that. Alex wasn't abusive in the normal way of things. He was controlling in a world where it was considered necessary to keep people alive and the business running as it should. Her hand slid down to her throat, and she clutched the base.

"Like I said, I don't need details. I just need to know if you want my help and that there won't be any blowback for my club. As long as those two requirements are satisfied, I'm good."

"I am the only one at risk, and I need as much help as I can get to stay under the radar," Tasa hurried to reply. If Jazz had any ideas of how to keep her well hidden, she was all ears. "What do you suggest?"

"The Squad has a bar, where I bartend. There's no better place to hide out than in a biker bar full of burly men who are into breaking the law and protecting vulnerable women. As much as I'd love for you to continue working here, they're in desperate need of waitresses. Even if you don't have much experience, you're obviously a quick learner and a hard worker. There's the additional perk that the Squad Bar isn't in the center of the city and that you'd be working nights."

"You work two jobs?"

"Pfft, I make jack at this job. I like to keep busy, and I need the extra money. The Squad Bar is starting out, so the tips aren't great there yet. But it's still better than here, and I have faith that it'll grow. Their bar is perfect for a city like

Poughkeepsie. We have lots of different indie scenes."

"You really have no qualms or reservations about helping me. Are you for real?"

"Yeah, I am." She gave a slight, self-deprecating, almost shy shrug. "My father was a jazz drummer, and growing up, we had people crashing at our place for one night to play a gig or for months to jam or record with my dad. It's in my blood to assemble a ragtag of people around me."

"I'm in. At least until the spring. Then I'll have to hit the road again." It'd give her time to gather more money to start her new life while lying low until it was time to head north for the workshop.

"Another perk is that it'll be even easier to pay you with the Squad than it will here. Bikers are allergic to asking questions."

Tasa turned to wipe down the counter and deposit the dirty dishes into a large plastic bin. "Thank you, Jazz. You've saved my life."

"Come on, go put the dirty dishes in the back and grab your shit. My car's parked on the street."

"Will do," Tasa replied as she hoisted the container on her hip and made her way into the kitchen.

Bouncing around as she got ready, Tasa was giddy with a surge of new energy. With it came nerves. That was only natural, but meeting Jazz and getting a job was the universe telling her she was in the right place. Any lingering doubts were swept away. She'd made the right decision, and her only duty now was to revel in it and enjoy every second of her newfound life. She was ready for whatever came next.

CHAPTER FOUR

TASA FELL IN love the instant she walked into the Squad Bar. It had the feel of an old-style dive bar or speakeasy. The scent of old wood hit her as she walked out of the bright sun into the dark interior. Everything was made of wood: the floors, the wainscoting of the walls, and the long, well-used bar. A row of booths lined one wall, and groups of tables and comfy chairs were spread across the floor. The Squad logo, painted on a plaque mimicking spray paint, hung above the bar, a bike dangled from the ceiling by a series of chains, and some Harley paraphernalia was scattered on the walls.

No frills. The opposite of the way her mother had decorated her apartment back in New York. Without gimmicks or over-the-top embellishments, it felt … homey. Yes, that's the word she'd use. It was like coming home after a long day at work. Daylight glinted through the large windows in the front of the bar but lost its fight against the darkness emanating from the wood and bare-brick walls. Stuttering halfway across the large room, any blade of light petered out on the old, scuffed planks of the floor.

Jazz brought her to the Bar a couple of days after they met. Although she was nowhere near as competent a waitress as a barista, she figured she'd learn on the job. The first day, she'd trailed another waitress and helped Jazz behind the bar. She'd quickly found her place among them. Many of the other waitresses were biker bitches—a term that had struck her as harsh at first. After hearing them call themselves "bitches" with such pride, time and time again, the term grew on her.

But one person took her breath away. The manager of the Squad Bar. Whistle was his name. The air in the bar shifted when he showed up from the back after Jazz had gone to talk to him about giving her a job. Jazz said it was just a formality, since they were desperate for responsible waitresses, but nerves roiled her stomach in knots.

Tasa was at the bar, organizing the bottles of liquor, when she felt heat coming from behind her. Tossing a glance over her shoulder, her gaze locked on the beautiful set of eyes of the man walking beside Jazz. They were a unique blue green, the color of tropical seas, outlined by thick lashes as black as the midnight sky. Her mouth dropped open of its own accord.

Whew, now, that's a striking man.

Besides stunning eyes that could stop a person in their tracks, the rest of his face was exquisite, with a body to match. He was tall, a head above hers. His broad shoulders topped a torso that tapered to slim hips. From the shirt that clung to his chest beneath his cut, she noticed his muscles stood out boldly, as if carved out of marble. Colorful tats snaked down both of his arms. How did someone get to be born with all the boxes checked off?

Then he opened his mouth to talk. His gravely bass voice had a slight lisp at the end of some of his words, reminding her of older members of her own family. Although she was certain he wasn't of Romanian origin, he had a familiar air about him that she couldn't quite pinpoint.

Jazz was talking directly to her, explaining that everything was settled, including a cash payout every week, but Tasa was too distracted to focus on her. It was pathetic how she couldn't seem to tear her gaze off Whistle's face while her friend rattled on.

When Jazz made the introductions, Tasa only managed to stumble out a greeting. God, she'd never been tongue-tied in her life. Yet, she didn't miss how his eyes lingered on her face for a long moment, as if trying to figure something out. It made her nervous on more than one level. First, there was the "oh shit, does he suspect something?" layer. Then there was a squirrely feeling in her chest, followed by a ticklish feeling in her core. Both were bad harbingers of things to come. If simply meeting him was this disturbing to her peace of mind, what would happen when she had to work an entire shift with him?

"Hey there," he said, holding out his hand.

Tasa looked at his large hand in horror but, girding her courage around her, she gently placed her hand in his. An electric jolt shimmied up her arm. What the hell …? Instantly, she took a step back and yanked her hand away, but his fingers only tightened his grip on her.

One of the waitresses called to Jazz, who tossed an answer over her shoulder, and while her friend was distracted, she distinctly heard him murmur in a gravel-filled voice, "Aren't you a pretty one?" The words drifted low over her, leaving her feeling a little light-headed.

They were followed up with an appreciative look that coasted over her face and down the length of her body. Wherever his eyes lingered left a blaze of fire behind. Her breasts suddenly ached, as if they were full, and her nipples turned into hard pebbles.

Tasa's spine stiffened.

This man was a danger. Any woman was at risk around him, but Tasa had more to lose than most. Namely, an independence she'd barely gotten hold of, and at great expense. He was a rabbit hole she ran the risk of falling into and never getting out. She couldn't afford that.

Tugging her hand out of his grip, she hissed under her breath. He heard her and threw his head back in a guttural laugh that had red heat simultaneously racing up her throat and rushing down her belly to pool between her thighs. Jazz turned back to them, but Tasa had already stepped away a couple of steps. Eyes slitted, she nodded tightly, whipped around, and fled behind the bar as the other waitresses flocked to his side. Ugh.

Determined to ignore the roiling in her belly and the lust swirling in her head, she clenched her teeth and focused on her tasks with intense determination. On more than one occasion, she felt a set of eyes warming the side of her face or the back of her body. Only once did she give in to her curiosity and followed the source to collide with that unrelenting set of turquoise eyes. Her heart slammed against her ribs, followed by a warm flush over her skin. A moment passed between them, eyes bolted on one another, before she tore her gaze away. It was both wondrous and torturous. It was incredible to feel that kind of sexual energy with a man, especially one who looked like Whistle, but it was hopeless because there was no way in hell she could hit that the way she liked. Just her luck that she found a man who set her afire and was completely off-limits.

THE MOMENT WHISTLE laid eyes on that tasty little package, Tasa was standing on her tiptoes, reaching for a bottle of whiskey on the high shelf of the bar. Her back was to him, but he'd already clocked her shapely figure. Damn fine, with a heart-shaped ass to die for. It only got better once she turned around, her big dark eyes landing on him as Jazz pointed her out. He couldn't keep his feet from stalking toward her.

She spoke through a pair of ripe, lush lips, not that he registered half of what she said because he was riveted on the nuances of emotions flittering across her face. Her face was so expressive. Her wide doe eyes, the color of chocolate, tilted up at the corners, a little bit feline. When he stepped closer to shake her hand, he noticed intriguing flecks of green in her irises. People waxed poetic about his eyes, but he could honestly say he'd never met a person with eyes as vivid as hers. There was a sharp intelligence in them.

Then there was her pert little nose and a pair of swollen lips that were begging to be wrapped around his cock. *Fuck.* He let out a little huff of disbelief. Thinking about her lips had gotten him hard in under a second. Irritation slightly pricked the back of his neck. He didn't normally lose control like this, especially over a woman.

She shook her head, causing her thick sable hair to

cascade over her shoulders and hide half her face. He dipped his head, not willing to break their eye contact. Her luxurious hair was long enough for him to loop around his fist, at least twice. His fingers twitched, and he had to hold himself back from the urge to do just that.

There was something about her that called to him with a speed he'd never experienced before. Despite his initial annoyance at getting a hard-on in public over a random woman, his gut told him to unearth whatever this was. His gut never failed him. It was easy enough to follow his instinct, what with the interplay of innocence, wariness, and naughtiness in those soulful eyes of hers. Paired with that sultry body, she was like a siren's call to the sailor within his soul.

He loved her reaction when he'd called her pretty. Like a spitting kitten that had been dunked in a tub of water. There was a spine in that woman. Attitude and grit. But also respect. With Jazz so close by, she wouldn't dare be rude to him, even though his comment had obviously riled her up. A man could tell a lot about a woman if he bothered to pay attention, and Whistle had been trained to read people at a young age. But before he could get into it with her, poke at her a little more, she took the first opportunity to slip away from him.

Run, little girl, run.

The fact that she darted away, especially after that electrifying touch, only made him want to hunt her down. If he was a better man, he should leave her alone. Hell, he should at least warn her. *Run as fast as you can, little girl, 'cause when I get a hold of you, I'm taking you.*

Was she right to be scared? Fuck, yeah, she was. The

hunter in him had reared its head, like a predator catching the scent of prey in the air. It'd be a shame for a woman that fine to slip through his fingers, and he had no intention of letting that happen.

There was something oddly familiar about that girl. He couldn't quite put his finger on. She wasn't Russian, of that he was certain. Yet there was a similarity to the women he'd grown up with. An air of innocence. A gentle smoothness in the way she moved. The way she cocked her head to the side as she watched him. Wary, yet inquisitive. Despite her caginess, she was a curious little kitten. The woman may like to pretend she wasn't affected by him, but when he stared at her long enough, her eyes invariably found his.

This unexpected interest in one specific woman should rattle him. God knows it'd never occurred before. But, truth be told, excitement strummed in the core of his chest. He was more intrigued than anything else. He'd never looked at a woman as a challenge, but this … well, this one was worth pursuing. And the fact that she hid and dodged his attention only whet his appetite. His inner beast licked its chops in anticipation of taking a bite out of that heart-shaped ass of hers.

CHAPTER FIVE

A BOUT A WEEK later, as the employees shuffled in for the evening shift, Whistle called them into the office, one by one, for a "conversation." As everyone milled around the bar, joking as they set the place up for happy hour, Tasa threw Jazz a worried look. "Are you sure everything's alright?"

"You've got nothing to worry about. There's a problem, but it began before you started, so he doesn't suspect you. What would be suspicious is if Whistle didn't bring everyone in for a little one-to-one chat," she murmured discreetly near her ear.

Tasa stilled.

"What is it?" she hissed. If there was a problem, she needed to know ASAP. No way did she want attention thrown on the bar, especially not by the police.

"Can't tell you the details, but someone's not playing nice."

Fidgeting with the strings of her apron, Tasa gulped. "Will the police get involved?"

"Nah-uh. That's not how it works inside a club. Traitors are dealt with internally," Jazz assured her.

Tasa nodded her head in understanding. That was

certainly the way she was familiar with. It was the way things worked in her family, and she was far more at ease with the idea of an internal form of justice. "Okay," she breathed out with relief.

"Tasa," came her name in a familiar, low bass tone that sent a delicious shiver up her spine. Widening her eyes at Jazz, who gave her a reassuring squeeze of the arm, she made her way to Whistle. He studied her carefully as she moved toward him. She noticed his eyes were a few shades darker by the time she reached him. Maybe it was the low lighting in the bar. He gestured for her to precede him down the dark hallway toward the splash of light spilling out of the open door of his office.

She paused at the entrance for a moment, taking in the small, compact space. The place was surprisingly tidy, with files neatly stacked in a steel-mesh divider and a desktop computer on the desk. Choosing one of the chairs facing the desk, she perched on the edge of it, waiting for him to close the door and take his seat. Instead, he motioned toward a small couch pushed up against the far wall. Silently following his direction, she skirted around a low table and took a seat right up against the arm of the couch, making sure to put as much space between them as possible.

He grabbed a few files, dropped them on the low table, and slid into the space beside her with the sleek movements of a large feline. Spreading his arm over the back of the couch, his leather cut creaked as he turned to face her. It was winter, but he wore a short-sleeve black T-shirt that showed off an arm of sculpted muscles covered with tats as intricate as lace. Even the knuckles of his fingers, tapping lightly against the top of the couch, were tatted. She didn't dare inspect them closely, but she was most certainly intrigued. In her world, tats were a man's calling card, stating his *familie*, his profession, even something as specific as the numbers of deaths under his belt. In the normal, civilian world, a woman could still learn quite a lot about a man from the tats he chose.

This was the closest she'd ever been to Whistle for more than a passing moment. Close enough for the distinct scent of leather, clean male, and his own cedar-based aftershave to waft up to her. She shrank back, to protect herself from the seductive assault of his fragrance, but despite her best efforts, her nostrils were suffused with that spicy warmth of his. Her mouth gaped open in a tiny, silent gasp. Inhaling sharply, she promptly realized her mistake when she took in a nose full of his scent.

His riveting eyes locked on her, and a small notch formed between his black brows.

He cocked his head to the side, a small, amused smile lingering on his lips. "You scared of me?"

"What? Of course not," she sputtered, feigning insult.

"Why are you moving away from me, then, baby girl?"

The abraded edge of his voice scraped over her skin like a rough caress. *Baby girl?* She gave her addled mind a sharp, little shake to slough off the lust weaving itself around her and choking her good sense.

"Um, I'm not. I was just making myself comfortable," she boldly lied, squirming a little in her seat as if trying to find just the right spot. A cacophony of sensations rioted through her, and she wasn't used to being assaulted by so many feelings around a man. What made her most wary was the inconvenient tug she felt in her heart. Because she could not, under any circumstances, get attached. It would upend her meticulous plan to leave for Montreal, and after the workshop ended, either stay with Madame Pierrette or go off and conquer the rest of the world. If she felt a magnetic pull right this moment, without knowing him well, what would it be like if she allowed for any intimacy? The first time she saw him, she was determined to keep him off-limits, but it became quickly apparent that this was going to be harder than she'd anticipated.

"You don't look comfortable," he noted. "Fact is, you look scared." He moved closer, causing another wave of his decadent scent to assault her senses. "Is it 'cause I'm a big bad biker?" he taunted in that lilting tone of his.

"No," she scoffed with a hard roll of her eyes. She tossed her head, flicking her hair over her shoulder for good measure. What kind of prim goody-two-shoes priss did she come off as if he dared ask such an absurd question. By no means was she scared of him, even less so because he was a biker. He was a Boy Scout compared to the cold-blooded monsters she grew up around. Her gaze scored down his front. Sure, he was *big*, but in no way did that constitute as *bad*. Angling her head, she spotted the shadows lingering in those vivid eyes of his. Intensity, yes. Maybe a woman who hadn't grown up as she had would've judged him as lethal.

Her? Meh, not so much.

"I'm not scared of you," she assured him.

He made a disbelieving noise in the back of his throat. A sexy-as-hell, toe-curling kind of noise that had her thighs clenching before she could stop it, and she had to consciously relax her muscles and sink deeper into the couch.

His phone vibrated, but he didn't flinch or move an inch to check it. He simply took it out of his back pocket, silenced the ringer, and laid it face-down on the table, his attention utterly focused on her the entire time.

His gaze roved over her face, questing for what, she had no idea. Then it dipped to the deep cut in the clingy long-sleeved shirt she'd borrowed from Jazz. Jazz had been right that showing a little cleavage, along with show-casing her butt in a tight pair of jeans, did wonders for her tips.

"Hmm, you should be a little scared," he murmured low in that gravel tone of his as he inched closer. "If you knew what I wanted to do to you …" He trailed off with a tiny, almost self-conscious shake of his head.

His movements were smooth and relaxed, but she had the distinct sense of being a prey in the crosshairs of a decidedly hungry predator. She didn't know him, but she'd be a fool to mistake this guy as a simple biker, and her *bunica* had certainly not raised an idiot. He may not be like the *mafie* killers of her world, but that in no way meant she should underestimate him. Beneath his relaxed posture were ripples of danger, and she'd been around enough savage men to recognize the signs.

He moved nearer still, and her heart tripped over itself as another wave of his leather-clean-male-cedar fragrance hit her again.

She cleared her clogged throat and cheekily asked, "Why's that?"

"I'm the big bad wolf. Could be bad for your health." He'd gotten so close that his lips were but mere inches from hers. "Or I can be good. Very good to you. Depends on how you wanna play it," he replied smoothly.

"I don't play games," she rasped out through her parched throat. Damn, the way he pressed close into her personal space was doing something awful to her, ratcheting up a whirlwind of nerves. Suddenly, she worried whether he was on to her. Was he somehow connected to or working with Alex and she'd had the wretched luck of falling in his clutches? Was she about to be expedited back to Sunnyside, all hope of freedom lost?

Licking her dry lips, she inquired, "Why don't you tell me what you're talking about?"

His fingers picked at a lock of her long hair and twirled it around his index finger. Tugging it, he brought her face closer to his and whispered, "We're a family here."

Okay, that's not what I expected. "Okaaay, and you're telling me this because?"

"Because I need to know everything about my employees. When Jazz brought you in and vouched for you, you became part of my family. There's a little thief in our family, and it's my job to catch it."

Leaning away until her spine smacked against the arm of the couch, she swore, "I promise you. It wasn't me. I don't have a death wish."

"Didn't say I thought you were the culprit. The stealing started before you showed up on our doorstep like little, lost orphan Annie."

Tasa tried tossing her head back in offense, but his hold on her hair yanked her back in place. She let out a little huff. "I'm hardly lost. I'm most definitely not an orphan, and I'm not a redhead, if you haven't noticed." *Shut up, Tasa.* Maybe if she held her breath and quit scenting him, she'd regain control of her faculties because she was babbling like a mindless idiot.

His beautiful ebony-black brows gathered over his porcelain skin. "In this family, we protect our own. That's what family does." He gave her lock another little tug. "You come to me if you have a problem, if you're in trouble, if you need … anything."

She swallowed hard; the sound audible to her ears. Of course, she couldn't tell him about her situation. He didn't know her from Eve, but he offered her protection because of her connection to Jazz, and she appreciated the gesture. He was either unbelievably cocky, or he was *that* confident in his abilities. Tasa had long ago learned to trust her instincts and her gut told her to lean in toward the latter. If she was right, and this was the kind of man with the means to protect her, it would go a long way toward making her feel safe. After independence, safety was her second priority. And if she wagered a guess, she'd say this was a man who didn't speak out of turn, who didn't boast or preen.

It was the first time since leaving New York that, connected to him by his hold on her hair, her fears melted away like ice cubes on the hood of a car in the blazing summer sun. In that instant, she made the decisive choice to stay in Poughkeepsie and the Squad Bar. She didn't want to bring her brother to their doorstep, but if she hid out for a few months and moved on in the spring, they'd surely stay under his radar.

"I'm not in any trouble," she replied, the touch of his fingers as they raked her hair, scraping her scalp, and pulling her head back, shot electricity straight to her core.

"Mm-hmm," he replied, clearly not believing her. "Seems like I'll have to earn your trust to get a confession out of you. Don't worry, I'll eventually find out every damn thing I want to know, but I'll give you time."

"How gracious of you," she snapped. She might trust him to protect her, but he better not hold his breath for her to crack. No way was *that* going to happen. It dawned on her that he'd been watching her, probably more than the few times she'd caught him staring. She had the odd sensation that she'd been in his sights since the instant she walked through the Bar doors. He may have kept his distance, but he'd been circling her for a while like any good hunter.

She got the uneasy feeling that, having pricked his interest, she wouldn't simply melt back into the woodwork. His curiosity had been ignited, and from the way he looked at her as if she was a meal to be devoured, one slow bite at a time, he wanted her. She knew a predator when she saw one, and this one was on the prowl.

There was a game to play here, and while she hadn't picked up on that fact until it was too late, now her best bet was to play it. And she was going to lap up all the sexually driven attention that came her way. She'd milk this for all she could get. Dispose of that pesky hymen and learn what good sex was really like, because there was no doubt in her mind that Whistle knew his way around the female body. Just their little back-and-forth, testing and teasing, had her thrumming with desire. She was seconds away from melting into a puddle of lust.

"So, how do you expect to *earn* my trust?"

Looping his fist around her hair once, twice, he dragged her close enough for their breaths to intermingle, hot and heavy. His eyes dropped to her lips. Impulsively, she licked them glossy and wet. His scent hit her bloodstream like she'd gotten drunk on the finest, strongest *țuică*, a plum brandy from the old country. His stare, along with his hold on her hair, made her nerves jangle like a caught gazelle.

She went limp against his hold, as any good prey would, and a rumble of approval reverberated through his chest. His lips moved down the side of her face to the shell of her ear. She felt his warm breath as he praised her, "Good. Good girl."

Sharp teeth raked along the curve of her ear and nipped her earlobe. Her eyes squeezed shut, and her thighs clenched hard. Jeez, that was hot. Her cheeks flamed at his compliment, and suddenly, she very much wanted to do exactly whatever this man wanted of her. She wanted to hear the praise coming out of those gorgeous, sculpted lips of his. The very ones that were now skating down the side of her throat. She drew in a ragged breath when his teeth took hold of a sliver of skin and inflicted another nip. Balling her hands, she kept as still as she could, afraid that if she made a sudden move, this fantasy would *poof* … disappear. Because his controlling maneuvers were a wet dream in action.

His other hand smoothed its way up her ribs until it cupped her breast. Tasa never expected to be approached by him, much less touched like this. She was no slouch, but that didn't mean she was in his league. With his looks, he could choose anyone he wanted, and while, sure, she may have fantasized about him more than she'd ever admit aloud, she was too much a realist to anticipate any of *this* happening. But happening it was, and he was moving on her fast.

He hadn't expected any resistance, and she didn't give him any. On the contrary, he'd pried open a Pandora's box by touching her. He'd triggered lust that played out in a filmstrip of explicit images in her mind's eye, of what she wanted him to do next. Kiss her, slide his big hand down her torso and settle between her legs, perhaps. She leaned into his touch until her breast was firmly against his palm, prodding him to move faster still. Answering her prayer, his fingers curled around her tit and squeezed.

Thump.

The knock on the door startled her out of her trance. She tried pulling back, but Whistle's hold on her tightened, keeping her in place.

Brilliant blue eyes locked on her as he called out, "What is it?"

"Puck's on the line. From jail. He said he tried calling your phone, but you didn't answer," came Jazz's voice from the other side of the heavy wood door.

"Alright, have him call me again. I'll pick up," he replied.

"'Kay," she confirmed. Her feet shuffled for a moment before her footfalls retreated down the hall.

"Saved by the bell," he noted coolly as he turned the ringer back on his cell phone. "But this conversation isn't finished, Tasa. I've got my eye on you, so brace yourself. You won't get away so easily next time."

Struggling to draw in a steady breath, Tasa scrubbed a hand through her hair. She felt, oh, so naughty, and it wasn't because she was holding out on him by keeping her secrets.

Staring down on her intently, he demanded, "Nod yes

if you understand."

Her head nodded on its own accord, although she wasn't quite sure what he was talking about. The fog of lust hadn't quite cleared from her brain. Was he talking about her secrets? About sex?

Taking her by the nape, he steadied her head, thumb lodged beneath her chin. "This discussion is not over. Not by a long shot. This—" he flicked his finger between them, "—has just begun, and I have ways of breaking down your resistance. You've been given fair warning."

A slight tremor coursed through her shoulders and sputtered down her spine. *Holy hell, he sounds just like my family.*

"Now, go scurry away like a little rabbit while you have this reprieve."

Tasa narrowed her eyes at him, tugging her head until he released his hold. "I'm not an animal," she balked.

He let out a guttural chuckle that vibrated down to her clit as he said in a rough tone, "Oh, I could tell you were spirited the moment I laid eyes on you, princess."

Her body jolted. *Princess?* Of course, to anyone in her circles, there was no doubt of who she was. A *mafie* princess. But what did he suspect?

Having caught her reaction, Whistle's eyes tapered into slits. Taking hold of her tresses once again, he whispered against her lips, "I see you, baby girl. You may dress in Jazz's clothes, but that's not the world you came from. You're as luxurious as they come, like a mink stole. Soft, expensive." His hand cupped her breast again and tapped her aching nipple. "Lush."

His phone rang, and Tasa jumped, breaking their

staredown. Leaping at the opportunity, she scrambled off the couch, lunged for the door, and ran out of there as fast as she could. Whistle's husky chuckle followed her mockingly as she scampered down the hall and hurried to get ready for her shift.

AFTER DISCONNECTING FROM his call with Puck, Whistle leaned back against the sofa, tapping his cell phone on his thigh. Chortling to himself, he replayed the speed at which Tasa had vaulted to her feet to escape. He shook his head to himself. As if she had a chance in hell. He wasn't lying when he compared her to mink. Her hair, wrapped around his fist, was soft, heavy, and glossy like the finest fur. It had taken a significant amount of effort to let go of it when they'd been interrupted. Putting effort into letting go of a woman? That was new, but he'd known she was different from the beginning. Even now, after ten minutes of talking to Puck, his cock hadn't completely returned to normal.

He'd kept an eye on her throughout the week. Whistle let out a grunt. Like he could've stopped himself. Every time he was in her presence, his eyes were drawn to her. Surreptitiously, he checked her out from behind corners and columns. It was creepy as fuck, but he didn't give a damn. After plotting ways to brush up against her or strike up a conversation here or there, he'd had her right where he wanted her.

Tasa was game, thank fuck. He'd caught the interest in her eyes even before they were alone in his office. The way she'd track him as he crossed the floor, eyes darting away the instant he caught her gaze. Or the way she lingered when he was checking things at the bar. She may not fully realize it yet, but she was drawn to him as well.

Whistle hadn't gotten anything in life without hard work. His career as a young violinist came from five hours of practicing a day. Sure, for the past six years at the club, he'd fucked around, getting into more than his fair share of fights. They were more tests of loyalty to his new family. Didn't help that he loved himself a good brawl. But in his previous life, before the club, and whenever it really mattered with the Squad, he knew the meaning of showing up. The name of the game was diligence, with a heavy dose of stubbornness and arrogance in spades. It had worked for him with everything he'd achieved in this life, and it would work in nabbing Tasa as well.

She was a challenge, and not only because of the secrets she wasn't adept enough at hiding, but because she was as royal as mafia could get. Like the Bratva princesses of his youth, she was used to being draped in diamonds and Chanel, holding the finest vodka between her slim manicured fingers. While Tasa wasn't Russian, he'd bet the cut on his back that she came from a similar world. Which meant that if she was running, which she clearly was, then she was in need of protection. And protection from someone far nimbler at hiding than she was.

Someone like him.

If his hunch was right, then he was dealing with a virgin. Blood oaths were essential to any mafia world such as the one he'd been raised in. While not true of the Bratva, other mafia societies were particular about their women, who were protected and remained virgins until they reached a marriage age. Marriages were generally arranged, and ripping through the maidenhead solidified the couple and, more importantly, their families. It was archaic and borderline sick, but, hey, he didn't make the rules. He did, however, know when to follow them. In any clandestine world, abiding by a regimented set of laws was paramount. It's what kept the savages from devouring each other and what kept their world in the shadows and below the radar.

A blood pact was irrefutable and unchangeable. A husband may cheat a thousand times over. Hell, a wife might have her fun as well. If she survived the retribution for adultery, she'd find herself still bound to her husband until death. There was no such thing as divorce with a virgin bride. If he did what he planned to do, was he prepared to keep her for life? Fuck, yeah, he was.

The way he felt about her had been different from the get-go. A week of watching her and then being with her alone in the office had solidified what he already knew. This woman was special. His gut knew it. Despite oozing sultriness, she was an innocent, and for the first time, it mattered that he would be her first.

A possessiveness griped him by the throat. His cock would be the first to split open her tight pussy. The first it would pulse around as she came with pleasure. He'd revel in watching the lips of her cunt spread around his bare cock the first time he pressed in. Watch as he withdrew, rivulets of pale-red streaking up and down his cock. Watch her slick cleft tighten around his shaft as she arched her back and bucked out her orgasm. As their combined come dripped out of her when he pulled out for good. Because he wouldn't leave until she was dripping from release.

WHISTLE'S WAR

Plus, the look in her eyes was undeniable. She was going to lose her virginity regardless, and he'd be damned if it was to anyone but him.

To another man, fucking her and keeping her might be two different things. It wasn't only the blood she'd shed that made her his. It was loyalty with a capital "L." He may hate Igor, his father, and both of his older brothers, who were made in his depraved image. He despised the cruelty they stood for and the acts of callous violence they engaged in. But true loyalty transcended evil. It couldn't be tainted by their bloody hands. It was as pure as that girl's hymen.

He'd broken his oath to his Bratva family as an act of loyalty to his soul. When he crossed the invisible line from the dark shadows of the Bratva to the sunlit sidewalks of the real world, his one recurring mantra had been "loyalty." Loyalty was the old women in babushkas sitting on wooden crates, selling homemade blinis. Loyalty was his grandfather pouring black tea from the old samovar, its metal hammered from before the Bolshevik Revolution. Loyalty was the thread that underlies the very fabric of society.

Dropping the tattered, frayed thread of clan loyalty on that fateful night on the beach, he'd found it again when he first stepped into the clubhouse. He'd recognized it instantly. It was as if he'd picked up where he'd left off in Brighton Beach, the night of his last kill, when he offed the owner of the corner fruit-and-vegetable stand for not fulfilling his loan terms as quickly as his father expected. Even though Whistle had gone to elementary school with the man's daughter, Anya, for Christ's sake.

That night, he'd announced to his father that he'd never kill senselessly again. Throwing the knife into the

55

crashing waves, he sloughed through the cold, wet sand and climbed onto the boardwalk, where he stomped on the wooden boards to shake off the grains of sand.

Stalking off, he never looked back. A honed weapon who knew how to kill at the drop of a hat, he swore he'd never kill again unless there was no other alternative.

Ever the cunning bastard, his father had let Whistle go in a calculated chess-inspired move to regain his queen. With him gone, his father hoped to re-take his place at the center of his mother's affections. She was the only person that cold fucker ever loved. Since it gave Whistle freedom, he didn't disabuse his father of his delusion because she could never love him again after discovering what a monster he was.

When he looked at Tasa, it was as if he'd tripped on that pesky thread again, picked it up, and recognized it for what it was. Loyalty. She had his, whether she wanted it or not. She was certainly in need of it. He'd understood instantly that she was running from someone. Hell, it was his story after all. He'd recognized the signs. The twitch of an eye when he talked about finding out her secrets, or the nervous jolt when he'd called her princess.

His protective instincts had been roused, and he was well aware that once that happened, he was all in. There'd be no staying in his lane. He'd tear down anyone who tried to hurt her.

Mine, his soul called out, and no real man turned away from the Russian soul within calling out for their woman.

CHAPTER SIX

"**S**O, WHAT HAPPENED?" Jazz asked, her hand reaching out to steady Tasa's quivering body. Peering into her face, she asked with concern, "Hey, are you okay?"

"Yeah, yeah," Tasa stammered out, slipping away from Jazz, and going behind the bar to put away the dried glasses.

"Okaaay," her friend said with a trace of doubt in her tone. "I know what this is. It happens often enough that you shouldn't be embarrassed." Tasa glanced up at her in confusion. "Whistle has that effect on women."

A laugh punched out of her. Good God, was she that obvious? While she was rattled by the way he wormed into her soul and the very real risk that he'd ferret out her secrets, she was far more concerned about the way her body reacted to him. She wouldn't be able to rebuff his attentions. The possessive gleam in his eyes was another worry. The whole point of cutting herself off from her entire family and Nina was to become independent. Then again, perhaps it was a figment of her imagination. He was a biker, for Pete's sake.

Grabbing a cloth, she forcefully rubbed a glass clean of any residue smudges. On the plus side, now that she was an independent woman, she could finally get rid of her virginity. She didn't have to worry about Whistle having antiquated notions of honor with respect to virgins. He wouldn't know about that, much less accept the notion of a blood bond that having sex with a virgin would trigger in her world.

Besides her curiosity, she was another step in her new lease on life. He obviously believed in that song and dance about "family" that he'd given her, but Tasa was more than confident in her ability to keep her secrets close. She was used to men underestimating a woman's power, and of all the times in her life, she could not afford to crack now. Not with her freedom on the line.

Something in Jazz's tone, a strain of wistfulness when she spoke of Whistle, had Tasa turning her attention back to her friend. *Oh, no. There's history between them.* How had she not thought of it before?

"You seem to know a lot about Whistle and his effect on women. I'm assuming you two were together?"

"Me and every other bitch in the club." She snorted. "Plus half of the city of Poughkeepsie."

Tasa pursed her lips. If Jazz was attached to him, then she'd have to re-assess Operation Lose The Hymen with him.

Focused on Tasa, Jazz must have seen the look on her face because she shook her head vehemently in response. "No, no, you do what you want. And you want him. I can tell. Hate to say it, but more importantly, he wants you, and Whistle gets what he wants. Especially when it comes to women," she concluded.

"Oh, yeah?" Tasa scoffed. She wasn't a dog to be collared and leashed by a man.

Jazz's hand landed on Tasa's arm. "Seriously, Tasa. I've known him for years. We're more like friends with benefits. Whistle isn't the kind who settles down with one woman. If you want to hit that, then hit it. No skin off my nose. The essence of being with Whistle means to share him. It's the way of the Demon Squad, and more importantly, it's one of Whistle's rules."

"I don't want any drama," she fretted.

"Please, bitch. I'm the last person to start drama. I say it like it is, and I'm telling you, there's nothing between me and Whistle. We're good friends and we've fucked. That's all."

Damn. Having been kept tucked away as a virgin to the point where even when she'd had the chance with her vocal instructor, she still walked away with that intact, she was a little envious of Jazz's free-spiritedness. It was something she aspired to. Casting her head down, Tasa scraped off a little bit of scum from the bottom of a pint glass. There was more. She'd seen the way Jazz's eyes followed Whistle around. She may not be willing to admit it, even to herself, but Jazz had caught feelings for him.

"I don't know …" she hesitated.

"Tasa," Jazz warned. "I'm not into that societal bullshit when it comes to relationships. That's society's way of keeping women down."

Tasa huffed out a little laugh. Jazz didn't know the half of what kept women down. If she thought monogamy was "societal bullshit," what would she think about arranged marriages?

"What I love about the Squad is that everyone's free to

do what they want. Whistle's clear with every woman he's with. They don't have claims on him, and he makes no claims on them." She arched her brows. "Are you sure that's something you can handle?"

"Oh, I'm more than sure. In a few months, I'll be on my way. I'm not setting down roots in Poughkeepsie when I've barely begun my life's adventure. I want to travel the world. I definitely don't want to be locked down to some dude at the age of twenty. Sheesh, that would be a travesty."

"Okay, good. Then, we're on the same page."

Tasa blew out a little sigh. This was already getting complicated. There were enough unattached men out there that she didn't have to get stuck on Whistle. But the image of his eyes, the turquoise deepening to a darker shade as they locked to hers on that damn sofa, shimmered in her mind. She had the uneasy suspicion it'd be a travesty *not* to indulge in him if given half a chance.

"Let's see, Jazz. Who knows if anything will happen," she returned, as she walked farther behind the bar.

"Don't worry about that," Jazz hummed behind her. "It's happening."

TASA SHOULD'VE HEEDED Jazz's warning.

If she had, she wouldn't have been caught off guard after her shift was over. The last of the kitchen staff had come back from disposing the garbage bags in the dumpster in the back. Throwing up his hand for a goodbye wave, he ducked out the back door, leaving her alone.

Exhaustion dragged at her muscles. Without a ride, Tasa would have to wait for the bus, in the freezing cold, to get back to the apartment. Untying her apron, she pushed open the door leading into the storage room to dump it in the basket of dirty linens. She flicked the switch. Once. Twice. The light didn't come on. Groaning, she turned the switch off, propped the door open, and with light from the hallway, rummaged around until she found a carton of bulbs. Dragging a stool toward the bare light socket swinging from the center of the ceiling, she unscrewed the burned-out bulb. She may be a princess, but Tasa had prepped herself for the real world. Rebuffing her mother's insistence that she have a servant, aka a snitch, at the apartment she shared with Nina, she'd learned to keep the place clean and do her own damn laundry, thank you very much. An ole itty-bitty light bulb? Pfft.

Suddenly, a body blocked half the light coming from the open door. A gasp rushed out from her parted lips. She clutched at her chest.

Whistle.

She let out a long sigh. *That's right, Whistle's often at the Bar.* If she recalled correctly, he sometimes slept there in his quest to catch the thief.

Blinking down at him, her eyes adjusted to the additional darkness. "Jesus, you scared the living daylights out of me."

Backlit from the glow in the hallway, there was a halo crisply outlining his head of inky curls. He took a step inside and his broad shoulders and solid torso cut off more light, plunging the room in darkness. A shadow across his face hid his brilliantly colored eyes, but a bright slash of light illuminated the upward tilt of his lips into a smirk. Goose bumps skittered down her arms.

Prowling toward her, he griped her hip to steady her, searing her skin through the thin material of her skirt and tights. Glaring up at her, he complained, "You shouldn't be here alone, in the darkness, teetering on a shaky stool."

To prove his point, he shook her lightly, and the stool wobbled beneath her. Her hands flew out and grasped his shoulders for stability.

Letting out a nervous giggle, she chided him breathlessly, "Stop it."

"Go on, finish up. I'll make sure you don't fall."

"Fine," she huffed out and finished switching out the bulbs.

"Give it to me," he said, palm out. She handed him the dead light bulb, and he tossed it onto a shelf. "Something I've been curious about," he began.

"Oh, yeah? What's that?" she asked, although her voice resembled more of a rasp. The air between them had shifted into something dark, much like the dimly lit room they stood in. She was tempted to reach out and touch, to rake her fingers through his enticingly soft curls. Her heart hammered against her breastbone.

Suddenly, a hand landed on her calf. She let out a little gasp. It glided up to the back of her knee before halting. His thumb caressed the spot. Back and forth. Back and forth. A rushing sound flooded her eardrums as heat spiked in her core from the intimacy of that small, light caress.

"Been wondering if you were turned on earlier today. In the office."

"What? No, o-of course n-not." *Grrr.* That sounded

ridiculously false, even to her ears. She'd never been great at lying. Omitting things, no problem. Bold-faced lies, not so much. The truth of the matter was that she'd been wet, on and off, since she left his office. Even now, she knew she should stop breathing because his beguiling scent of leather and musk was twining itself around the rational part of her brain and squeezing the life out of it. If she weren't afraid that the lack of air would tip her off the stool, she'd have taken the chance.

His palms lifted off her, and she whimpered in protest, swaying a little on the stool.

He immediately returned them, one wrapped around the back of her thigh. "See how this is gonna work, right? You answer honestly, and you get what you want. You lie, and you get punished."

"Punished?" she squeaked out.

"Oh, yeah. It'll be more than removing my touch. Lying to me is never a good thing, Tasa." His voice dropped into what could only be described as a sexy growl. "Can't abide liars. That's not the way toward a healthy relationship. There are rules to being with me, and disciplinary action is the best way of making sure those rules are understood. And followed." *Relationship? Rules? What the hell was he talking about? Disciplinary action. Hmm … the last one's the most interesting.*

"Alright, let's start again."

"I was being honest," she protested because he was already arrogant as hell. She wasn't about to add to what was surely a huge ego, if she could help it.

The hand around her hip curled tighter, but the other one slipped off her and landed hard on her right buttock.

"Oww!" she cried out.

"Still don't get it? You lie, you get a corrective touch. You speak the truth, and … well …" He trailed off as his hand slid up her leg and rubbed the spot he'd just walloped over her panties. Another sexy growl. "Damn, I feel the heat coming off you from that one tap. Imagine if I smack that ass until it's cherry-red." She jerked in his hold. "Responsive, aren't you?" His fingers slipped under her panties and gripped her buttock. He patted it lightly. "Cheeky little thing is in need of another love tap. Bet it's a nice shade of pink for me already."

Her entire body felt as if it'd gone up in flames, heat licking at her skin like she'd been plopped into the middle of a bonfire. Hips twitched against her will; her body wanted to follow his commands like a marionette. His fingers kneaded into her flesh, and she had to suppress a moan. Her head swiveled around to look at him, but his face was hidden in a dark shadow, and she couldn't tell what he was thinking.

"It's a simple ask, Tasa. Alright, let's start easy. Do you like what I'm doing to you right now?"

Her eyelids dropped to half-mast, and her mouth gaped to take in deep breathes of air. Did she like it? Was that a real question, or was he simply taunting her? She'd expected to have sex. What she hadn't expected was for him to seduce her, to school her, to play her like a musical instrument.

Dizzy, she stuttered, "Y-yes." Seriously, that was the best she could do?

"See, that wasn't so bad."

Suddenly, her skirt was lifted and tucked into her

waistband, cool air rushing past her heated skin. Yanking down her panties, he sunk his teeth into her butt cheek. A little yelp escaped. Then, his tongue lathed it all better.

"Now, let's go back to my original question. Where you wet earlier?"

"Yes," she replied, stronger this time as anticipation of a reward flooded her.

"What a good little princess you are. Fuck yeah, you were wet. I could practically smell your cream from where I was sitting, and all I wanted to do was to spread those thighs and get a look at that little pink gash of yours. Sink my tongue in your tight wet hole. Bet it was ripe for me, wasn't it, baby?"

She blinked down at him, stunned. Did he just say those words to her? Never had a man spoken to her like that. And, boy, it was hotter than she'd ever thought possible.

"Yeah, it was," he repeated, his hand cupping her pussy, middle finger toggling her clit. "So fuckin' wet," he murmured against the skin of her ass as his thick finger sunk in deep, past the second knuckle. His eyes fell to half-mast, blocking out even more of his irises. His mouth dropped open as he rasped out, "Your tight cunt's squeezing the fuck out of my finger. Imagine what that hot, silky pussy will do wrapped around my cock."

She shifted a little on her feet, widening her shaking legs to adjust to his thick finger. It wasn't the first time she'd been fingered, but it'd been a while. He pulled out and then added another digit on the way back in. The sucking noise of his thrusting digits was the only sound in the dead silence of the room. He curled a finger that hit a spot she'd been looking for, in like, *for*ever. She'd long come to the conclusion that she didn't own one, like normal women, because months of messing around with her vocal teacher or on her own had led to nothing. Apparently, it'd only been under wraps, waiting for the man with the magic fingers to find it.

Her body shuddered, and she shook on the stool. "Whistle, I'm going to fall." Her hands grabbed at the socket and light bulb.

He chuckled darkly. "Better hold on tight, baby girl, 'cause I'm not nearly done."

"What if someone comes," she breathed out. She thought they were alone, but anyone could walk in. She didn't want to be caught by a coworker with her skirt up and her panties down, ass exposed to the world.

She felt him stiffen behind her. As if insulted, Whistle ground out, "Are you fuckin' kidding me? No one will ever see you like this but me. This is for me, only *me*." There he went again, using possessive words that muddled her brain. But she couldn't focus on those words when he played her body like a virtuoso. Between his fingers curling inside her, his thumb strumming her clit, and his teeth and tongue tattooing her ass, she came within minutes. Back arching, a throaty cry ripped out of her throat. Pitching forward, she clung onto the socket with both hands, praying it didn't break off, as waves of intense pleasure crashed over her. A frenzy overtook her as she banged his fingers, riding them hard. He did something, grinding down harder, and her body jerked in place. She squeezed her eyes, tightening her grip around the socket as bright fireworks exploded behind her eyelids.

Her pussy clenched harder, milking his fingers, and he murmured, "That's right. Let that good little pussy come."

Oh God. That deep growl of his when he spoke brought a shudder down her spine. Unable to hold on any longer, she blindly let go of the light socket, and her butt slid down and landed against his chest.

Pulling his delicious fingers out of her, he wrapped an arm around her waist, holding her close as his thumb played with her while aftershocks ricocheted through her like bullets. She stared blurrily at his forearm, tendons shifting as he adjusted her.

Gasping for breath, the stool finally toppled over, and she was swept into his arms, panties dangling off one shoe.

CHAPTER SEVEN

F UCK, WATCHING TASA come apart was a thing of beauty. Sure, Whistle had made many a woman come, but he'd never felt anything like the pride puffing up his chest at knowing he'd put that blissed-out look on her face. If he had to guess, this was her first orgasm. Knowing he'd brought her to those heights filled his heart to bursting.

And it was just the beginning. Imagine what he could do when he got his tongue or cock inside her. He'd felt the thin membrane when he'd fingered her, and like the scent of the kill, it had forged an intense desire of possession inside him.

Whistle carried her to the bar and sat her bare ass on a stool, skirt still tucked into her waistband. The stunned expression on her face made him want to pound his chest in triumph. He restrained himself, barely. Grabbing his bottle of *Stoli Elit* from the freezer, he poured two shot glasses of vodka.

Holding it up, he toasted, "To your first orgasm," and slammed it back.

Tasa's head whipped in his direction. Her mouth parted, eyes sparkling, the speckles of green particularly bright at the moment. He regretted he'd pulled her out of her daze. She looked fucking sexy as all hell, hair mussed up and eyes glazed over. He loved the way she lost control and her curves fell against him when she tipped off the stool, and he relished carrying her soft body as he walked to the bar.

"How did you know?"

He gave a little shrug. "Educated guess. You confirmed it."

"Ahh." She picked up her glass and sipped it daintily, her little finger dangling in the air.

Christ, what a princess.

"So, you're Russian?" she said casually. Too casually. But Whistle didn't have anything to hide. Not anymore. Not like her.

"I am." He gave her a straight stare. "What are you?"

She fidgeted in her seat. Realizing she was sitting bare-butt, she made a tsking noise and stood up to bring her skirt down.

"Don't," he intoned, his voice scratchy with want. He liked knowing she was bare and available to him, her cream painting the insides of her thighs. He fucking envied the top of that wooden stool, knowing her ass was sitting on it. Couldn't wait till he had her cheeks filling his hands while she sat on his face. All that sweet, sticky honey of hers dripping down on him. *Patience, motherfucker, patience.*

Her pert nose scrunched up. "Don't what?"

"Don't pull your skirt down."

"What the—" Smart girl, she didn't fight him or even bother finishing her question. Eyes flaring with lust, she simply settled back down slowly.

He moved around the bar and wrapped his hand on her

knee. Squeezing lightly, he ordered, "Spread your legs open so I can see the little pearl I made so needy and wet."

She took a sharp intake of breath. A sign that she liked his domineering talk was that her little clit swelled even larger.

"You didn't think I was done with you, now, did you? Tut, tut, tut. I'm not that much of a saint."

Her eyes dropped to his package, where he was sporting a hard-on he'd been struggling with since she ran off. She wasn't going anywhere until he said so.

"You're a hot little thing, aren't you, baby girl? It came off you the instant I got close, like your scent of honey and everything sweet." Leaning in, he nuzzled the wisps of hair on her temple and murmured, "How do you want it next? You wanna bounce on my cock or have me tongue that little clit of yours?" His lips drifted down to her throat, following the movement of her muscles as she gulped.

Then his hand fell, slipping between her thighs, and cupped her. "Fuck, that feels good."

Moaning, she dipped her head forward, her lips brushing against the bristles of his cheek. Her head snapped back, and her gaze got caught up in his. The golden-green highlights of her brown irises glittered as he brought his head up to cover her lips with his. He pressed his mouth against hers, pressuring her to open, but she wouldn't. She wanted to, he could tell by the way she fidgeted under him, but something was holding her back.

She twisted away and rasped out, "No kissing."

His nostrils flared. Narrowed eyes shot off sparks of fury. *What the fuck?* His soul roared out. Although his heart was thrashing about in his chest like an enraged animal battering against prison bars, his brain clicked in place. Why should he care? He was a biker, for fuck's sake. He didn't care about something as ludicrous as *kissing*. Granted, she was an enigma, but he'd ferret out her secrets soon enough, and he'd get her underneath him even sooner. He shouldn't care, but his soul seethed at her no-kissing rule. She was his, dammit.

Pinching her chin, he turned her face toward him. Chewing her plush bottom lip, Tasa blinked up at him. He didn't try to hide his feelings, and after having read his expression, she promptly broke eye contact and tried to twist away from him, but he wouldn't allow it.

"I don't like to be told what I can and cannot have," he snarled, feeling particularly irate at being foiled in anything that had to do with access to her. He hated to be denied. "I *take* what I want," he seethed.

"Sheesh, let go of the ego already. It's not a reflection on you, Whistle. God, believe me when I tell you, you're the sexiest man alive, but it's not something I can do," she replied, eyes pleading for understanding, which he did not have. Understanding and pity were not high on his list at that instant.

"Why not?"

"Does it matter?" she shot back.

It shouldn't matter was the underlying commentary beneath that simple question, but the hand cupping her pussy tightened possessively. His eyes flicked away from her. Unfortunately for both of them, it did matter. He'd never felt this way about a woman. So primal and inexplicable. He didn't know her well, but that didn't seem to matter, because he knew one thing clearly. Once he fucked her, she would be his for good. And fuck her, he would. She didn't want to kiss him? She wanted to preserve some barriers between the two of them? Fucking fine, then. Kissing or no kissing, he'd proceed with phase one of his plan and railroad her by using her attraction for him against her.

Go ahead, keep your kisses. He'd make sure she'd come to regret it on her own and beg him for them. Anyway, there was more than one kind of kiss for her to get addicted to, and he planned to leave her as mindless for him as a heroin addict in withdrawal.

His gaze returned to hers. "It doesn't." He reminded himself he hadn't yet earned her trust. As of now, there was nothing between them. No foundation. No conversation, even. Nothing but this moment.

But that would change if he had anything to say about it. Until then, she could keep her little show of control.

"Okay." She breathed out a pent-up sigh of relief.

"You don't want to kiss. Not a problem, but understand this, princess. I command the rest of you, especially this tight cunt." He tightened his hold on her hot pussy. "And you're not leaving this office without getting marked."

"Marked?" she squeaked, confusion entering her eyes. "W-what does that mean?"

"You'll see," he warned, a low edge to his voice.

"But why?"

"Because, Tasa," he replied in disgust. "You're so wrapped up in your secrets you don't notice other men crushing on you, but I'm not the sharing type."

"That's ridiculous," she huffed out. "Sure, we flirt and

tease each other, but no one's taken any notice of me besides *you*."

He swiped a hand over his eyes. With the curves she was sporting and those tilted cat eyes that had specks of green embedded in deep brown, she thought no one noticed her but him? Christ, she was oblivious.

Eyes flashing back to her, a muscle ticked in his jaw. "It's not up for discussion."

"If we're laying down rules, then maybe we should define a little bit more what this is—" she cleared her throat, "—between us."

His middle finger strained forward, parting her lower lips and putting a kind of pressure that had her twitching under his ministrations.

"This is us fucking, whenever and however we want." He bent his head, his lips sweeping across hers. "I'm warning you, I'll want it a lot. I'm a demanding asshole. And take care, make sure you keep this only for me."

"I didn't think you claimed anyone, in any fashion." Pulling slightly away from him, she raised her chin proudly. "But if that's how you want it, then it goes both ways. As the only girl and the youngest in my family, I've never been great at *sharing*. Jazz told me you never commit, so I would've done the open thing to be with you, but if you're going to put a limit on me, then it will have to be mutual."

He almost laughed. It hadn't occurred to him that he may want another woman. Sure, let her think otherwise. It was an easy give, but he'd make it seem like it was a fucking sacrifice and build off of it at a later time.

"It's a huge ask, but I'll concede it, for you," he emphasized with a chin lift in her direction. "For as long as this lasts between us, it's just the two of us."

"Alright, I'm good with that."

With a sardonic twist of his lips, he asked, "Ready?"

Without waiting for a reply, he pressed her thighs wider and moved between them. Lifting her off the stool, he waited until she was steady on her feet and pulled her shirt up and over her head. Dropping it on the bar, he placed his hand at the base of her throat and caressed down to cradle her full breast in the palm of his hand. Nice. Flicking a pert nipple over the delicate silk mesh of her bra, he unclasped it and stole it off her.

Bending over, he sucked that little bud deep in his mouth. Her fingers gripped and clawed at his shoulders. The little digs of her kitten nails urged him on, but he wasn't going faster than he intended. He rolled the other nipple between his thumb and forefinger, once, twice, a third time before pinching hard. She wheezed out a little scream. More surprise than pain, he guessed by the sound. Then his tongue swept over it to make it feel all better.

Stepping away, he ordered, "Place your hands on the bar."

Hands on her waist, she cocked a hip out and complained, "I'm sick and tired of taking orders. From anyone, Whistle. Just in case it's not obvious, that includes you."

He prodded her in the shoulder toward the bar. With a loud huff, she slapped her hands on the wooden bar with a resounding thud. Moving in behind her, he bent over and whispered against her ear, "If you're a good girl and do what you're told, I'll make it worth your while."

"What, with money?" she scoffed. "I may need money, but I'm not a whore."

A disgruntled noise came from the back of his throat. "No, Tasa, with pleasure."

She sucked in a harsh breath.

"I don't want to hear you talk that way about yourself. Ever. Unless you wanna feel leather stripes against your ass."

Without realizing it, she'd divulged that she was in need of resources. Soon, she'd learn that he'd take care of her every need.

"Trust me," he said in a low rumble.

A frown puckered between her brows. Her hands slipped off as she looked at him over her shoulder.

"Hands. On. The. Bar." A hint of impatience laced his tone.

She inhaled a shaky breath. Slowly, she lifted her hands and placed them, palms flat, on the smooth, worn surface of the bar.

"Good, princess," he breathed, his hot breath fanning her cheek. "Tonight, I'm not fucking you like the princess you are, the way you deserve to be fucked. With candlelight and roses. Our first time won't be like what you should have. I'm taking you how *I* want. And I wanna hear you screaming my name, loud and fuckin' clear."

A shudder overtook her shoulders at his command. Damn, she was a perfect dirty little girl. Pressing kisses along the side of her throat, he bit, nipped, and sucked until he'd marked her as promised. He was nothing if not a man of his word. Hand rubbing her pussy, he inserted one finger and then two, stretching out the little crevice of her tightness. Tasa was as untried as they got. Christ*fuck*, it was going to hurt. Whistle was by no means a small man. Her slick heat might coat his fingers completely. She might be primed for him, what with her earlier orgasm, but there was no doubt that she was a virgin.

Unbuckling his belt, he asked, "You on birth control?"

"Yes," she breathed out as her walls quivered around his fingers.

He flicked her little clit. "Good, I'm clean. We're going bare."

"What? I don't know if that's a good idea."

"I've got no cause to lie to you, Tasa. I'm a man of my word, and I've never gone without a rubber before, so I know I'm clean, but if you want, I'll use one."

"Never?"

He shook his head.

A notch toggled between her brows for a moment but then smoothed over. "Why now?"

His eyes pulled up to the ceiling. Was he willing to admit what a pig he was? Fuck yeah, he was. His gaze returned to her, and he held her eyes. "Because you're a virgin. I've never had a virgin before, and I wanna see your blood streaking my cock. Now you know. I'm a fucking savage, and it turns me the fuck on."

"Holy hell," she breathed out. "I got goose bumps everywhere."

"Yeah, that's cause you're as *filthy* as me, baby girl. So, we good?"

"Yeah."

"Thank fuck." He wanted to feel her, every inch of her, with nothing between them. She'd imposed enough barriers between them, and he was intent on reducing as many of them as possible. What he didn't tell her, what she didn't know yet, was that no one else was ever going in after him. He'd be her one and only. That was the other reason he was going bare. She'd be his one and only as well.

Pushing his jeans off his narrow hips, his cock jutted out, ready to play. Sliding his hand down her ribs to the nip of her waist, it smoothed over the curve of her luscious ass. He spread her pussy lips open and notched the crown of his cock at her opening. Swiping the flared tip back and forth at the entrance of her slick heat, he let out a shuddering breath. He pressed up, breaching her tight flesh, watching it stretch under his invasion. *Fuck*, the tip of his cock buried in her was a sight of goddamn beauty. And no doubt about it, she was *tight*. Tight enough that he could feel the press of her strong inner muscles, committed to keeping him out. But there was no way that was happening.

Tasa tensed up, so he nuzzled his face in her sweet, honey-scented hair. Damn, he just got a whiff of what she'd taste like on his tongue, and he was more than eager.

But one thing at a time.

Cooing near her ear, she began to relax again, and just as she did, he took advantage and drove in an inch. Then another. Her flesh clamped around his shaft, fighting his penetration. Digging into his reserve of patience, he blew out his breath.

"Princess, you've got the tightest cunt I've ever had the privilege of fucking."

"Whistle!" she cried, although she was more turned on than shocked by the rapid rising and falling of her chest.

"Fuck, but it's true," he grunted. Although, he'd already broken through the seal of her hymen, she was still incredibly tight. He controlled his thrusts, keeping them strong enough to shove through her resistance while measured enough to minimize her pain. "Babe, you have to relax and let me in."

"It doesn't bother you …?" she panted out, her fingers gouging the wood, leaving behind long, ragged tracks. "That I'm a virgin?"

"The only thing that bothers me is that I might hurt you. But nothing's gonna stop me from drilling into that tight heat, princess." He thrust in again, hard. "*Nothing.*"

It was obscene almost, the way his thick dick crammed inside her tight channel. He pulled out and caught sight of the streaks of blood. *Fuuuck.* Swerving her around, he grabbed her ass and hiked her up around his waist.

Against her lips, he said through clenched jaws, "You might have to kiss me, this one time. I need you to relax. You're too tight, and I need you as relaxed and open as possible so you'll let me in and take your mind off the pain."

Her eyes flared wide, and she looked away. After a few torturous seconds of gnawing at her bottom lip, her eyes flashed back to him. "This one time?"

"Yeah," he rasped and immediately dipped his head. His tongue parted her lips easily. Her taste was intoxicating, like the finest vodka. She groaned against his mouth, laving and sucking at his tongue. Fuck, she sure knew how to kiss. He felt another gush of desire coat his dick. She was ready.

Taking her hips, he tilted her up and pushed in again, this time going all the way until his balls rested against her ass, catching her pained cry in his mouth. Finally bottomed out, nothing felt as good as Tasa. He scoffed at most traditions of his youth, but the primal beast residing in his chest was roaring to beat its chest in triumph. He'd never known anything like this before, but deep inside, the protector reared its head, sniffing the air as if it had caught the scent of its mate. Whistle had always had a penchant for loyalty and there was no denying it. She was his.

Once in, he froze. Not moving a muscle, he broke their kiss and croaked, "Fuck, baby, are you okay?"

Her nails clawed into his shoulder as she flexed her newly stretched inner muscles around his shaft. He groaned into her shoulder but held still until she released a gust of air over his nape.

"Okay." She nodded and gusted out, "Now."

"Brave girl," he murmured near her ear.

After taking one last moment to revel in the victory of breaching her, he picked up an easy rhythm. Tweaking her clit, he had her swiveling her hips in a circle eight meant to drive him insane. His thrusts got deep and stronger. He buried his face in her hair, clamping his jaws together to hold on.

Lifting his head, he growled, "Tell me, Tasa, tell me what you want."

"You … I … want you," she replied raggedly between pants.

He pulled out, leaving her pussy clenching on air. Her head flew up. "What the—"

His cheek came flush against hers and snarled in her ear, "What. Do. You. Want?"

His breath fanned over her cheek.

Her nostril flared. "Your cock. Now. Fuck me with your cock. Hard."

"Thatta girl."

His hand tangled in her hair and tugged it back as he speared her with his cock, hard and deep.

"Hold on," he warned, thrusting and withdrawing, his pace ticking up faster and faster.

"Harder," she screamed.

So the princess liked a stab of pain.

Tongue sweeping between her lips again, his cock stretched her, pummeling the walls of her glorious clutch as he fucked her rough and raw. Miracle of miracles, the proof that she was made for him came with the intensity of her climax. Her entire body tightened as her flesh rippled against his. Her head tore away, and she screeched out his name as her fingers scored down his sides and tore at his shirt. As her tight sheath pulsed around him, and with his balls slapping against her ass, he shot into her. Moaning into the dip of her shoulder, his teeth latched on and bit down as he spilled his hot come. That had to be the hardest he'd ever come, and he was no stranger to fucking hard.

Unlatching her flesh from his teeth, he dropped his head, the slickness on his forehead melding with the sheen of perspiration between her perfect tits.

It was done.

Now, she was his.

Forever.

He hoped she had a clue of what his ownership meant.

CHAPTER EIGHT

HO-LY. SHE'D DONE it. She'd finally lost her virginity. Their harsh breaths blended together in the silence of the empty bar. Tasa pried one eye open and glanced down at the ebony curls of Whistle's head as he caught his breath against her chest. Wow, if this was sex, then she was down for lots more of it. A small niggling thought snaked into her brain that it was only this good because it was Whistle, but she shoved it roughly away.

She could do this, as long as she didn't kiss him again. She could have sex and not fall for him. Not get so attached that she wouldn't be able to leave him when the time came. As long as she swore to herself that she'd do whatever was in her power to keep that one barrier to intimacy with him. If she allowed another kiss, then it was equivalent to waving a white flag. It'll be undeniable proof that she'd fallen down the rabbit hole and given up her dreams. For a man. Which was not happening.

Thus, the rule.

He lifted his head, and she got momentarily lost in his translucent exotic eyes. A languid, gushy, warm feeling meandered through her body. Her eyes fluttered closed. She was so tired she wanted to drop wherever she was and go to sleep.

"I have to get home."

"I'm taking you."

"No, that's not necessary," she insisted, pushing against his chest.

He caressed the side of her face. "If there was a good place, I'd keep you here to crash, but I've been sleeping on a cot or the couch in the office. No way I'm putting you there. I know where Jazz lives. Not only am I taking you home, but I'm staying over. You shouldn't be alone tonight."

"I don't know about that …"

"It's a Friday night. Jazz left for the clubhouse after her shift, and I'd stake my life on her staying over there with one of the brothers. It's past two o'clock, Tasa. You're not going home alone, and you're not staying there alone either."

She was no stranger to protectiveness. Maybe, at some point in the future, she'd argue for the sake of it because his authoritative tone was irritating, but it was late and she was exhausted. After a crazy shift, having her first orgasm while hanging onto a light bulb, and losing her virginity, she was wiped out. If she was honest with herself, she'd admit to wanting to spend the night with his divine body wrapped around her.

"Alright, alright."

After cleaning up in the bathroom, she dressed and found Whistle waiting at the back door, tapping his keys against his jean-clad thigh.

Thrusting a helmet in her hands, he asked, "Ever ride before?"

"Yeah, my twin has a Ducati."

He grunted in disgust and shoved the door open for her. His bike was a Harley of some sort. As Nicu had taught her, they were the Cadillacs of bikes. Her heart shifted in her chest. This was the longest she'd ever gone without talking to Nicu. Damn Alex. If he'd been more understanding, she wouldn't have had to run and cut off all contact with her family.

Settling in behind Whistle, she breathed out deeply and soaked in the vibration of the seat beneath her as the loud pipes rumbled, and they were off. She was surprised when he nailed the throttle and the bike went from zero to sixty in seconds and they were racing down the empty Pough-keepsie streets toward her apartment.

By the time they arrived, her body was thrumming with excitement. It'd been a couple of years since Nicu had driven fast with her on the back. She got off on rubbery legs, and Whistle's hand shot out to steady her. Chuckling, he followed her up the path to her apartment building, his eyes sweeping up and down the street, inspecting every shadow as she fiddled with the key.

"Shit lock," he grumbled as he flicked his finger over the handle when she opened the second door into the vestibule.

"Well, there are two doors."

"Doesn't matter if someone gets to you while you're stuck between them."

Not bothering to answer, she simply rolled her eyes and took the stairs to the second floor. They entered the apartment decorated in what she'd call boho chic. Besides the haphazard collection of Ikea furniture, Jazz was into music, and the centerpiece of her living room was shelves of LPs and a record player. Jazz posters of legends like Thelonious Monk and John Coltrane graced the walls.

Throwing her coat on the couch, Tasa walked straight back to her room, stripped, threw on a silk nightie, and let herself fall backward on the mattress and box spring that lay on the floor. On the walls was Jazz's dedication to women jazz singers, starting with Bessie Smith and ending with Nina Simone. She threw an arm over her eyes and let her tired and well-used body sink deep into the mattress.

Letting out a sigh of relief, she shouted out, "You can stay over, but don't think we're going to do anything but sleep. I'm exhausted."

She lifted her arm and peered over toward the doorway of her room. Whistle was leaning against the doorjamb, his hair tousled from the ride. Folding his arms over his chest, he rumbled, "No worries. I know you must be sore and bruised from the way I pounded into you."

"Oh my God, you did not just say that," she rebuked as she leveled him with a bruising look. Although she ruined her flawless expression of annoyance when one corner of her lips ticked up.

Pushing off, he prowled toward her as he stripped his shirt off. Her mouth went dry. Did she say she was tired? She should take that back because every cell in her body was humming with giddiness. She wanted to lick up and down the solid, sculpted six-pack of his torso. Devouring the sight of his chest, her eyes slowly focused on his tats.

She shot off the bed.

"What the hell are those?" she screamed, her index finger pointing to the tats below his clavicles. Finger shaking, she stammered out, "W-what are you?"

His eyes flicked down to the eight-pointed stars on his chest, near his shoulders, and he stalked up to her. "You know these?"

"Yes, I know them. You're not only Russian, y-you're Bratva. Worst yet, *Vory*."

His hand grasped her arm tightly and dragged her toward him. "How do you know?"

How could she not know his tats were a calling card for being inducted into the upper echelons of the powerful Bratva mafia? The eight-pointed star was for a thief of high standing. What did this mean? She thought she was with *bikers*, not more mafia. It made no sense for a biker to have tats like his.

Stalling, her eyes flitted nervously around the room. "W-what?"

"How. Do. You. Know? Are you from Brooklyn?" He stared down at her and shook his head. "No, that doesn't make sense. It's been too long. They cut me loose a long time ago, and they let me live. There's no point in killing me now."

"I-I'm not Russian."

"Who are you?" He twisted her around, her spine slamming against his chest, one hand wrapped around her throat. "Tell me, Tasa. If you know about the Bratva, then you know we don't fuck around. Tell me everything you know before I drag it out of you myself."

"Okay, okay," she rushed out. He slowly released his hold on her, and she backed away slowly. Heart pounding out of her chest, her eyes raced from one end of the room to the other as thoughts assaulted her from all sides. Fight?

No, he was too strong. Run? He was too fast. *Okay, okay, stay calm.* She had to face him and find out what he was and what he knew. Then she'd go from there.

Taking in a large gulp of air, she confessed, "I'm Romanian *mafie*. You pegged me right when you called me 'princess.' I'm a runaway princess. A-are you ..." She swallowed. "Sending me back?"

"Fuck no, you're mine. If you're Romanian, then you know you're tied to me for life."

"WHAT?! Oh, hell no, no, no. I'm not, Whistle. I am *not*. I just got away from under their thumb."

Panic clawed at her throat, suffocating her. She whirled around, left, right, left, trying to figure out if she could grab some clothes and run.

He grabbed her arm and yanked her into his chest. Shivering, she thrashed in his arms, but he only tightened them, pressing her closer into him. She began sobbing because there was no way she was getting trapped again.

"Calm down. Calm the fuck down. I'm not going to force you to marry me. But I'm not going to lie to you either. You know the truth as well as I do. It's blood you shed for me. Virgin blood. For Romanians and Italians, family ties are paramount. If it comes to a showdown between me and someone else, then you're mine. Mine to protect." He caressed her hair. "Mine to set free."

What does that even mean?

"How did you even end up in a biker club?" she asked, her gaze skating down his chest to the rose that told her he had been incarcerated when he was a minor. Her eyes hopped from one animal to the next. Tigers and wolves, but his wolves looked nothing like the Lupu wolf head.

Across his left pec, he had a huge dark Demon Squad tat that seemed to cover up an earlier tat.

Staring down at her, he let out a sigh. He shuffled them over to the bed and lay down, pulling her on top of him. Her ear rested against his heart, the *thump-thump* rhythm, strong and steady. How could he be so calm? How was he actually *alive*, was a better question. The Bratva didn't let anyone out of their brotherhood.

"My father's Igor Popov."

"I've heard of him. He's kind of a bigwig in Little Odessa."

"Yeah, he is. What's not common knowledge is that he was sent in exile to America for having married the love of his life, who was from an old aristocratic family, a family line so long and powerful it survived even the Soviets. My mother represented everything that was the opposite of the Bratva credo. My father could've gone far in the *Vory*, but he had the misfortune of falling in love with a woman. After marriage came the baby in the baby carriage.

"As you probably already know, a true *Vor* must be without family, without wife, and most definitely without children. It's more acceptable to violate the code for one's personal criminal gain than to take on a woman permanently. Knowing he'd doomed himself to a life of a low-ranking criminal, he accepted exile from the Motherland and built a life here. A life and an organization he could control with an iron fist."

"So, you grew up Bratva."

"Yes and no. I was able to escape, until I turned fifteen, in the violin. I was Nikolai Popov."

Her mouth dropped open. She raised herself up on her

forearms, inspecting his face carefully. *The* Nikolai Popov? She was in bed with a child prodigy. Everyone had heard of him. He'd disappeared off the scene years ago, rumored to have burnt out. Then he'd vanished into thin air, with speculations of suicide. "You're Nikolai Popov? People think you're dead. You were a god in those circles. I mean, your mom made Tiger Moms look like a litter of suckling kittens."

He huffed out a small laugh. "Funny. That was the plan. I was inducted at fifteen, in juvie by sixteen. Nothing, not even the violin, would stop the Bratva from claiming one of their own. I *had* burnt out on violin. Somewhat. It's a complicated story better left for another day, but after years of being cuffed to a violin by a ruthless, striving mother, I became a man. Only to find myself trapped with the Bratva."

Uhm … yeah, she could completely relate to being trapped by a suffocating *mafie* society. She had it bad, with controlling male relatives and arranged marriages, but she could well imagine how hard it was for him, a boy. Girls had to give up their hymen to their husbands, but boys … well, the expectations were much more extreme. Boys were expected to kill as proof of loyalty. To kill as proof of strength. It was barbaric. Building tears burned the back of her eyeballs.

Staring down at his hands, he snarled, "I didn't want these hands to turn from creating beauty to bloodying people." He turned stark eyes back to her. "I realized I'd only succeeded in changing one jailer for another, so I ran off. Of course, I told my mother because, let's face it, I'm not a monster, and she would've never survived my death, but I had to get free. I was picked up by a couple of Squad brothers and put under their protection. My father eventually found me, but he never did give me up to her."

"Have you never seen her again?" Tasa couldn't imagine never seeing her family again. She intended to return, at least for visits, once Alex had given up his plans for her.

"No," he replied darkly.

"Why not? You're beyond her power now." Unlike her, he could come out in the open. His mother no longer held sway over him. Besides, it'd been years since he'd played. It was preposterous to think he could regain the heights he'd reached, should he even want to.

"True. Toxic I can handle, but she's beyond toxic. More like obsessive, ya know? Guess that's where I get my doggedness from. Once my father tracked me down, Prez, the president of the Squad at the time, made a deal with him. I stay away, and he doesn't kill me. It was his only chance to win back the wife he'd lost after she discovered what he was really like. With me out of the picture, he thought he had a chance. Good luck to the old bastard."

While Tasa might be highly critical of her family, she also knew how good she had it. That didn't mean she was going back to Queens. She had a mission to accomplish and a point to prove to Alex, but she knew that once they'd ironed out their differences, he'd welcome her back. For visits only. She had no intention of returning permanently. As bad as Alex was, he wasn't a vicious madman. His mother sounded like she was struggling with mental health issues, which wasn't surprising, married to Igor-*fucking*-Popov. She wanted to spit on the floor in disgust at the brute's name.

While Alex was glad her brothers followed him, he wouldn't have forced them into the life of the *mafie*. After the bloody retribution of Tata's assassination, which Tasa thoroughly approved of, he hadn't used violence for the sake of violence. Whistle's father sounded like an ogre. It broke her heart at what he'd had to endure because she knew more than most what that entailed. Even knowing that, he could've easily experienced worse than she imagined.

Biting into her bottom lip, she wanted to reach out and caress his hair. Curl into him and give him comfort, but she couldn't. Not yet. Their discussion was far from over.

CHAPTER NINE

"**Y**OU HEARD MY story. Now, it's time you told me yours, Tasa." Whistle paused a beat, pulling himself up until his back was propped up against the wall. She scrambled up to her knees between his splayed legs. "The whole story. Don't leave out any details," he insisted.

Avoiding his gaze, she fiddled with the buttons of her powder-blue silk nightie. Damn, but the woman was sexy. Yet, he refused to be distracted. He'd told her more about his life than he had to most of his brothers, even Hoodie. The time for reckoning had arrived, and she wasn't going to get around it.

"Come on," he nudged her, pushing against her shoulder.

She took a deep breath as if rallying her courage. Her eyes drifted off him to the far corner of the room. They grew misty as she began, "My full name is Tasa Lupu, of the Lupu clan, the premiere Romanian *mafie* family this side of the Atlantic. My father was assassinated when I was twelve. At that time, my oldest brother, Alexandru, became the head of the clan. Until last week, I was finishing my last year at Juilliard and got into a tad bit of trouble with him."

Her eyes snapped to his. "Nothing out of the ordinary

for a twenty-year-old," she hurried to add, as if he didn't already guess that she was a good girl. "But he insisted that I either commit to pursuing a serious career in opera or accept an arranged marriage with the son of one of his associates. I withdrew from my last semester, got half of the tuition reimbursed, and fled New York."

"You've been gone for how long exactly?"

"Just over two weeks ago."

"Have you seen anything out of the ordinary?" he interrogated her.

She shook her head. "Nothing. He has more contacts in Paris and Milan than he does outside of New York City. On the spur of the moment, I got off the bus heading for Montreal and met Jazz. We hit it off, and one thing led to another. My plan was to stay here for the winter and then hit the road again in the spring."

Hit the road in the spring? Try over my dead body. He sucked in a breath and slowly exhaled to gather his self-control. *Down, boy, down.* Taking one final deep inhalation, he reminded himself he could handle anything that came up in the future but to stay focused on the here and now.

"Have you been in contact with anyone from home?"

"I texted my grandmother and my best friend with a burner phone to let them know I was okay. I didn't want to start a war if anyone thought I'd been kidnapped. I destroyed the phone afterward and haven't been in touch since."

"How badly does this *associate* of your brother's, or his son, want the marriage?"

An associate can mean anything. Different scenarios

flew through his head. Maybe her brother owned money and Tasa was being bartered to forgive a loan. If so, then Alex wasn't letting her go for shit. It could be that a business deal was embedded in the marriage contract and one couldn't go forward without the other. If so, then Alex would still need her. Or the marriage contract could be a ceasefire of a turf war. If she was lucky, it was a marriage made for intangible reasons, such as uniting families for name recognition, alliances, connections, or even genuine affection. Those were more malleable, giving her brother some wiggle room. Because these marriages had little to do with the bride and groom and everything to do with the families.

"I'm not irreplaceable, if that's what you mean. Cristo, the son, is in love with another woman. I've known him most of my life, and I can assure you he's not weeping over me. Who knows, maybe he can even marry the girl he loves. His father isn't particularly attached to me, either. His primary concern is an alliance with Alex. I figure one of my brothers will have to take my place and marry his daughter to make up for my betrayal. Most likely my twin, Nicu. He's Alex's lapdog, whereas Luca, my middle brother, is not so … pliable."

"So," Whistle mused. "If you were worried about a war, that means Alex will be worried for your safety, not simply for what he lost with your disappearance. How close are you two?"

"Not very, but that doesn't matter. He cares for me, and more importantly, he feels responsible. More than responsible. The oath he made to my father on his death bed might have something to do with that," she murmured, picking off non-existent lint from her nightie.

Yeah, a death oath was a real thing and not to be taken lightly. Youngest mafia princess and sister of the head of the family? Alex was definitely on the hunt for her.

"Wow, not a big thing at all for a mafia son," he deadpanned.

"Oh please, Alex is a driven individual. He's been that way since birth. As the oldest, he was prepared to take on the business. Not that I'd underestimate what he did after my father's death. He had to work his butt off to consolidate power and prove he was a capable leader. But he's a busybody who thinks he knows what's best for everyone. God help the woman crazy enough to fall for him. It's never occurred to him to *not* rule my life or make decisions for me. Time was ticking, and I had to make a bold move." She gave a shrug. "Once I graduated, my freedom would be curtailed completely."

If Alex was as Tasa described him, driven and bossy, then he was coming after her. There was no doubt on that score. *Fuck.*

"Funny, if I didn't have a mother who lived through me and pushed me to become an accomplished violinist, I wouldn't understand his drive to have you pursue the opera."

"Alex couldn't finish college because he had to take up the mantle of greatness, but both of my brothers are pursuing degrees while working for the family. Opera, music, art, culture in any form is revered in my family. Since I'm the one with the most talent, which, believe me, doesn't say much, he decided early on that I could take that as an alternative to marriage."

Tasa gave a belabored sigh. "And once Alex makes a decision, he doesn't deviate from it. In my teens, I threw myself into singing, but Juilliard was an eye-opening experience. Being around people who had both a God-given talent and the drive to succeed, I realized I didn't have what it takes to compete. I didn't *want* to compete."

Her eyes drifted down to her fingers laced tightly together. "Actually, I started taking experimental dance. Even switched majors behind Alex's back. That's the other reason I left." She pursed her lips. "I got into a program in the spring. In Montreal. It's an incredible opportunity, but my family would never understand. Experimental art is not culture to them. It signals only two things: bohemian excess and poverty." Her eyelids fluttered as she traced a line in the blanket. "That's another reason why I can't kiss you. Because I have to leave by May for the workshop."

So she had goals. He already knew she wasn't intending to jet-set around the world like a socialite, but his chest puffed up with pride that his girl had dreams. Modern art fit her to the T. Breaking boundaries, seeking freedom of expression in new forms. It was an adventure, as opposed to the rigidity imposed by a traditional art form like opera. His woman was an artist to her core, like Hoodie.

Taking her arm, Whistle hauled her over to his chest. Her sable tresses spilled over his arm and spread across the pillow. "It takes courage to leave everything behind and strike out on your own. You have something special that they don't see. Spirit. Grit. I saw it in you from day one. You may be more like Alex than you think. Leaving your world behind and going for what you want shows true strength."

"Maybe that's why Alex and I always butt heads, but my desire is for the freedom to explore, and that's something he simply can't understand."

"No, many people can't understand until it's taken from them. Then again, not everyone needs the same amount of freedom. That's why bikers created their own societies, with their own set of rules. True freedom makes the average person uncomfortable. The space we need just to breathe feels like chaos to others. Like you, I refused to be shackled by either of my parents' expectations. If I had to go on the run for the rest of my life, if I had to die for it, so be it. I'll never take away your right to self-determination, Tasa. Your freedom is safe with me, but I do have one condition. Your safety. Once I'm sure you're safe, you can continue on your journey."

He swallowed. Damn, those were hard words to say. He prayed that they'd find a way to be together. He wanted her heart. He didn't want to tie her down like a prisoner, like Igor had done to his mother. He'd prefer she stay, but he'd let her fly with the hope that she came back to him.

Her head shot up, eyes narrowed on him.

"That's unnecessary," she cried out as she propped herself up. "I can take care of myself."

"That's the deal I'm offering. Honestly, you don't have the clout to counter my one and only rational demand."

"I just got out from under one over-bearing man. I want to be free, and I'm not your responsibility," she insisted.

"The fuck you aren't," he growled. "I told you, you were mine to protect and mine to set free, but I can't set you free until I know you'll stay alive to enjoy it."

"This isn't your war to fight, Whistle," she snapped. "It's mine. Mine alone, and that's how I want it to stay."

"The hell it isn't mine. The instant you let me into that tight paradise of yours, the moment I popped that precious cherry, you became mine. Don't doubt that for a second. I'll take whatever measures necessary to keep you safe, and I don't give a fuck if you hate me. I killed my first man at fifteen. A man who didn't deserve to lose his life, but it was either him or me. I'm a ruthless bastard to the core. Don't let this soft biker persona fool you."

"Soft *biker* persona," she scoffed. Her lips twitched. "You do realize that's an oxymoron."

"Not if you grew up Bratva, it's not," he threw back. "I've been a prisoner of others. I've been locked up behind bars, in juvie and then in jail. I have no intention of keeping you leashed to my side like a good little mafia *wifey*, but your brother did you a huge disservice if you believe you're not in danger. It's not as simple as waltzing out of New York and starting new, whether in Poughkeepsie or Timbuktu. He *will* find you, have no doubt on that count. And when he does, I'll be there to protect you and fight by your side."

On one hand, he commended Alex on doing such a good job of taking care of her. Her brother's guardianship is what had made her who she was, but if Whistle had to rip those rose-colored glasses off her, so be it. She wasn't going to get hurt on his watch. That was *never* happening.

"What does that even mean? *Protect* me," she spat out.

"It means doing whatever I need to do. It's not just about you, either. Even if he doesn't touch a hair on your head, and that's not a guarantee, he'll enact revenge on anyone who's helped you. That means Jazz. The club. Me. That's my family, Tasa, and I will protect them till my last, dying breath."

Fucking hell, she needed to see what was at stake. The instant she'd walked into the Squad Bar, hell, the moment she took Jazz's help, she threw others in the mix.

"Jazz?" She swallowed. Licking her lips, she repeated, "The club? I hoped, prayed it wouldn't come to that … or that I'd be gone before he found me. If he ever found me."

Christ, she was naive. He had to hand it to her brother that he'd cared enough to protect her from the ugliness of their world and keep her innocence intact. She didn't automatically assume Alex would hurt anyone, and her immediate concern was for others. All signs of a woman who'd been raised in a loving household. No abuse or manipulation. Unlike his, which included a healthy dollop of cruelty sitting on top of a foundation of exploitation.

He brought her back down against his chest. "It's not an unreasonable ask. Once I'm sure you're safe, you can go on your way," he murmured into her hair.

The way his fingers dug into her haunches as he made his promise, he wasn't entirely sure he could let her go, but he'd give it his best shot. While he was certain her first instinct was to flee Poughkeepsie like a bat out of hell, Tasa was also smart. Once she calmed down, she'd accept that it was best to hold down the fort with a crew of bikers and him by her side.

"You must've known he'd come after you," he prodded.

"I thought I was clever enough to escape," she rushed out in frustration, hands clenching against his chest. "After enough time passed, I planned to contact him and hash things out between us but …" She let out a sigh of frustration. "You're probably right."

Pressing her fingers into her closed eyes, a long breath rushed out from her parted lips and she finally consented, "Okay. For now."

"You're making the right choice, girlie," he praised her.

That concession had taken the last bit of energy out of her. Swept away by exhaustion, Tasa's eyelids bobbed and drooped heavily. Reaching down, she dragged the throw, folded at the bottom of the bed, over them and nestled against his side.

Glancing at the digital clock on the nightstand, which blinked out that it was past four a.m., she asked, "Don't you need to take your clothes off?"

"If I take my pants off, I'll end up fucking you again, so no."

"Thoughtful move on your part," she mumbled as her eyelids fell and she dropped off to sleep.

Whistle looked up at the lights from the passing cars coming through the window. Long beams spread across the ceiling before suddenly blinkering away. While he'd slept with women, he didn't cuddle much. Holding Tasa was a different experience. He was almost relaxed, knowing that she was safe in his arms.

From the first, she'd wormed her way into his heart. Now, she was becoming his heart. Whatever hurt her, hurt him, and there was no way he'd allow anyone to hurt either of them.

CHAPTER TEN

WHISTLE WOKE UP from a dream where he was inhaling the scent of honey. He was in his grandfather's *dacha* outside Moscow, wiggling his fingers to reach the honeycomb nestled in the bottom of the jar of honey. Shifting closer toward the delicious scent, his dream morphed from that innocent boyhood memory to the dirtiest fantasy of plunging his cock into a tight, wet hole while smearing his face in a pool of honey that smelled like Tasa.

His cock brushed against something, and pain slashed through his sleep, almost making him yelp. Disorientated, it took him a moment to wake up and realize that he was sporting the hardest morning wood of his life. Glancing down, he was appeased to find Tasa, dead to the world, one leg and an arm flung over him possessively, like an octopus.

Rotating his head to the side, right into her nest of tangled locks, he took a deep inhalation of her scent and let out a groan. Thank fuck, he'd kept his jeans on, even if they were currently strangling his cock. Otherwise, awake or not, he'd be balls deep inside her. But she was his, whether she was ready to admit it or not, and he took care of what was his. That pussy of hers was definitely his, and it needed rest.

Settling deeper into the warm nest of their bed, he followed the cracks on the ceiling for a while, not wanting to disturb her sleep. Normally, the morning after fucking a woman, he woke up to the sound of his teeth grinding together. Even though he gave the bitches the option of staying over didn't mean it wasn't a trial to be a stand-up guy. He never felt the inclination to fuck them again, he just wanted them out so he could get on with his day. But whenever he woke up irritable, he reminded himself that the bitches were as much a part of the club as the men and deserved to be treated right.

This conviction came from the years he spent watching over his mother. She may have been a pain in his ass, but her melancholy had seeped into his blood. He'd made an oath to treat the women who passed through his life with respect and he was willing to tolerate a little discomfort to that end.

His gaze coasted over Tasa's head and down her spine to that cute, pert ass of hers, twitching under the sheet. He clapped a hand on one tight ass cheek. The fact that he didn't want to hustle her out of bed, didn't even want to rouse her, was additional proof that she was different. He kept still, hoping she would continue dreaming her pretty little dreams. He liked her head on his shoulder, her arm wrapped around his middle, and her leg strewn across both of his, pinning him down.

She intrigued him with her intoxicating mixture of innocence and fire. With that fierce backbone beneath a ripe sultry body. Who could hold out against such a combination? Sure as hell not him. The latent protector within him had marked Tasa as his. It'd been well-honed by his mother, but the inclination hadn't hit him so hard since he cut himself off from his past life.

Whistle cursed low when the air coming up the pipes of the radiator in the old tenement building banged up a racket before letting out a hiss of warm, steamy air. Like the sleeping princess she was, Tasa didn't wake, and he relaxed again. Inhaling her sweet fragrance, he was transported back to the summers of his boyhood when he'd been carted off to his maternal grandfather in Russia.

Eventually, she stirred, interrupting his reverie. Her eyelids quivered for a few moments before popping open. Warm brown eyes focused on him, and her lips spread into a satisfied smile.

"Hi," she said in a throaty voice that went straight to his choking cock. Her gaze glided over her body, and a flush of self-consciousness flagged her cheeks as she realized she was draped over him. She moved to disentangle herself, but he placed a staying hand on her back.

"Hey, you," he said. "You sleep okay?"

"Yeah." Her eyes roved over his face. "You've been awake for a while."

"Not too long," he fibbed. Truth was it hadn't been long enough.

Lifting herself up on her elbows, she inspected his tats. Gliding her fingertips over them, she took in the details, likely contemplating what they meant. His jaw tightened as that delicate, innocent touch of hers made his muscles jump. He followed the path she'd taken over his various tats and wondered how much she'd guessed of his life. She already knew he'd been inducted into the Brotherhood, but did she know the rose meant he'd done time as a teen? By the way her eyelids batted quickly, he'd say yeah.

He blew out at low sigh. Time to move her thoughts away from the past. The past was dead to him, and he was dead to the past.

Turning her onto her back, he popped open the buttons to her nightie and spread the shimmery silk aside to display her gorgeous tits. Topped with stiff cherry-colored nipples, they made his mouth water. Her chest was rising and falling by the time he'd finished his inspection. His knuckles grazed down one side of her breast. Then he cupped the underside of one of her heavy tits and brought it to his waiting mouth.

Her head fell back at the contact but snapped right back up as if she couldn't miss a second of watching him. She thought she could keep a part of her soul intact, tucked away from him, by not kissing? *Think again, my little princess.* There was more than one way to skin a cat, more than one pair of lips to suck. Tugging at her clothing, he displayed her long, toned body, with the nip in her waist and the swells of her beautiful hips.

Her fingers darted for his jeans, but he batted them away. "Not yet, baby. Let me taste you first. Spread wide and show me that pretty pussy of yours. Show me where you let in my cock yesterday. Your first and only cock."

"God, you are so bad," she groaned but didn't hesitate to follow his command.

Good girl.

"Mm-hmm." His fingers parted her lips, and he rubbed against her slickness, nudging slowly until she gave a little wince. Pulling out, he said, "This morning, I get to have a good, long look," finishing in his head, *at what I own.*

"Pretty and pink." *And mine.* "So tight and wet." *And to do with as I want.*

"You're only gonna get wetter," he promised darkly as he leaned in and buried himself in the sweetest of musk and honey.

Her breaths came out short and choppy as he braced himself for the first hit of her on his tongue. A growl emanated from his chest. One taste made him greedy for more. He lapped the flat of his tongue against her opening, devouring what he could.

His shoulders knocked her legs wider as his tongue dug in like a ravenous beast, gorging on her. Besides her wet little cunt, all pink and perfect for him, was her taste. *Addicting.* The mewling noises and sounds of desperation she made were music to his ears. What she wouldn't let him do to her mouth, he'd take out on her pussy, exacting his revenge on her clit. Her delicate hands found his hair as she tossed her head from side to side. Gently, he pressed his finger inside her tight hole, and by then, she was slick and too far gone to feel any discomfort.

Finding that spot was easy as fuck, and within minutes, her thighs were shaking around his head. She was shuddering and flinging her body every which way as she climaxed on his tongue like it was the Second Coming. Her screams of pleasure could've broken the sound barrier and taken out his eardrums if he hadn't been so caught up himself.

The instant she was done, he shifted her until her head tipped over the edge of the mattress. Her glazed eyes blinked up at him, mouth wide just the way he wanted it.

"Next time, I'll let you ride that climax out longer," he said by way of an apology as he ripped down his zipper and finally, *finally* released his poor, tortured cock. "I know I worked your untried cunt last night, but I need *in*. Now," he grunted out as he plunged his dick inside her open mouth. She moaned around his cock, the sensation jolting up his shaft, through the rest of his body and ending in a shudder of his shoulders. Thighs splayed open, she played with herself, fingering her little pearl.

Fixated on that flushed part of her, his gaze took a while to return to her lips. To him plundering her wet, hot mouth, that tongue of hers swirling around whatever she could get access to. She was by no means an innocent when it came to blow jobs, but he needed to take her throat.

"Relax your throat and breathe through your nose," he instructed.

Thrusting hard and fast, his control slipped as she made little gagging noises, interspersed with moans. He would've been hard-pressed to stop, but her hand grabbed onto his hip and egged him on. Her tits jiggled with each thrust of his cock, urging him to go faster just to see them shake again.

Fuck, he was losing it. The wet heat sucking sounds of her mouth were too much. Fisting her hair, he yanked her head farther down and back, and fucked her throat until his come shot out and he came with a roar. Stars burst in his field of vision as if he'd been whacked against the side of his head. It took a few moments of straight-up blacking out before his vision returned to Tasa's fingers in her pussy.

Bending over her, he latched on to her clit and sucked it in deep before giving it a little bite. She came with a keening noise around his cock and bucked underneath his mouth as she came.

That was the most perfect fuck, without being buried in pussy, he'd experienced to date. He stumbled back a step, his dick slipping out of her mouth, and dropped to his knees in front of her.

Panting, Tasa began to ramble. "Would you like me to make you breakfast, or do you need to go right away?"

He laughed gruffly. Delirium must be setting in because any old shit was coming out of her mouth. He could relate as feeling slowly returned to his extremities. "You can make me breakfast. After, we're going to the clubhouse to talk with my president, Kingdom."

Her wet fingertips settled on top of her chest as she stared up at him from her upside-down position. She bit down on her plump bottom lip, making Whistle suppress a groan, and gave a consenting nod.

"There's no reason to be nervous," he assured her.

"There's every reason to be nervous. He could decide to send me back."

"Doubt it. Kingdom's old lady works with survivors of domestic violence. There's no way he's gonna send you back into a situation where you'll get hurt."

"Alex would never hurt me," she affirmed.

"Kingdom doesn't know that. Since you don't want to be returned to your brother, I suggest you don't offer up that tidbit of information," he counseled. "Come on, I'm starvin'."

"Oh!" Her eyes lit up as she rolled over onto her stomach, her pert ass cheeks taunting him and he couldn't help giving one a little swat.

"I'll make you a Romanian omelet like I make at home," she said excitedly as she sat up and crawled to the edge of the bed, her tits swaying with each movement. His cock twitched to attention. He'd just finished coming but every move this woman made was sexy.

"What is that?"

"Basically, an omelet with meat in it. Ham, sausage."

"Sounds good," he said as he lifted to his feet and stretched his arms above his head. Her gaze went to his chest, but she quickly averted her eyes and sashayed out of the bedroom buck naked, her hips twitching in the most mesmerizing way.

Whistle grabbed a quick shower before rummaging around in Jazz's chest of drawers for a clean T-shirt. Jazz had male roommates before and enough brothers stayed over that he figured he'd find a cast-off shirt. He donned one with the Demon Squad logo that Hoodie sold on the club website. Dressed, he followed the mouthwatering scent of eggs and meat into the living room and sat at the counter that separated it from the kitchen.

Tasa had tied her hair up in a messy bun. She was wearing a pair of black leggings that hung to her curves just right and a Juilliard sweatshirt. Dressed as casually as he'd ever seen her, she still rocked it. He liked it better, knowing that a mafia princess like her would never walk out the door without being dressed to the nines. There were appearances to be upheld as the only girl of a powerful family.

She slid a plate in front of him with a fluffy omelet, bits and pieces of sausage and ham sticking out. A cut tomato, a few slices of cucumber, and a couple of slices of toast lined the sides of the plate.

"You need to keep your strength up now that you've given yourself the job of being my knight in shining armor," Tasa quipped as she turned away to brew coffee in a hammered-copper *turka* pot. He watched as she stirred vigorously. When the foam rose, she pulled the small, long-handled pot off the heat source and poured a bit of foam into a small porcelain cup before returning the pot to the stove. Carefully, she did this several times before handing him a perfect cup of Turkish coffee. His eyebrows lifted. The aroma of the dark brew wafted up to his nostrils. It'd been a long time since he'd had a cup like this.

"Don't kid yourself. That's the farthest thing from what I am," he tossed back at her after following her motions for a while. "Finding a woman I want to fuck on the regular doesn't mean I've been redeemed from being a mega asshole."

Tasa huffed out a disbelieving laugh. "You're sure sounding like an asshole now." Nodding to the cup, she said, "I added a touch of sugar."

He was pleased with her correct assumption of how he liked his coffee. Taking a sip, his eyelids dropped to half-mast as the grainy, full-bodied flavor hit his taste buds, bringing him back to childhood. "Haven't had a cup like this since I left Brooklyn. Ya know, the sign of a good wife is how well she brews her coffee."

Tasa rolled her eyes. "My family owns a café, and while I've tried modernizing it, I haven't been able to break through to the crew of old men who come in every day for their Turkish coffee. Believe me, I didn't learn for the sole purpose of pleasing a future husband."

He shrugged his shoulders lightly. "Still. Not a bad skill to have."

The omelet and coffee made him realize how much he

liked for her to prepare a meal like this. It was something he could get used to.

TASA TURNED AWAY from Whistle to hide her pleasure at his compliment. After taking a sip of her coffee, she dug into her omelet. It had turned out pretty good, but she was vexed with herself that she was preening like an idiot over a measly little compliment. She cursed her mother's influence. Why else would she melt because he'd praised how she made coffee, of all things?

Narrowing her eyes, she cast a glance over her shoulder. Whistle scooped a forkful of omelet in his mouth. His eyes slid closed as he made an obscenely sexy moan, like he couldn't get enough. Warmth pooled low in her belly. *Damn him.* What the hell was happening to her? Sure, she was a good cook, but she couldn't remember feeling this way from the plain act of feeding a man. Of course, she loved it when *Bunica*, her grandmother, praised her, but she loved that woman to the end of the world and back.

There was an easy comfort between them, and it would be so natural to fall into being with him. That messed with her head because she was a woman with a plan. Not just the workshop in Montreal in the spring, but bigger plans of discovering the world, whether with travel or dance or both. Who knew, maybe she'd end up in a traveling dance troupe. Or a circus. The point was that her life wasn't meant to pause in Poughkeepsie with a sexy biker forever.

The sounds of scraping boots outside the front door interrupted her ruminations. A key scratched against the metal casing of the lock outside. The internal working of the lock turned, and the front door swung open.

Jazz stood frozen at the entryway, keys dangling from her index finger. Mouth agape, she took in Whistle, sitting at the counter, shoveling food in his mouth like it was his last meal.

Stumbling forward a little, she quickly recovered, snapped her mouth shut, and greeted them with a far more chipper tone than Tasa had ever heard her use before. "Hey, guys!"

"Hey, Jazzy," Whistle returned fondly.

Jazz locked the door, looped the keys on a hook by the door, and strolled into the apartment. After dropping her bags and tossing her coat over the couch, she approached Whistle, who brought her in for a hug and a quick peck on the head. A pang hit Tasa square in the chest, causing her to back up a step. It was such a foreign sensation.

Jealousy? Tasa shook the cobwebs out of her head. God, no. She'd never been jealous of another woman in her life. Of course, she'd been envious of Nicu and the reams of freedom he had at his disposal, but she'd never felt jealous of another woman before. It must be the fact that she'd lost her virginity with him; lust had messed up her brain.

Last night and then this morning, she'd been riding high and the wave of jealousy rattled her. She had absolutely no claim on Whistle. She didn't *want* a claim on him, either. Right? *Right. Absolutely. I'm not looking for a man.* She couldn't afford to fall for this guy—or any guy, for that matter—and she'd best remember that fact.

Shutting down the tumult of feelings lurching inside her chest, Tasa turned toward Jazz with a huge smile. "Hey, girl, how was your night?"

"Good, crazy good," she replied with a lopsided grin.

"How was the clubhouse last night?" asked Whistle.

"Poppin'. You missed a great time, Whistle," she said with a little moue as her fingertips ran down his chest.

Tasa's jaw tightened. She had to consciously unclench her teeth and relax her body. *Well, shit.* Alarmed at her reaction, her appetite fled. Finishing her coffee, she turned her attention toward the sink and attacked the pile of dirty dishes like their existence was a personal assault on her sanity.

"Never seen you stay long enough to eat breakfast, Whistle," Jazz observed slyly. "If I'd known, I'd have made you my famous sweet-potato biscuits and coush-coush, an old Creole recipe of my grandma's."

"Would've never passed it up if I knew you'd cook me a real Southern breakfast," he teased back.

Out of the corner of her eye, Tasa watched as Jazz leaned into Whistle. "Not just any old Southern recipe, but a Louisiana Creole recipe."

Tasa's fingers curled around the sponge she was holding, squeezing the life out of it. Wrenching the tap of hot water to full force, she concentrated her entire attention on the dishes before she smashed them, one by one, against the wall. Despite trying to block out their conversation, bits and pieces still filtered up to her over the rush of water.

Abruptly, there was a block of heat at her back. Her pulse accelerated, heart jumping to her throat, as Whistle leaned over from behind. One hand curved around her hip, leaving a brand on her sensitive skin. A whiff of his musky scent swept over her as he brushed her hair to the side.

Dropping his empty dish into the sink, he crooned softly against the curve of her ear, "Finish up and get ready, baby girl. We've got to go."

Crap, Jazz was only a few feet away from them, checking her mail on the other side of the counter. Distracted, a dish slipped from her soapy hands and clattered against the bottom of the sink. A low chuckle whispered over the skin of her exposed nape, making her hair stand on end.

Curse that man for the way he affects me.

CHAPTER ELEVEN

TASA FINISHED UP the dishes as Whistle went back into her bedroom to make a call to Kingdom. The instant he was out of sight, she abandoned them and leaned over the counter toward Jazz.

In a hushed voice, she gritted out, "I'm so sorry Jazz. He wanted to take me home yesterday. After I was done, no one was left in the bar, and he insisted. I tried dissuading him."

Tasa cringed. She was rambling on, but in no way did she want to mess up what she had going with Jazz. Besides being her roommate and co-worker, besides the fact that Jazz had helped her out of the goodness of her heart, Tasa considered her a friend. She'd grown up in a closed, somewhat stifling society, where everyone knew each other's business and not everyone was to be trusted. Besides Nina, she didn't have any true girlfriends. She loved her brothers, especially her twin, but it wasn't the same as having feminine companionship.

"I'm not trying to steal him away or hog him or anything," she finished and blew out a breath. This was embarrassing.

"Girl, chillax. I already told you; it's all good. Whistle's a free agent. Enjoy him while you can. He may have stayed for breakfast, and that's different for him, but he's not a stayer." Her eyes turned serious; an expression of pity briefly rippled over her face. "You know that, right? Tell me you know that."

Although Jazz's words hurt Tasa to the core, she understood her friend was looking out for her. On more than one occasion, Whistle had told her she was his but he also seemed to accept that she'd eventually leave. *So that means it will end, right?*

"I know, and I don't want you to think I'm simping after him. I swear, I didn't mean for *any* of this to happen," she insisted with a slash of her arm in the air. "He says he wants to help me."

Jazz grabbed and squeezed her hand tightly. "That makes sense. He helped me when I first came around, but don't mistake that for anything more. I fell for him a little after he took me under his wing, and it went *no*where."

"I know," she replied, squeezing her hand back. Jazz wasn't saying anything new, but her excitement after their incredible sex, along with their conversation from last night and breakfast this morning, took a nosedive. They'd shared a level of intimacy she hadn't experienced with the vocal instructor from last semester. That had been pure sexual exploration. Without emotion, without the connection she felt with Whistle, without heart.

Whistle brought out a side she hadn't experienced before, hadn't even known to expect with a man. But when it happened? *Pow!* It hit her like a Mac truck, and she realized that she was tied to him for as long as he wanted. Since that would inevitably end, she'd hang on for the ride until he tired of her. As long as she tamped down that newly discovered jealousy, bred from a frightening sense of possession, and didn't get attached, she'd survive. She had no other choice because she had her own plans in the works. Yet there were feelings between them now. After only one night together. Confusion, fear, and embarrassment were bundled together in a complicated mess of a knot in her tummy.

Whistle sauntered out of the bedroom, completely dressed, and she scurried back to finish the dishes in the sink.

THE PROSPECT HELD the door of the clubhouse open for Tasa to enter. Whistle gave him a chin lift and looped an arm around her shoulders. Her eyes darted around, taking in the long bar, the groupings of couches and tables, a pool table near the back, surrounded by a lot of empty space. It had a similar feel as the Squad Bar, with the bare-brick walls and lots of wooden accents, but less intimate. This was a larger space with pockets of comfiness in the groupings of furniture, but one got the sense that it was a place of business and headquarters to a larger organization.

The bitches' eyes were the first to zero in on her. She felt as if all the female eyeballs snapped toward her at the same time. She recognized a few faces from the Squad Bar. There was a variety of reactions, but they all coalesced into shock the instant Whistle's arm fell around her shoulders. From one of the islands of couches rose two women. They made their way toward them gingerly as if she and Whistle were aliens, dropped out of the sky.

The older of the two, a stunning, statuesque lady a decade older than Tasa, spoke first, "Hey, Whistle, who do you have with you?"

"Hey, Sage. This is Tasa. She's a waitress at the Squad Bar. We're here to see Kingdom."

"Hey, Tasa." The woman immediately turned to her, giving up all pretense of being interested in Whistle and stuck out her hand. "I'm Sage, the president's old lady. This is Sammi."

Whistle dipped his head and murmured in Tasa's ear, "She's a princess like you, but of the Squad."

Sage's eyebrows lifted high at his comment, but Tasa nodded slowly. "Hey, Sammi. I'm Tasa."

"So, what's going on here, Whistle?" Sammi asked, circling him like *he* was the trapped animal for once. Tasa was starting to like these women. They were no-nonsense, like any biker bitch, although neither of them dressed like bitches. Sage was a professional woman, whereas Sammi looked like she'd stepped right off a runway, draped in designer clothes that would have her fitting right in the Romanian *mafie* circles.

"Whistle, don't answer any questions. They're circling around you two like vultures. Come the hell over here and leave them alone. They're gonna find out what they want without your help. Best leave them be and get a drink," bellowed out a man from the bar.

Sammi rolled her eyes. "Thanks Cutter, but we don't need your interference."

"You sure as hell don't, but he does," the man named Cutter said with a snort. "Get the hell over here, I said."

Whistle shook his head. "Welcome to my daily hell with these assholes. Are you going to be okay?" he asked, a look of concern in his eyes.

"Of course," she replied without hesitation. His gesture was sweet, but she was more than capable of standing on her own.

"I'll be fine," she stressed, placing a hand on his arm.

"Protective," said Sage.

"Handsy," Sammi piped up.

"Fuck," muttered Whistle before lifting Tasa's tresses in his hand and sliding them over her shoulder. With a last knuckle grazing down her temple and along her jaw, he leaned in and murmured, "I'll have a drink with that fucker and then we'll see Kingdom, 'kay?"

She swallowed. His attentiveness touched her in a place that almost had her tearing up a little. "Yeah," she breathed out.

"Holy. Shit," Sammi broke in, a pair of saucer-wide eyes darting from Whistle to Tasa, and then back to Whistle again. "Am I hallucinating? Did I just drop into an alternate universe?"

"Come with us, Tasa. Do you want anything to drink? Coffee? Soda?" asked Sage. Tasa shook her head and allowed the women to guide her to the couches where they'd been sitting when she entered the clubhouse.

"How do you know Whistle?" Sammi asked as she crossed one leg over the other, fingers laced around her one knee. She batted her eyelashes innocently, but Tasa wasn't fooled. Since Whistle left her with them, fully knowing their goal, she figured it was alright to answer.

"I started waitressing at the Squad Bar over a week ago

now. Jazz is my friend and roommate."

"Jazz is a sweetheart," commented Sammi.

Sage leaned in, watching Tasa perceptively, and inquired, "Annnd, she's good with this?" Her hand fluttered between her and Whistle, sitting at the bar.

Tasa eyed him carefully. His head swiveled around, sensing her attention on him. Grinning, he reassured her with a sexy wink before turning around to answer a question posed by one of his brothers.

He'd caught her. Sighing, Tasa's shoulders drooped. Focusing back on Sammi, her eyebrows knitted together. "Good with what?"

"With you and Whistle?"

"Why wouldn't she be? Whistle and I aren't together or anything," she returned sharply, and then snapped her mouth shut, somewhat surprised by her rudeness. She murmured softly, "Sorry, I didn't mean to snap."

"Oh, this is too much," said Sage with a light chuckle. "Payback for all those times he made my life a living hell with his brawling, his middle-of-the-night arrests, and those eight a.m. bail hearings." She gave a little air pump. "Yes!"

"What are you talking about?" Tasa bit out.

"Just that Whistle has never—and I'm not exaggerating when I say never—brought a woman to the clubhouse, put his hand around her shoulder, or caressed her face the way he did just now. I don't care if he had sex with her once or a hundred times, he's never paid attention to a woman unless it was exactly an hour before he planned to have sex up until first thing the next morning. He may be a total screwup in every other part of his life, but he's extremely disciplined when it comes to how he treats women."

Leaning a little forward, Sage's voice dropped an octave. "Down to the minute."

Tasa's laughter rang out. "He's the farthest thing from a screwup I've ever met. That man is a god in certain circles." Did they not know who he was? Nikolai Popov. How clueless could they possibly be?

Sammi's eyes blinked, her lower jaw dropping to her chest. Sage, who had a bit more finesse and restraint, suppressed a laugh, but her eyes lit up with mirth.

Okay, they must not know. If they didn't know on their own, then Whistle must not have told them. Considering where he'd come from, that wasn't such a bad thing. She sure as hell wasn't about to out him. Deep gratitude filtered through her soul. He'd told her things he'd obviously kept from people who were as close to a surrogate family as he'd ever had.

"A god, you say?" queried Sage with a wide smile. Okay, maybe Sage knew. She seemed to have read between the lines. "He's told you about his past, I see. This is becoming more intriguing by the second."

"What past?" interjected Sammi, but Sage waved her question away, and Sammi leaned back, seeming to know better than to interrupt with questions.

"Whistle is a complex man," declared Sage.

"He is?" stuttered Sammi.

She nodded sagely to her friend. "He is. He's a man with a past, and I'll leave it at that. These past several years with the club, he's been working out his issues, discovering himself. I've come to the conclusion that he isn't one who trusts easily, and besides catching up on time lost during his non-existent childhood, he was constantly fighting and trying the patience of every brother in this club to see if they were worthy of his loyalty. But you, Tasa. You, he seems to have taken to instantly. You, he's chosen to confide in." Her tone changed subtly during her little speech, a harder edge tinting it toward the end. "That's not something to take lightly, and I'd like to make myself perfectly clear. Whistle is important to us. We'd do anything to protect him."

Tasa drew back from Sage's blunt warning. Whoa. Mama Bear just charged out of nowhere. Sage laid a gentle hand on Tasa's knee. "Sorry, I got a little carried away. Not quite sure where that came from. Must be the pregnancy hormones," she explained away as her other hand rested on her large belly. "Hope I didn't scare you."

"A little," she replied honestly. She barely understood what was going on. Jazz had warned her to brace herself for the inevitable ending of her and Whistle, but Sammi's shock and Sage's warning suggested that Whistle treated her differently. She didn't know what to think. Her heart screamed, *yes*, while her brain shouted back, *hell no*.

Meanwhile, she was stressed out about her imminent meeting with the president of the Demon Squad. He held her future in the palm of his hands. He could either let her stay, let her go, or throw her back into the den of wolves that was her family.

"It may not seem genuine, after practically biting your head off, but I do sincerely welcome you into the club," said Sage.

"I wouldn't be so quick to do that," she muttered.

"Why not?"

"Well, I'm in a … situation, and Whistle brought me

here to talk to Kingdom about my predicament. He may send me back to where I came from."

"Oh, I can assure you he will do no such thing without my say-so," she replied confidently as she inspected her nails. "Does Whistle want you to stay here?"

"I … yes, I believe so."

"Then, that's what's going to happen. Whistle has never asked anything of the club. He may be a pain in the ass, but he's a loyal brother who's done whatever's been required of him. If he wants something, then I'll make sure he gets it."

"You sound like his guardian angel."

"That's an apt description, I suppose. I swear, I've spent so much time getting him out of jail and other kinds of trouble, I feel like his big sister. I've grown quite fond of him over the years."

Tasa's head lilted to the side as she studied Sage. She had the standing and demeanor of a queen. It was very different from her own world, where women were taught to follow along and do what they were told. Her mother was one of the few women involved in certain aspects of the business, and yet, she'd deferred to Alex in everything. Tasa didn't know much about bikers and clubs, but if nowhere as bad as the mafia, they were by no means a model of gender equality.

Yet, Tasa believed Sage. She spoke truthfully when she blithely stated that Whistle would get what he wanted. The subtext being that Sage would get it for him. Tasa wasn't exactly used to seeing a woman of strength in action, and she had to admit, it was impressive. First Jazz, now these two women. She got the sense that this was a place where she could grow into the kind of person she fantasized about. Strong and independent but with the backing of a supportive family ... of a man. It was obvious how much Sage loved Kingdom. Her eyes took on a distinct sheen when she spoke of him.

A hand landed on her shoulder, and Tasa jumped. Her gaze shot up and found Whistle's stunning eyes looking down on her warmly.

"Hey, I'm done with the beer, which was a barely disguised session of twenty questions. The brothers are shameless. I checked, and Kingdom is free to see us. Ready?"

"Yeah," she said with relief. His hand slipped off her shoulder, leaving her aching, even from that simple touch. Nodding to the women, she thanked them and hurried to follow him.

"Whew, that was a little intense," she confided as she caught up and walked alongside him past the bar and toward a hallway.

"Don't let them rattle you. They're curious, and Sage has been through a lot with me. She's taken a liking to me for some reason. The hours she puts in my cases whenever I get arrested has fucked with her brain cells."

Shaking her head in disbelief, Tasa admitted, "I don't see Nikolai Popov getting into drunken bar fights."

Whistle chuckled. "I shed him a long time ago."

"Can you ever shed who you were as a child?"

"With every fiber of my being, Tasa," he replied, his voice as jagged as shards of glass. "Not only did I have a lot to catch up on, but I had a flood of rage inside me. It took years to loosen its hold on me. I was partially joking about

Sage, but she figured me out before anyone else in the club. Not only does she know who I was and my background, but as my lawyer, she had access to every file with my name on it. That included my stints in juvie, because no one bothered to have them sealed, but hospital records as well."

Tasa halted in the middle of the hallway. Her hand stayed Whistle. He turned toward her, and her eyes coasted over his face, catching little nicks along his hairline. The harsh light from the overhead fluorescent lamp illuminated things she hadn't noticed before. One little, barely visible cut slashed the top of his eyebrow. There was another on his temple. Running her gaze down his arms, she found various scars covered over by dark tats, some of them as straight as a surgical knife. She shivered. "Jesus."

"Don't worry about me, princess. I'm a survivor. And unlike the people who called themselves my family, I'm part of a *real* brotherhood in the Squad. Being able to count on each other is how we survive. I'd protect anyone here with my life, which is more than I can say for my so-called blood brothers." He paused before confiding, "And you're part of that family, now."

His words rang loud in the hallway, ricocheting off the walls and roaring in her ears. Her heart stuttered in her chest. She believed him. By the fierceness of his expression, his vivid eyes narrowed in determination, and the set of his angular jaw, she knew he'd do anything for her. She didn't know what she'd done to deserve the loyalty of such a strong, fierce man, but she knew she could trust him.

Honor-bound oaths she understood, but like Jazz, Whistle had no reason to help her. It humbled her to her core. She'd been over-protected her entire life, but she'd also been taught that no one but family, family bound by blood, could be trusted. Anyone outside of their circle was highly suspect. Even within their circle, there were moles and snitches. Family was the only thing you could count on. Over time, she'd discovered the flip side that family could also be repressive.

Now, she learned that some people could be trusted despite the lack of blood bonds. Tasa's gaze drifted over to Whistle as they resumed their walk alongside each other down the long corridor to Kingdom's office. Sure, she'd lost her virginity to Whistle, but he wasn't helping her because of that. He'd *chosen* to follow that rule, and not simply because he happened to be the one who tore through her hymen. For reasons she couldn't quite put her finger on, he felt protective of her. Maybe it was the commonalities of their situations, that he'd been where she was.

Either way, he was the epitome of loyal. Once you earned his trust, he'd never waver.

"Come on, we shouldn't keep Kingdom waiting," he nudged her forward.

CHAPTER TWELVE

IN FRONT OF the closed door of Kingdom's office, Whistle grasped her hand, brought it to his lips, and kissed her knuckles. Nodding, Tasa clasped his hand tightly and moved behind him.

"Don't be afraid," he assured her gently. She didn't know Kingdom, and he could see how it might be daunting, but Whistle had trusted him with his life on more than one occasion. And with the training Kingdom got from Sage regarding survivors, he wasn't going to throw Tasa back to the dogs. Of that Whistle was certain.

But he understood her fear.

"It's my life," she stated in a strained tone.

"I'd never let anything happen to you," he promised as he tugged her into his side. Hooking an arm around her neck, he pressed a kiss to her temple. Since she'd banned kisses on her lips, he made sure to kiss her everywhere else, as often as he could, to crack that barrier wide open. He couldn't wait for the moment she melted against him, unable to help herself from kissing him back.

Knocking lightly, he turned the knob at the sound of Kingdom's voice. Kingdom was VP when Prez, the former president of the Demon Squad, had peeled Whistle off the sidewalk as a runaway. He knew Whistle's story, having been involved in the negotiations for his release with his father. The man was brilliant. He had the mind of a criminal but the heart of a vet. If anyone could help Tasa, it was Kingdom.

Turning into the comfortable mancave that was used as an office, he brought Tasa before his president and proudly introduced her. "Hey, Kingdom, this is Tasa."

He remained quiet, giving his brother time to scrutinize his woman and come to his own conclusions. There was no swaying the man. Ever since Sage and her law partner, Greta, took on helping survivors, the entire Squad had dedicated themselves to the endeavor. Kingdom would help, either for Whistle's sake or because she was a woman on the run. If one or the other wasn't enough, hopefully, the combination would cinch it.

Taking in a bracing breath, Tasa stood tall and extended her hand. "I'm pleased to meet you, Kingdom."

He rose behind his imposing, big-ass desk and shook her hand with a grunt. Giving Whistle the stink eye, he bit out, "She yours, Whistle?"

"She is." He spoke firmly, chin set. Squaring his shoulders, he blew out his chest.

Waving them to sit down, he turned his attention back to Tasa. "Whistle already gave me a summary, but I want to hear it from you. And I mean, down to the smallest detail. Don't leave a damn thing out thinking you can spin a story any which way. Don't even try to lie. I'm a military weapon, honed to precision in the dust bowl of Iraq. I'll catch you in any lie you lay on me."

Swallowing, her throat worked, and Whistle was momentarily distracted by the love bite he'd left on her long, slender neck from this morning.

"My name is Tasa Lupu—" she paused at the slitting of Kingdom's eyes, "—of the Lupu clan. Romanian *mafie* out of Queens, New York. Alexandru Lupu is my brother."

"How can you prove you're a Lupu?"

Whistle yanked the collar of her Juilliard sweatshirt and exposed the tat of a wolf baring its teeth on the curve of her breast. Whistle wasn't the only one sporting a calling card tat. It was a quick peek, but the distinct mark was enough to prove her legitimacy.

"If you know the Lupu name, then you know that each of us has the mark of the wolf. Lupu means 'the wolf' in Romanian. Those who are born in the life, and those who pledge themselves to the life." She glanced down at the area of her tat. "People like me, who were born into the clan … our tat is a slightly different shade, but a *Lupu* is a *Lupu*."

She paused and chewed on her plush bottom lip, ruminating over something. If *Lupu* tats were anything like Bratva tats, they were inescapable.

"Go on," Kingdom prompted.

"I'm the youngest of my family and the only girl. My oldest brother, who is the *şef* …" She waved her hands. "It's like the equivalent of a boss or don. He recently forced my hand over a situation we'd been wrangling over for some time. Namely, my future. After finishing college in the spring, I was to be married off to the son of one of his close associates, Cristo Popescu. I did the only thing I could think of and escaped. By chance, I got off a Greyhound bus in Poughkeepsie and met Jazz at the coffee bar where she works. We hit it off, and she generously invited me into her home and got me a job waitressing at the Squad Bar, where I met Whistle," she finished.

"Now, this is an important question, Tasa, so think before you speak. What would your brother do if he found you?"

Tasa pursed her lips together as her brows drew together in thought. "Honestly, I'm not sure." She glanced down at her hands and cleared her throat before answering, "I-I'm not a virgin anymore, and it's standard for a marriage contract to include a clause for virginity." Her eyes darted to Whistle and then to Kingdom. "I'm no longer an acceptable bride for Cristo."

"Damn straight," interjected Whistle.

Kingdom gave him a crippling look for interrupting his interrogation. Whistle shrugged and shot him a cocky, unrepentant grin. What? So he was crowing.

Tasa dropped her gaze to her lap again. Whistle clasped her hands in his big one and squeezed them still to give her reassurance.

"At this point, I'd wager he'd consider it an insult to force him and his father to accept the marriage contract. Would my brother force me to marry one of his soldiers or lock me up at home till the end of time? I don't know the answer to that."

"Would he exact corporal punishment for your ... indiscretion?"

"If you're asking me whether he's been physically abusive toward me in the past, the answer is no. But then again, I've never countermanded an order like this before, so I'm treading on unknown terrain."

"Are you scared of him?"

"Of course, I'm scared of him. I want to be free. *Free*, Kingdom. I don't know if you know what it's like to have another person dictate your life, but I want to choose my own destiny. I walked out on my entire family in exchange for a chance at freedom. There's no reasoning with him on this matter. We've had so many arguments, but he knows no other way. In his mind, I'm his responsibility until I'm married to another man, and he must 'protect me from myself,' as he repeats so often."

Tasa's eyes broke away from Kingdom's. They welled, but she stiffened her spine and swallowed back her tears. Whistle interlaced their fingers together, squeezing to let her know that he was there for her. She was a brave one, for sure. Her stifled tears tugged at his heart, but he refrained from interrupting. *Hold on, baby, I'll take care of you.* After they were done, he'd take her home and lick her pussy until she couldn't remember her own name, much less this conversation.

"Have you seen anything unusual? Anything that tells you he may have found you already?"

She shook her head resolutely. "Not yet. I've been trained to be aware of my surroundings, of course, and I've been diligent, but I haven't spotted anyone suspicious. I haven't gotten that prickly feeling on the back of my neck like I have in the past when someone watched me."

Kingdom drummed his fingers on the wooden desk, his eyes fixed in the distance. Returning back to them, he declared, "You're under our protection while I find out more information about your brother."

"Please be careful. I don't want him tipped off to where I am, and I don't want you getting on his bad side. If anything is out of sorts, he'll pursue it relentlessly."

"Don't worry about us, Tasa. I've got one of the best military-trained trackers the Army's ever produced at my disposal. I'll discover what I need without your brother being the wiser. We're keeping this between us for now, but I promise that I'd cut you loose before sending you back. You left him for freedom? I sure as fuck am not going to yank it from under you. That's not how it works with the Squad."

Whistle's heart brimmed over with pride at his adopted family. *God*damn, this was why he'd left the Bratva and turned his life over to these motherfuckers.

A sigh whooshed out of her, her shoulders sloping forward in relief.

Lifting her eyes to his president, she whispered, "Thank you, Kingdom."

His lips twitched as his eyes found Whistle's. "I see why you like her," he noted with an approving nod. "Seems like our youngest is finally starting to grow the fuck up. You're gonna have to keep your wits about you, Whistle. No fighting. No jail."

"That shit's over with," he vowed. No way would he risk getting separated from Tasa, especially now. In fact, not ever again. He wasn't missing one day of being with this woman.

"One last thing, Tasa. Do you know what being under my protection means?" Without waiting for her response, he went on, "It means you follow whatever I say, whatever Whistle says. No questioning it. And before you huff and puff and complain that it's like being under your brother, I promise you that it's not."

"I'd never say that," she interjected.

"Good, because it's for your protection. We're taking over, for now. I'm assuming you know what orders are?"

"Yesss," she replied, gnawing at her bottom lip.

"Then, follow them. I'm not interested in controlling any other aspect of your life but for one: safety. Believe you me when I tell you I'm a busy man. I have a baby that's gonna pop out of my old lady any day, so I'm putting the safety of my *entire* family on the line for you, not only my Squad family. In exchange, I expect complete obedience on this one point."

She tapped her foot softly against the floor. "Are you sure it's not better if I leave Poughkeepsie?"

Lunging forward, Whistle snapped, "No." *No way in hell is that happening. No way.*

Her eyes zipped from Whistle to Kingdom, looking for answers.

Kingdom gave a little shake of his head as a warning to Whistle. "That decision has already been made. A man's only as good as his word. I said you're under Squad protection until I do my due diligence and make a decision to the contrary." Slapping his hands on the desk, he said, "We're done here. Now, get the fuck out 'cause I've got shit to do." His eyes ticked up to the clock on the wall. "You guys should be getting back to the Squad Bar. How's it going there, Whistle? Catch the thief yet."

"Not yet," Whistle groused about that sore spot. "Whoever it is, the fucker's crafty as shit. The cameras haven't caught anything, but the inventory keeps coming up short. I'll find the bastard, have no fear, Kingdom. And when I do, I'll personally make sure to send the right message out."

"Once you find him, first thing you do is contact me. Don't need you going Red Mafia on his ass."

Lifting to his feet, Whistle pulled Tasa up to him. Cradling her against his side, he let loose a grin. "You got it boss-man."

CHAPTER THIRTEEN

WHAT A FUCKING day.

After meeting with Kingdom, Whistle steered Tasa into his old room in the clubhouse, which was luckily still unoccupied, and took her again. It crossed his mind that he should hold out until night but, at the last minute, decided against it. Thank fuck she was game. After what amounted to years, off and on, of being incarcerated, he was used to interrupted sleep, but his feet were dragging by the time he'd dropped Tasa back at her apartment and got to the Bar. It had been a long-ass day.

Trudging into his office, he checked the time on his cell phone. He had about an hour before getting Tasa and bringing her to work. The days of her taking the bus were over. Her protests suggested that he was overreacting, but fuck it, if it put his mind at ease, he wasn't going to overthink it.

Head against the back of the chair, he'd gotten a few minutes of shut-eye when there was a knock at his office door. Eyes closed, he shouted out, "Come in."

Lifting his head, he caught Jazz walking in. With a grunt, he dropped his head back and shuttered his eyes once more.

Suddenly, a pair of hands were sliding down his chest. One hand kept going until it cupped his crotch.

"I'm busy, Jazz."

"With what? You're awake," she replied in a coy tone.

"Not now. Not in the mood."

"I can put you in the mood, baby," she crooned in a sultry tone that made his skin itch. Her fingers began unbuckling his belt. "I can make you feel sooo good."

He laid his hand on top of hers, halting its progress. "Chill."

Exhausted and trying to catch some z's before another long night, he was not in the mood for chick drama.

Her fingers pushed against his hand a little, testing him, but he held firm. Finally, his eyelids slid open, and he let out a sigh. "What the fuck, Jazz? You makin' a pass at me or you tryin' to save Tasa?"

"Both," she joked.

"Not funny." Shaking his head, he ordered, "Quit it. Nothing's happening between us."

Perching on the arm of the chair, she looked down on him with a little pout. "Why not? Don't we have a good time together?"

Not so good that he'd sacrifice a woman he wanted like Tasa.

"We have," he agreed. "But things have changed."

"What's changed?" She lifted a mocking eyebrow at him. "Don't lie to me and tell me you've fallen for her."

"Stay in your fuckin' lane, Jazz. This is none of your business," he growled. Jazz had no fucking clue who he was. At least, Tasa did. The thought eased his anger somewhat. At least she knew his past, knew who he was, and knew to take what he said seriously. Jazz was overstepping. "I don't have to justify anything I do to you, and I sure as fuck ain't gonna talk about it with you."

"Please, Whistle. Don't tell me her pussy's made of gold. One's as good as another."

"And you would know that, how?" he asked with a chuckle.

"I've been with women."

"Alright, I respect that, but I'm not talking to you about Tasa." He wasn't a wet-around-the-ears kid. He sure as hell wasn't going to jabber on like a teenage girl with her bestie. Just because he wasn't a total dick with the bitches didn't mean he had a pussy.

"It's only been twenty-four hours, Whistle, and you're already treating her differently. Staying over is normal, but eating *breakfast* afterward? Hell, you only keep women overnight to satisfy some rule of yours, but the second the sun rises, you jump out of bed like your ass is on fire."

"Your point is?"

She lifted her chin obstinately. "I've already warned her about what to expect from you."

His chest went tight, fear slicing through his gut and dropping acid inside. Sitting up straight, he knocked her off his armrest. Leaning forward, he glared at her and demanded, "What in the fuck is that supposed to mean?"

"Are you seriously asking me that question? You're a biker. I couldn't let her fall for you. I had to explain how it was at the Squad. Bikers share women; they don't stick around, and they don't get attached."

Whistle cursed under his breath. Clenching his jaw as he reached deep inside himself for patience with this woman he'd long considered a friend, he quipped, "There's something called an old lady, Jazz. Think you've heard of the term, no?"

Jazz stumbled back a few steps, her arm shooting out to steady herself against the wall.

Eyes bulging, she croaked out, "Is that what she is?"

He swiped his hand over his forehead. "Fuck, Jazz, I'm not discussing this with you. You need to stay out of our business. She's under my protection. Kingdom's protection. This has nothing, and I mean *nothing*, to do with you, and I sure as hell don't want you meddling. You better stop running your mouth with Tasa."

"You really think this has nothing to do with me?" she asked in a low tone.

Christ*fuck*. He'd long guessed Jazz crushed on him, but what was getting her panties in a twist? She didn't like to share him when they fucked, but she didn't seriously think she was in the running to be his old lady? "You always knew the deal between us, Jazz," he said carefully.

"That was when you treated everyone the same," she spat out. "That's changed, and if anyone's meant to be your number one, it should be me."

His eyebrows lifted. This was fuckin' news to him. He didn't want to be crass, but hard pass on that one. Jazz was great but he'd never shown her extra attention. He'd made damn sure of it, for fuck's sake. To avoid this very situation.

Crossing his arms over his chest, he stared her down in a way he'd never needed to before. But this petulant shit had to stop. Right. Fucking. Now. "How do you figure that?"

"Because I've been with you from the beginning. I've been with you the most, and I've …" She swallowed hard. "… wanted you the most."

Aww, fuck. He didn't want her to hurt. "Jazz, baby. That's not how this shit works—"

"It is," she cried out. "I-it should be. Fuck, Whistle, you must know how I feel about you."

He did now. He might've before but figured if he didn't acknowledge it, it would go away. Jazz was a good friend, and he didn't want that to change, but hell would freeze over before anyone fucked with his plans for Tasa. He finally found someone who made his stomach flip. But the woman had the kind of baggage that could tear them apart, and he needed to build as much of a foundation between them as possible in as short a time as possible.

A long moment of silence stretched out between them.

"I do now," he mumbled. "I never played games with you, and I'm not gonna start. Truth is, I don't feel the same as you. Regardless of whether I met Tasa or not, our relationship wasn't gonna turn into anything else than it was. I didn't realize how deeply you felt, Jazz. If I had, I would've made better choices. I thought my position was clear."

Wringing her hands together, she hissed out, "If Tasa hadn't shown up, you would've grown to feel the same way."

"No," he replied firmly. He had to make her see reason and fast because he couldn't have a saboteur in his life.

Raising to his feet, he took her chin between his fingers.

Shaking her head a little, he swore, "Tasa has nothing to do with this. Nothing, and I mean *nothing* will change how I feel about you. You have a special place in my heart, but I'm a man who knows what I want, Jazz. No one's gonna persuade me differently. Have I ever shown you to not know my mind? Especially when it came to women? No matter how the brothers act with the bitches, I have my own set of rules, and I follow them religiously. Regardless of what any other brother does, I treat women the way *I* think is best. Always tried to treat you with respect, and I'm doing the same now by telling you to keep Tasa out of this. My feelings won't change. Feel me?" he finished with a last little shake of her chin before releasing it.

Once free, her head whipped to the side, her high cheekbones flushed a shade darker than her natural skin tone. Her pride was wounded, but he was satisfied she understood his stance.

"I'm not saying this shit to humiliate you," he said, taking a softer tone. Placing his hands on her shoulders, he squeezed. "I care for you, Jazz. Always will."

"Just not the way I want," she rasped out.

"Not that way, no. I'd never lead you on. Believe me, you don't want a man who can't match your capacity for loving him. I've seen what it does when love isn't reciprocated, and you deserve much better than that. You deserve the best. And you'll get it. There's a man out there who will see you for the treasure you are and worship the ground you walk on. You deserve that man." He let out a soft sigh and ended, "But that man ain't me."

She huffed out a little disbelieving laugh. "Yeah, right."

His jaw clenched, and he could feel that telltale muscle jumping from irritation. He had to end this right away. Not leave one fucking stone unturned.

"You don't have to believe me, but it won't change my final decision. However, there's one thing you need to do. You've got to promise me that you'll stay out of my way when it comes to Tasa."

Jazz's gaze was glued to the floor. Taking her chin again, he lifted it until they were at eye level. "I'm not playing, sweetheart. Don't fuck with what's mine."

Her eyes flickered closed for a brief moment, and she expelled a sigh. "Okay. I won't do anything to sabotage you. Yes, I wanted you, but I wasn't lying when I said Tasa and I are friends. What are your intentions with her? Where you serious before?" She squeezed her eyes shut for a moment. "When you talked about an old lady?"

He admired her ability to switch tacks. She was always quick on her feet, and her concern for Tasa was authentic. Granted, with his record, he wasn't too surprised that she'd question him even though his pride took offense. But he stifled it and kept tight reins over his temper. Not that he was going to get into it with her. He didn't owe her a damn thing, and she wasn't Tasa's fairy godmother, regardless of how protective she might feel. It couldn't touch how protective *he* felt toward Tasa.

"I'm not discussing her with you."

Squaring her shoulders, she pleaded, "She's my friend, Whistle. We talk. She comes to me for advice, and I can't just shut her out. It's not the way we communicate, and … she'll become suspicious if I close down on her."

Fair enough. He didn't want Tasa to get scared off and run if Jazz's behavior changed toward her. "Your job is to support me with her. I may not know the details of how the future is going to play out between us, but what I do know is that she's mine, Jazz."

His tone was more of a growl by the time he finished, but he had to make sure Jazz understood.

"If you fuck with her head, you're directly fucking with me, and I won't take kindly to that. Don't think I won't eventually learn about it. Nothing stays a secret in this club. Even without that, I'll eventually know because I'm gonna be her everything."

Her eyes were swimming with sorrow and resignation, but Jazz wasn't stupid. She'd have to have a death wish to countermand his order.

"Yeah, okay," she replied with a sharp shake of her head.

Releasing her, he took a step back and repeated, "Okay."

He swiped his cell phone off the desk and checked the time. "I've gotta go. I'll be back in twenty minutes with Tasa. Hold down the fort, will you?"

Shrugging on his biker jacket, he patted the pockets to make sure his keys were there and then strode toward the door.

Pausing with his back to her, he checked over his shoulder with a narrow-eyed look and confirmed, "We good?"

Her shoulders slumped forward, dejection etched across her face, but she replied in a strong voice, "We're good."

With a final firm stare, he nodded tightly and walked out.

He was gonna get his woman.

CROSSING THE PAVEMENT to his bike, Whistle swiped his phone open and tapped Cutter's number. Christ, he needed to talk to someone. Puck was in the slammer. There was Hoodie, of course, but Hoodie didn't do relationships, even if Whistle sometimes caught him checking out Jazz. Of course, no one noticed Hoodie besides Whistle, what with the way he clung to the walls like he was trying to meld into them.

The instant he heard Cutter's "Yo," he barked out, "Any leads?"

"Brother, it's been half a second since Kingdom gave me the lowdown on you and the new girl. Could ya let me catch my breath?"

Whistle blew out a breath and relaxed the tension building in his shoulders.

Hearing the frustration in Whistle's exhalation, Cutter demanded, "What is it?"

"Fucking Jazz just declared her un-fucking-dying love for me, that's what."

Since Puck was in jail, Cutter had been coming around the Bar. At first, Whistle was certain it was only to check up on him, but he'd been helpful of late and had finally started treating him like a man. Whistle grudgingly admitted that maybe it was because he was acting like one, for once. Now that Cutter and Greta, his old lady, were going strong for a couple of years, he'd relaxed the level of assholery he liked to lay on thick.

"Rough. But Jazz knows better than to think you'd get serious over anyone … oh, I see. It's this new girl. Aww, you sweet on her, brother?"

"Considering you follow Greta around like a pussy-whipped fuckhole, I wouldn't be making fun right about now."

Ignoring his gibe, Cutter replied, "It's like that, is it? You got a real thing with her?"

Whistle grunted his assent. "Maybe."

"Man, Jazz has been in love with your ass since she stepped foot in the Squad clubhouse."

"I knew she was crushing on me but was it that bad, man?"

"You're blind, brother. She definitely caught feels, but she's a big girl. She's not going to fuck with your girl. Jazz may be many things, but a vindictive bitch is not one of them. She's decent to the core. Gonna make one of the brother's a good old lady one day."

"Hmm," answered Whistle noncommittedly. "I don't need any fuckin' drama when this thing between Tasa and me has barely started. She's skittish as is. Her brother's already a huge problem, and we don't even know half of what he's capable of."

"You need me to put a prospect on her?"

"Not yet. She'll catch on to him in a hot second. She's grown up in the life, so she knows how to keep an eye out for herself. Her mistake is that she thinks she's gotten away for good. The mafia's reach is legendary, and let's face it, when the chips are down, they rally together. For a price, but they do it. Poughkeepsie is historically controlled by La Cosa Nostra, and those Italian fucks would slit their mother's throat for the right price."

"If you're smart, you'll take advantage of her situation to get closer to her," Cutter advised.

"That's the plan, but I want to know if you find anything, ASAP," he insisted.

"Will do, brother."

Huh, Cutter didn't growl at him for taking a forceful tone. The man was starting to respect him. Either that, or he was taking pity on him since he recognized someone as pussy-whipped as him.

CHAPTER FOURTEEN

WHISTLE HAD STAYED over again last night, just as he had the night before that, annnd the night before that. If she didn't know better, Tasa would think he'd moved in with her and Jazz the past week. Only Jazz was nowhere to be found. Whether she was uncomfortable with the situation or was giving them space, Tasa had no idea, but she was too self-conscious to bring it up. She wasn't naturally timid, but this was her first kind-of-relationship, and she was uncertain how to proceed. *Mafie* princess meets ex-Bratva biker. Not exactly a Bumble coffee date.

Whistle and she had not defined whatever they were, other than the fact that "it" was monogamous. It was a relief, in a way. Otherwise, she might be forced to put distance between them, and she wasn't ready to do that.

Regardless, there was one undeniable truth. He no longer camped out at the Squad Bar. Instead, he was in her bed. Every. Single. Night. And the things they did in there? Every sexual fantasy come to life. He was domineering in the bedroom, that was for certain.

He was domineering *outside* the bedroom as well, especially when it came to her safety. Once again, she found herself abiding by a set of rules dictated by a man. Although it was frustrating, it wasn't nearly as suffocating as with Alex. First, there was Kingdom's warning of what he'd put on the line to help her out. She wasn't about to repay his kindness by being difficult.

Then there was the fact that Whistle didn't trample on any of her other choices. He'd rationally explained the reasoning behind his demands, something Alex only did when they were in the throes of ugly, gloves-off argument. Whistle treated her as an equal and took into consideration any alterations she suggested, even if he didn't necessarily follow them.

Like the situation with the bus.

Tasa loved the bus. Taking the bus had been a revelation to her. For the first time, she wasn't living the life of a coddled child. She loved the jostling of people making room for one another along the narrow middle aisle. She felt like part of the flow of humanity as everyone went about their daily lives. She loved the way people gave up their seats for the elderly or for pregnant women. She enjoyed people-watching or simply stared out the window as she glided along the city streets. She loved the rocking of the hulking metal contraption, the halting forward lurches when it had to brake suddenly. It was the reason she didn't catch a ride with Jazz in her car when Jazz worked an earlier shift at the Squad Bar.

She'd been disappointed when her bus-riding had to come to an abrupt end, even if it was replaced by a ride on the back of Whistle's bike. Wrapping her arms around Whistle and leaning into him as he navigated the streets was thrilling, but she missed the solitary peacefulness of public transport.

At least, Whistle had explained to her the risks of waiting for the bus, in plain sight of anyone, especially late at night. It made his mandate easier to swallow, even if he hadn't been swayed by her argument that riding in the daytime would be safe enough. On one hand, she hated having her freedom curtailed, but on the other hand ... she sometimes felt exposed when she walked on the street. Every once in a while, an itchy sensation crept up her spine. Surveying her surroundings, she never found something out of the ordinary, so she ultimately dismissed it as simple nerves.

Although they hadn't discussed whatever was happening between them, Tasa was smitten at sharing her space with him. There was something special about living with Whistle. Of course, there was the sex, but it was about the small intimacies they shared. Like the Hungarian torte, made of layers of almond meringue dough and buttercream spiced with cognac and vanilla, that she'd baked him on one of their days off.

After pulling the torte out of the oven and letting it rest, she was cutting into it as he came through the door after running errands. Taking the slice she handed him, he tilted his head left and right in an adorable manner that mimicked a little boy. She giggled as he inspected it carefully before sitting down at the counter, taking a careful forkful and popping it into his mouth.

A low moan rumbled out.

"Good, right?" she beamed as she asked.

"Holy. Fuck. I was trying to figure out what it was, but I don't think I've had anything better. Not even my grandfather's Russian honey cake."

"I told you I grew up running around in a Romanian café. My grandmother made the desserts. She came from a region with Hungarian influences. Besides Hungary, she can make any dessert from Germany and Eastern Europe." She dug into her slice and hummed with satisfaction. "Not as good as my grandmother, but it'll pass."

Giving him a curious look, she asked, "What's a Russian honey cake?"

"Not sure what's in it except honey and sour cream, but it has layers like this. Sour cream featured in most Russian dishes I ate when my mother packed me off in the summers to my grandfather. Before the violin took over my life," he revealed. "Brings me back to the warm summer days I spent in the garden with my grandfather."

"What about your brothers?"

His eyes sobered as he looked down at his plate. "My brothers …" He shook his head before picking up the thread of his story. "The rift began with my mother. I know exactly how it went down. She fell for my father's looks, but when her sensitive, aristocratic soul learned that her Igor was a ruthless thug, she was devastated. She lost first one, then two sons to him. When she had her "oops" baby, she claimed me as her own. I'm pretty sure I was the product of rape, but I have to give her credit, she hung on to me ferociously. They'd made a pact: I was hers until my induction. The short answer is that I never got a chance to get close to my brothers." He gave a little, somewhat resigned shrug. "They didn't seem to mind. They already had each other."

His mother had poured her life and soul into him and his violin.

Tasa's lips drew down. She didn't like this image of Whistle, a lonely little boy in a big mansion, isolated with his mother and a violin. "What about after your induction?"

Whistle let out a mirthless half laugh, half huff. "After my induction, things got bat-shit crazy. I was torn between two worlds. Playing a concert at Carnegie Hall in midtown Manhattan and killing people hours later in the alleys of Little Odessa. My father welcomed me, but my brothers resented me. Then I ended up in juvie. Couldn't handle the double life, and I'd do something stupid and get caught. For two years, I was in a vicious cycle that took me in and out of prison. More than anything, jail ruined my music career. The days behind bars with no violin. I was a fucking mess, caught between my parents fighting over me."

"That's why you love being a biker, don't you? Because you're free to be you." The Squad and their closeness was certainly another reason that tempted her to want to stay.

"Yeah, there's no pretending when you're a biker. No trying to fit into the normal world. No faking it. By the time Prez found me, I'd killed more men than some inmates on death row. I mean, the Squad left illegal business ventures behind, but I am who I am."

He raised his hands, staring at them as if he could still see the blood dripping off them. "I don't have to pretend to be refined and cultured when I've bloodied my hands like a common thug. I'd have PTSD if it wasn't for the fact that my father and brothers never hid what they did and that I was under orders to kill." His gaze flicked up to hers and held. "Not the kind of order one ignored, know what I mean?"

Oh boy, did she ever. Tasa may have been shielded from certain aspects of her family's life, but the Lupu family were proud of who they were and how they got where they did. Her hand slid over the counter and covered his. She channeled as much love as she could in that touch. Anything to lift away even one of the demons weighing down his soul.

"Let's face it, there's no way in hell I can live a normal life. Even when I played, I wasn't a normal kid. But I'm more of my father's son than I'd like to admit because I have no interest in a civilized life." He spat out the word civilized in a tone of disgust.

Done with his confession, he jabbed his fork into the torte slice on her plate, having demolished his portion.

"I'll make you a honey cake," she offered softly. "Although I can't promise it will taste anything like your grandfather's."

The corners of his gorgeous turquoise eyes crinkled. Emotions she couldn't quite read flashed across his face. "If it's anything like this, it'll be delicious."

A warm pool of gooeyness hummed in her belly. He was loyal to his core. He'd even bestowed that undying allegiance on his father for a time, even if the bastard didn't deserve it. Granted, he hadn't had much of a choice, but she guessed that he'd done it as a tribute to his position in the Bratva. If Whistle had stayed, he would've become the soldier he was expected to be. For his sake, she was glad he'd escaped and found the Squad, where he'd been given the chance to discover and live his authentic self.

Tasa saw the shadows spelling out that he was a man capable of great violence. Then he turned his gaze toward her, and warmth entered those lagoon-colored eyes of his, giving them a darker hue. Despite his scars, he'd never hurt her. It came out in so many other things he did for her. The way she woke up every morning, with him curled around her back protectively, like a shield. For whatever reason, he'd chosen her, and she was grateful for it.

There was a shift in the air, and she followed him with her eyes as he sat on the couch and patted the seat beside him. His eyes smoldered, desire burning holes in her. Holes that quickly filled with her own red-hot lust. A jolt of exhilaration shot through her and she joined him.

Fiddling with the top button of her flimsy silk top, she slowly plucked it free. Her fingers slid down to the next buttonhole and slipped that one open.

"What are you doing?" he asked gruffly.

Her eyelashes fluttered. "Undressing."

He growled low, his legs spreading to give himself room. Glancing down, she understood why, and her pride soared that she was able to affect him so quickly.

Another button popped out.

Then another.

Scooping her hair in her hands, she raised her arms. The movement naturally split the blouse open, displaying her dark-red demi-cup bra.

Dark energy thrummed inside her.

"Closer," he demanded.

Coyly, she leaned in and licked his lips but then pulled back abruptly.

Slipping his hand between her thighs, he shoved her skirt out of the way and spread her legs. She promptly lifted her butt off the couch for him to hike it up. He groaned at her matching panties before dipping his hand inside.

"Fuck, princess. Such a hot little clutch you have for me."

He spread her slippery lips, his eyes glittering extra bright.

"Get up, sweet girl. You're gonna learn to ride cock today."

She let out a squeal of excitement, her hands darting to his buckle and making quick work of freeing his hardened shaft. Eager, she straddled him, curling her fingers around the sides of his cut as she bore down on him. She fought through the soreness and the natural resistance of her body. They'd had lots of sex, but it hadn't been that long since she was a virgin. She speared herself on his cock, taking him deeper and deeper until he was fully sheathed inside her.

Besides his fingers lightly grasping her hips, he gave her total power, and she was going to take advantage of the rare opportunity. This was the first time he wasn't controlling every move. Seated on him, it felt incredible. She was totally impaled, pierced by his thick girth, and she felt oh-so sexy.

Stripping her shirt off, he unclasped her bra and whipped it free. Her breasts bounced a little, and he palmed them roughly, tweaking her nipples in a way that had her arching her back, seating her even deeper. She gasped sharply at the friction. She might be sore, stretched, and chock-full of cock, but the edge of pain was erotic. She was hooked on him. It charged her with drive and determination. She lifted off him until only his flared tip spread the cleft of her pussy.

"Such a sweet little cunt you have for me. Such a good

little cunt. Who owns this pussy, Tasa?"

"You," she breathed out as she swooped back down until she was impaled once again before rising back up. Good God, the friction. Her jaw dropped open. Panting, she lifted up and bore down until she got a rhythm, bouncing on his cock. Her breasts jiggled in his palms until his hands dropped to her hips to guide her movements.

He looked up at her through his too-thick black lashes, and their eyes locked. The way they watched each other was painfully intimate. It was like a bridge, made of steel, binding them together, joining them as one. Unblinking, the backs of her eyes burned. His searing look tore her chest open. It was like a physical touch, plunging into her soul and seizing it within his fist. She'd never felt this bare and exposed. Never felt this close to another human being.

It suddenly dawned on her. *This* was making love. He was making love to her. Nothing else mattered but that moment. The world could have exploded around them, and they would've remained in their own little cocoon.

Eyes fastened on each other, he pumped into her, finally taking back control. His hands tightened, and then he boosted her up until only the crown of his shaft remained inside her. He slammed her down until he was balls deep. This sensation, on top of the many others that had built inside her, toppled her over the edge and she released a scream. His eyes shifted to a darker tint.

His hands snaked to the front and played with her clit. He nipped and suckled down her throat, then from one breast to the other, branding her with his marks.

"Feed me," he growled.

She pushed her breast into his mouth as she bounced

away on his cock, riding him for broke until her brain blitzed out. Expelling a harsh breath, she was taken over by a rush of sensation. Suspended in time and space for an instant, then she slammed back down to earth and rolled into another climax. Sparks flashed in front of her sightless eyes as pleasure zapped through her. Her body seized up, and she bit out another scream into the flesh of his chest.

As Whistle raced toward his own finish line, she waded through the aftershocks rocking her and gasped out, "Whistle, I want your c-come. O-on my tits."

His breathing came out harsh as his eyes shot up from where they were joined to her face.

"Fuck," he swore gruffly. With one last brutal down-stroke, he lifted her off and rumbled out, "On your goddamn knees."

Heat swept over her, flushing her skin. She scrambled down just as he began jerking himself off. God, what an image. Her chest rose and fell over the harsh pulls on his cock. His shoulders squared forward, the tendons of his neck strained, and the veins of his biceps popped out. Seconds later, his come sprayed across her torso, up to her collarbone, and down to her belly. The hot ropes of seed blistered her skin. She loved watching the zigzag marks he'd left dripping on her. Leaning forward, she wrapped her lips around the tip of his cock and sucked off the last drops. More come spurted in her mouth, and she yummed around the saltiness.

Pulling off his cock with a wet pop, she rubbed his come into her flesh, reveling in the stickiness and all that it meant. Rubbing *him* into her, becoming one with him. His piercing blue eyes grew heavy and fell at half-mast.

"Fuck, that's—"

He cut off mid-sentence, left speechless. Good. Rising to her knees, she buried her face in his chest, inhaling his spicy scent. His arms hovered for an instant before wrapping around her and bringing her tightly into his chest.

She felt him everywhere. He'd either touched, kissed, bit, or fucked every inch of her.

Every. Inch.

Inside out.

He'd staked his claim. Her body was his.

CHAPTER FIFTEEN

WHISTLE PLANTED A kiss on the crown of Tasa's head. Pulling her into his lap, he rubbed his lips into her hair. He loved seeing her totally at ease with him. Here she was in his arms, mostly naked, with his come drying on her tits. He wanted to crow in triumph but feared shattering the moment and risking her getting self-conscious.

Basking with her in his arms, he said, "We need to leave here."

Tasa lifted her head, her eyes found his. A cute, little furrow appeared between her brows. "I like it here with Jazz."

"Jazz isn't going to come back as long as I'm here, and I need to watch over you."

Although Jazz had kept her distance, this was her place. It wasn't right to flaunt his relationship with Tasa in her face. While she hadn't done anything to sabotage them, he didn't want to risk it. The best thing was to find another place, just him and Tasa. While it was true that he had to watch her, he wouldn't have been able to stay away if he tried. So another apartment was the only solution.

Tasa was so used to being watched that she didn't question him. It was a blanket excuse that automatically garnered her consent, and one he felt zero guilt in using. *Hey, all's fair in love and war, no?* His hand grasped her rounded kneecap. He rubbed a sensitive spot on the inside of her knee, in part to distract her but also because he liked touching her. She was so responsive that one small touch had her turning deeper into his chest, arching her back enough to signal her acknowledgment of his touch.

Her nose wrinkled in that adorable way of hers.

"She hasn't been here since you started sleeping over," she observed.

"No, she hasn't."

Tasa sucks in a breath. "Is she upset? With me?"

His hand dipped down her thigh, slipping underneath her skirt again, tracing the crease where her thigh met her pussy. "Don't think she's angry with you. It might be me. We had a conversation that didn't go the way she wanted."

"What does that mean?"

He shrugged. Whistle wasn't about to lay out the drama that had unfolded with Jazz. "Point is, it's better if we move someplace more secure and closer to the Bar so it's easier for me to check on it. This place is a fuckin' security hazard," he muttered, his eyes narrowing on the fire escape outside the window. "Already found a place and signed the lease. Got the keys. All we need to do is get furniture."

"Wow, you didn't even ask me? You already signed the lease," she said in bafflement as she pushed his hand off her pussy and drew away from him.

Guess she wasn't as pliable as he'd thought.

Rising to her knees, she said, "You're more than a bit pushy, you know that, right? There are so many boundaries you crossed. I don't even know where to begin. I'm not a child or your property."

He gave her a hard look. "There's one boundary I haven't crossed." He was talking about kissing, and she knew it. As for her mentioning the word "property," he figured she'd heard the term, what with working at the Squad Bar. After being made to feel like true property in a transactional marriage, he assumed it didn't have a good connotation. But this was neither the right time nor place to get into that discussion.

Rolling her eyes, she crossed her arms over her chest, plumping them up in a way that distracted him. The fact that she hadn't bothered to wipe off his drying come was hot as fuck.

"Don't tell me you're attached to this place?" he asked in an offended tone.

"Not necessarily this place, but that's not the point. It wasn't for you to make the decision on my behalf. I didn't leave my family to be pushed around by another man who thinks he knows what's best for me. And I like living with Jazz."

"Don't compare me to your brother. My only concern is your security. When it comes to that topic, yeah, go ahead and call me shameless. Guilty as charged."

Grinding down on her back teeth, she balled her hands as if she was holding back from walloping him for his arrogance. He got it. He could be a prick, but that didn't mean he was backing down. They had to move.

"And how am I going to stand on my own two feet, pray tell, when I have a man swooping in and making all the decisions for me?"

A pang of guilt hit him in the solar plexus at the hurt

on her face. He didn't want to deny her a sense of independence. Nor did he want to be compared to her brother. "Fuck, okay. You're right …" He scrubbed his face in frustration. "I might've been a little worried you wouldn't take to my suggestion, so I jumped the gun. I admit it. Should've come to you first."

"It's my first apartment, Whistle," she continued relentlessly. "After moving out of my family's home in Queens, I moved into an apartment chosen and paid for by Alex, and only on the condition that my mother decorate it. Ever see the Kremlin Royal Apartments?"

His forehead wrinkled. "Uhh … yeah, I think?"

"Well. That probably served as her inspiration. It's god-awful. This will be my first apartment, Whistle. I would've liked to be part of the process, you know?"

"Alright, alright, you've made your point," he grumbled. "But I stand by my point too. While I know you like living with Jazz, the less she's involved, the better. You trust your brother not to hurt you, but you don't know how he'll react to the people who helped keep you away from him?"

"He'd never hurt a woman. An innocent."

Whistle cocked a dubious eyebrow. "Really?" he drawled. "And you know this, how?"

Tasa's fingers curled into tighter fists, nails digging into the soft flesh of her palms.

"Truth is, you don't know everything about your brother's dealings. By eliminating unknown factors, we guarantee your safety, *her* safety, and strengthen our position."

He wrapped his hands over her fists, gently loosening them. Raising one hand to his lips, he placed an open mouth to the palm of her hand. "Does that make sense?" he asked in a gentle tone.

Blowing out a long breath, she agreed, "I suppose, but stop making decisions on my behalf."

"I'll do my best." He paused and then took up the earlier part of her response. "You suppose, princess? I think you can do better than that."

Fluttering her eyes and pursing her lips, she said, "Yes, okay, you're right. I'm sure you chose the location of the new place for a reason, and you've already installed cameras or what have you."

"Well, not me …" He winked. "More like Cutter and Flicker."

"Same difference," she grumbled.

Giving her bouncy ass a little slap that elicited a yelp, he ordered, "Come on, let's get in the shower before I add more come to those gorgeous tits. We have to pick up the truck from the clubhouse and hit a few furniture stores. Definitely getting a bed with a headboard so I can tie you up."

"Promises, promises," she quipped.

Fisting her hair, he pulled her head back and whispered against her lips, "That's a promise I intend to keep. The moment that bed is put together, the first thing on the agenda is leashing you to it."

Her chest began to rise and fall in a fast pattern.

"Test me, princess. I'm beggin' you to test me," he swore.

THEY JUMPED INTO the shower, where Whistle watched morosely as she scrubbed off his come. More's the pity, but he figured it was added incentive to spray on her later, once she was tied to their new bed. Afterward, they rode over to the clubhouse, got the keys to the truck, and went from store to store to load up on the basics.

Tasa wrangled with the salesman like she was in a marketplace in the old country. With her by his side, Whistle didn't think he'd pay full price for anything again in his life. She was such a contradiction. She'd been brought up with a silver spoon in her mouth, but she understood the value of a dollar and didn't take anything for granted. There was no sense of entitlement about her; she busted her ass every night at the Bar, she didn't squander her money, and she looked for deals like every day was Black Friday.

After loading up the bed of the pick-up truck with cardboard boxes of furniture to install and a thick mattress and box spring, he jumped into the cab and texted a couple of the brothers to meet him in front of the apartment. It was a small place, but he figured they didn't need much, and he'd let her decorate it and make it her own. It was part and parcel with his plan to get her invested in the place and give her more incentive to stay.

Hoodie and Cutter were lounging by the front door by the time they pulled up to the curb.

Taking the keys to the apartment off his key ring, he handed them to Tasa and then jumped out of the truck, calling out, "Yo, brothers, whattup?"

Tasa got out as well and greeted them with nods of her head. "Hey, Hoodie. Cutter."

"Whattup, Tasa?" singsonged Hoodie with a wide grin.

The kind of knowing smirk that made Whistle want to whack it right off his face. Peeking into the back of the truck, Hoodie asked in a mock-innocent tone, "That a mattress, you got in there?"

Tasa blushed. Muttering to herself, she hurried to the door and busied herself with opening it and figuring out a way of propping it open. Whistle had already told her the apartment number, so she left them to it and went upstairs to check it out.

He sighed inwardly as he watched her rush up the stairs, taking them two at a time. He would've loved to see her reaction when she first laid eyes on the place, but he was busy dealing with two assholes who were currently grinning at him from ear to ear. *Dicks.*

"What?" he demanded. "Come on, let it all out. I don't want you stressing Tasa with your teasing. She'd got enough on her mind."

"You domesticated now?" snickered Hoodie. "What's next? A bridal shower, you little pansy-assed pussy."

Crossing his arms over his chest, he leaned back against the side of the truck. "You done?"

Hoodie mimicked his stance and replied, "I'm not close to done, asswipe. Why the fuck you wanna tie yourself down to *one* woman? No pussy's worth giving up the variety."

Cutter snorted. "Says the brother who has no fuckin' clue. Bro, there's nothing like having the right woman under you. What's even better is when you've got to *work* to get her under you, knowing she doesn't want to be there, but she can't help herself 'cause your dick's that good. Knowing she has to surrender her feisty spirit 'cause your cock is dipped in fuckin' gold. There's nothing better than *that*."

"Or when she's screamin' your name, her pussy working you so fuckin' good. Damn, makes me hard just thinking about it," added Whistle. "Yeah, and the fact that her brother wants to take her from me. That just pisses me off and makes fucking her hotter. No one touches what's mine."

"So, she Squad property?"

"No, Hoodie, she's *my* property," he snarled.

"What about Jazz?"

"What about her?" Whistle shot back.

"What the fuck, Whistle? You know how Jazz feels about you. You've always been her favorite."

"Not anymore," he grumbled, remembering their last conversation.

Hoodie unfolded his large body and, in one quick move, loomed threateningly over Whistle. In an even, threatening tone, he asked, "You didn't hurt that girl, now, did you?"

Whistle's eyes widened. Hoodie never got upset. He shoved his friend's shoulder and said, "Knock it off. What's gotten into you?"

Hoodie fell back a step, but his eyes continued to burn.

"Answer me," he demanded in a tight voice.

"Fucking hell," Whistle cursed, scrubbing his mouth and chin. What had he missed here? Suddenly, he felt like he was walking in a minefield set out by his best friend. "I did nothing to her, Hoodie. Never led her on. Never lied to her. Never told her she'd be my old lady. *Never.* So back the fuck up and get off my jock, asshole. I've got some serious shit on my shoulders, and I don't need your drama on top of everything else."

Hoodie turned his head, looking chastened.

As he should.

Clapping his friend's shoulder, he advised in a low voice, "Look, brother, I never asked for anyone to be into me. If it makes you feel better, I got my payback 'cause I'm with a woman who fights me every step of the way.

"I know. You can't help the way you look any more than—"

"Christ, are you two done already?" Cutter broke in. "You—" he pointed at Hoodie, "—talk a good fucking game about not wanting the same piece of ass on the regular, but you're all up in his face over Jazz. You want that bitch? She's fucking free now, my brother, so it's on you from here on out." Gesturing to Whistle, he ordered, "Give him some slack already. He'd never intentionally hurt a girlie like Jazz, and he's in a hell of a fucking mess. Tasa's brothers are no joke."

Whistle's head whipped around to Cutter. "What'd you find out?"

"A fuck load, brother, and not much of it good. That brother of hers, the *Lupul*? That cocksucker's no joke. He's coming for her, have no doubt. She's the fuckin' baby of that family, and those brothers of hers are crazy-ass motherfuckers."

Whistle groaned. It wasn't what he wanted to hear.

"The three amigos made a name for themselves since their father's murder. First, they avenged him. Which was no easy matter. But did they stop there? Oh, hell no, they didn't. They kept up their killing spree until they controlled all of Queens, and that's a big-ass borough. They fought the Italians, the Colombians, and don't forget the Chinese. They scorched the fuckin' earth. Razed it to the ground. Now, they're the bosses of Sunnyside, Queens, aka "Little Bucharest." Thank fuck Tasa texted her granny to let her know she wasn't kidnapped. Would've triggered World War III up in there."

Fucking mother.

"What does he deal in?" he asked.

"Nothing's off-limits, but what they like to do most is fuck with people's money. Scams, white-collar Wall Street shit, financial crimes. Real upscale shit. The middle brother's some kind of financial genius. They're also into arms dealing, and when I say arms, I mean they can get their hands on anything. Flicker found one of their online catalogs of Cold War weapons. Tactical anti-assault weapons, missile launchers, anti-aircraft guns. If Iran wants a nuclear missile, they come knocking on Alex Lupu's door. They also dabble in drug trafficking and a scattering of other businesses. To keep diversified, ya know."

The throbbing in Whistle's head pounded harder as Cutter regurgitated everything he'd learned. Here he was, buying her crappy furniture and strutting around like a peacock when her brother was running industries worth billions. Lucky for him, his confidence bordered on the insane 'cause he was intent on locking this woman down if it was the last thing he did. Hell, Whistle wasn't just anyone. Once upon a time, he shared the rarefied air of a cache of highly coveted violinists from across the globe. That was no small feat. He'd single-mindedly, *obsessively*, worked his ass off, and if he did the same thing with Tasa, he'd have her in the end as well.

Fuck her goddamn brother.

Whistle glanced up to find Hoodie scrutinizing his face. Schooling his expression, he shook his head once, communicating to his brother to back the fuck off.

Shoving off the truck, he slapped its side. "Come on, let's get this shit inside."

Hoisting the mattress above his shoulder, Whistle glanced up the stairway and spotted Tasa's head dipping down between the banisters a few floors up.

Spotting him, she shrieked, "Oh my God, Whistle, the apartment is incredible. Come quick and meet our neighbor."

Hoodie chuckled at his expense.

Groaning under the weight of the mattress, he snapped, "Just hurry up, asshole."

"Fuck off, brother. You become manager of the Bar and you think you can shout orders?" Hoodie fired back.

Whistle heard the smirk in his tone. Damn, he wanted to throttle him. "It's fuckin' heavy, and we have two more floors to go, you prick. Fuckin' move already."

Getting to the third floor was a pain in the ass, but once he dropped the mattress to the ground, he caught Tasa as she ran into his arms. Wrapping herself around him was pure heaven. She introduced him to Maddie, a woman who wasn't a day shy of eighty. How she got up and down the stairs every day was a wonder. After the introductions, she waved goodbye to Maddie and urged him into the apartment.

Clapping her hands and giggling like a little girl on Christmas morning, she spread her arms out wide and gasped. "It's beautiful, Whistle."

He wasn't sure about that. There was nothing sleek or modern about it, but there was a comfortable, homey feel that he'd felt the moment he stepped inside with the building manager. It was a large open space, with one exposed-brick wall that morphed into a fireplace. There was also a huge bay window. The bright white walls were topped with old-fashioned crenellated molding along the edge where they met the ceiling.

The instant Whistle had walked into the kitchen he knew it was a perfect fit for Tasa, with its cheery yellow walls and new appliances. There were two bedrooms, each with a wall of windows.

Cutter came into the apartment and helped Hoodie maneuver the mattress into the main bedroom while Whistle followed Tasa into the smaller one facing the back of the building. Soft light flowed in through the row of windows in this quieter part of the apartment.

He walked up behind her as she swayed near the glass, looking down into the street below.

His hands fell to her shoulders and massaged them. "This place is yours."

Her head swung around, eyes wide with surprise.

"Yes, I'll stay here for your security," he clarified. "But it's yours. Your space to decorate as you wish. If you need time for yourself, I'll leave." She shook her head and tresses of hair slipped off her shoulder. He nodded yes. "I can go to the Bar or crash at the clubhouse."

He hoped—no, *prayed*—she'd make this place her own. That she'd get attached and remain past spring. Yeah, he was willing to use anything at his disposal to woo her to stay. It wasn't much, but whatever he had was hers. Like his heart. She held it in the palm of her hands.

"Babe, this is your place, too," she insisted.

"That's music to my ears, but everyone needs their own place. You've never lived alone, and you've got to experience what it's like to have that safe space where you can be you. To express yourself on these walls and make it your own."

She stilled. Her eyes roved over his face, staring at him hard. He felt it like a touch, but there was stark pain in them. Fuck, he'd overstepped. Assumed he knew what a complex woman like her needed.

Then her eyes went soft.

On him.

So, so soft.

Unshed tears gleamed in her big brown eyes.

She cleared her throat and said, "You give me gifts I don't even realize I'm yearning for until you offer them to me."

The breath he was holding in tightly, shuddered out of him.

"I can decorate for the first time in my own home." Wrapping her arms around his waist, she settled her cheek against his heart and hummed. "Thank you, thank you, thank you."

His stomach dipped. He raked his hand through her smooth sable locks, relishing their silky feel as they slipped through his fingers. He marveled at her, at the contrast of her steely core intertwined with strands of softness. These quiet moments, when she was tender and her heart was open—because he felt her heart reaching out to his— brought him to his damn knees.

CHAPTER SIXTEEN

TASA PAUSED BY the open door of the storage room; memories of Whistle teasing her with touches while she stood on the stool and hung onto the light socket rushed back. Jazz was rummaging around, pulling out bottles of liquor to bring out to the bar before they opened for the day. She'd arrived before her shift for the chance to talk to Jazz and get everything out in the open.

"Hey," she said softly so as not to startle her friend.

Jazz took a sharp intake of breath, grabbing her chest as her eyes swung over her shoulder to Tasa.

She took a hesitant step into the room. "Sorry, I didn't mean to scare you."

Jazz gave out a little chuckle. "No worries, I was so focused on going through the inventory, I didn't notice someone came in."

Tasa leaned back a little and glanced in the hallway. It was quiet for the moment. Hopefully, they wouldn't be interrupted. Taking another small step closer, she crouched down to be on eye level with Jazz. Her hands came together, and she wrung them as she took a deep breath. "I hope it wasn't too much of an inconvenience with my suddenly moving out …" she started.

Jazz held up a bottle to inspect it. "Nah, I'm used to people coming and going."

Was that a subtle jab? Did Jazz feel Tasa had abandoned her for a man? God, she hoped not.

"I wasn't really excited to move out, but it seemed like the best thing to do, for several reasons," she ventured to say. Taking a big breath, she blurted out, "I enjoyed living with you. I love having you as a friend, and I hope that Whistle and me being together won't ruin what *we* have."

She flinched at how ridiculous she sounded, but this was her first experience with having to navigate something as heavy as this with a friend.

Facing the wall, Jazz uncharacteristically avoided Tasa's gaze. She dropped the bottle back into the box and released a heavy sigh. "Whistle and I had it out." She darted a glance at Tasa. "He explained how he felt about you, about me and him. Congratulations, you've been able to do what no other bitch in the club has managed to do," she finished with a tinge of bitterness.

Tasa licked her suddenly parched lips. "I didn't mean for any of this to happen, Jazz. Believe me when I tell you I expected things to finish as you had predicted. It's as baffling to me as it is to anyone that Whistle and I are together."

"I questioned him about you and his intentions. He made it clear he was serious. More serious than I've seen him be about anything, and I've known him for years. What can I say, Tasa? Am I disappointed? Yes. Do I need time to lick my wounds? Again, yes. I was resigned to him never getting serious about anyone, so it was hard to see him with someone else when I've been there all along, but what can I do? The heart wants what the heart wants."

Tasa reached for Jazz's hand and gripped it tightly. "I never meant to upset you, and I hope you can forgive me for being part of something that hurt you. You matter to me. Other than Whistle, you're my closest friend here." She took in a deep breath. "But I understand if you need to step away."

"I was angry at him, not you. I am hurt, even though logically, I know it's no one's fault. I need time, but I'm not going to throw away my friendship with you over a man. That's not who I am."

"I understand," Tasa replied softly. While she liked to think of herself as a strong, honest person, she wasn't sure she could stand seeing Whistle with another woman. In fact, she was pretty sure she wouldn't be able to tolerate it one bit. "You have so many friends, Jazz. I depend on our friendship more than you do, but it wouldn't be fair of me to insist on it if it hurts you to be around me, or me and Whistle."

Patting Tasa's hand, Jazz gave her a sad smile. "I'll be alright. Your friendship is special to me also. Doesn't matter how popular you think I am. I just need a little more time, but I'll come back around."

"Thank you," she whispered back. Placing a soft kiss on Jazz's cheek, she raised to her feet and quietly backed out of the storage room. She had gotten more than she deserved. While, yes, she hadn't maliciously gone out of her way to hurt Jazz and honestly thought that she and Whistle would have a brief fling, she had ultimately chosen Whistle over her.

All she could do now was wait.

BESIDES HER FRAGILE friendship with Jazz, life since she'd moved into the new apartment was fantastic. Tasa was excited about having a space that she could arrange as she liked, and went all out with her decorating ideas. Whistle was there every night, occasionally spending it elsewhere to give her a little privacy after verifying her safety was assured. She didn't ask where he went, and he didn't share. Whether he crashed at the Bar, the clubhouse, or at Hoodie's, she didn't question it. Was she jealous? Worried? Both, dammit, but she sucked it up since he was making this sacrifice for her, not because he was trying to distance himself.

She also found she didn't like being alone very much. There were times when she swore she was being watched, but Whistle had secured the building, and she found nothing when she checked out of the apartment windows. Scoffing at these restless moments, she chalked them up to feeling lonely. Her mind was playing tricks on her. Or so she told herself.

Tasa found a dance studio, where she began taking classes with an instructor to get back into a routine. Six weeks of no practice, on top of winter break, had left her feeling rusty, and she had to get back into training. Her waitressing had improved, along with the rest of the staff at the Bar. Some people had been switched out for more seasoned employees, and others, like her, had simply gotten better over time.

About a week later, Jazz came back around, and they resumed their friendship. She even stopped by the apartment to check it out. The woman was a saint because there was no way in hell Tasa would've had the inner fortitude to do the same if she were in Jazz's position.

That self-awareness segued into the one blemish, the one thing that irked her in her new life. If she were to be honest, it more than irked her. It sent her into a tizzy fringing on hysteria that embarrassed her, especially since she barely managed to hide it from Whistle.

Jealousy.

Like a devious snake, jealousy had slithered into her heart. The club bitches flirting with him, she could handle, reasoning that if he'd wanted to be with any of them, he would've already been taken. The real problem was that Whistle was unbelievably attractive and garnered female attention wherever he was. *Aggressive* female attention. Some women had zero qualms about blatantly hitting on him in front of her.

And it ate at her.

Even though she firmly reminded herself that she didn't want to *own* him. Or more accurately, she couldn't afford to. If she did, then she'd have to be owned in return, and that could *not* happen. Absolutely not.

But tell that to her heart, a dumb, blind, and useless organ that acted out like a toddler at the most inconvenient moments. Such as when they were shopping for groceries together. In the store, Whistle demonstrated a severe lack of domestication by whispering in her ear all the things he'd do to her once they were behind closed doors.

"And when I say 'closed doors,'" he clarified, "I mean any set of doors. Car doors count. I'm going to lick and suck that little clit of yours till you're screaming my name and yanking my hair. Ya know, the way you like to do that? Guiding my mouth right over that sweet spot of your tasty pussy, just where you want it. I fuckin' love it when you grab my hair, wild girl. When you smear your juices all over my face when you come."

Giggling, she shoved at him as they pushed the grocery cart together. Figuring it was better to split up their tasks—otherwise, he'd end up dragging them out of there before they even got started—she tore the list of groceries she was holding in two, thrust the bottom half in his hand, and pointed him to the farthest aisle from her.

"Dairy section," she ordered with a jab of her index finger. "Get a gallon of whole milk. I'll meet you at the cashier," she finished with a touch of exasperation.

Tasa shouldn't have been surprised by what happened next. After all, she knew who he was. A sexy, New-York-Times-Square-billboard-worthy hottie. Whistle wasn't a regular, ole human-level hot. He was otherworldly, god-like hot. And a biker to boot. That was like catnip to even normal women, forget about the pushy kind. She should've known drooling women stalked him like a pack of zombies. *Should've, could've.*

She was in the baking section when she caught a glimpse of him walking past her aisle, closely trailed by a young, hot blonde-thing dressed in a skin-tight workout outfit. That was a woman on the prowl if she'd ever seen one. The blonde was around Whistle's age, and for some reason, that got her dander up even more. A woman with a bigger set of breasts than her, as well, proudly displayed in a push-up bra, leaving very little to the imagination.

Tasa cringed. She hated, utterly hated comparing herself physically to other women. Normally, she didn't. Except that her sanity went right out the window when it came to Whistle. Sighing to herself, she clenched her eyes and fists shut at the same time.

Jealousy exploded in a wave so powerful she stumbled back a step, her hand shooting out to grip a shelf. *Holy hell.* But did she fight it like a rational woman? Of course not. Instead, she leaned into the insanity, abandoned her cart, and crept down the aisle to watch the scenario play itself out. Clearly, she was a glutton for punishment.

Bobbing and weaving, she scampered from aisle to aisle until she caught up with them in the frozen section. Tasa got along with women exceedingly well. She normally considered herself a chick's chick. Until that moment. The situation unfolding in front of her eyes challenged that self-concept to the extreme.

Whistle was in the process of opening a refrigerated door when the woman's hand reached out and landed on his, stumbling into his side for good measure. It was so contrived Tasa rolled her eyes in exasperation. By God, but that hussy was brazen!

Whistle glanced down at the woman's hand gripping his. Stepping back, he removed his hand from the handle. With a wave, he gestured for her to go ahead and get what she wanted. And, boy, did she take advantage of it. Opening the door, she bent over, arching her back shamelessly, sticking her ass out for his perusal. To give him credit, his eyes skimmed over her in a cursory manner before moving away to grab something else. Tasa had to hand it to him; he didn't encourage her behavior in the least.

But the damned woman was not to be deterred.

Her next move was straight-up bold. Tasa's teeth clanged together audibly as she held herself back from tearing the woman's fingers off his bicep as she tested its strength, saying something ridiculous like, "Oh, you must work out a lot." Tasa couldn't read lips, but she got the gist of the comment.

A whirling dervish of violence spun around inside her. Her stomach curdled with disgust, but before she had a chance to intervene, Whistle starchily lifted the woman's hand off him. His beautiful face twisted into something dark, his perfectly sculpted upper lip curled. Whatever he said instantly put the blonde in her place because she shuffled back, stammering out fake excuses. Instead of listening, he promptly dismissed her with the turn of his broad back.

Tasa bit back a vicious smirk as he stalked off. She rushed back to retrieve her half-filled cart before he caught her stalking him. He found her and placed the items into the grocery cart. Plucking at his shirtsleeve, Tasa brought him in for a hug and grabbed his ass.

"What was that for?" he asked with a knowing twinkle in his eye.

Breaking away, she tossed her head and said, "What, I can't touch you now?"

A smirk spread over his lips as he questioned her, "Were you checking up on me a few aisles away?"

Busted.

But she refused to concede a thing. She widened her eyes innocently, clutched her chest, and mock gasped. "Who me? Never!"

"Mm-hmm."

As he moved off to continue shopping, she nabbed his sleeve and suggested gently, "We can finish together."

"Is that right?" he teased. "Can't have me out of your sight for more than five minutes, can you?"

"Not when every woman on the planet starts stalking you the instant you're away from me," she groused.

His hands fell to her ass, and he maneuvered her so she was right up against his front. Grazing her lips, he murmured, "You have nothing to worry about, Tasa. *Nothing.* Don't make me have to prove it. There's a public bathroom not far from here. Remember my promise earlier about closed doors?"

"You mean threat?" she fired back.

"Threat, promise. Different sides of the same coin. The option stands."

Moving closer until they were flush against each other, she could feel his erection pressing deliciously into her belly. She murmured seductively, "Why don't we finish up with the groceries. I want to reward you for being such a good boy."

"Done," he rasped out, gripping hold of her hand and tugging her down the aisle.

The weather had turned in the blink of an eye. They ran from the truck to the apartment door gripping their grocery bags as they were pelted by hail and sleet. After they'd put the groceries away, they stripped off their wet clothes and tumbled into bed.

They whiled away the rest of the day in bed. Whistle seemed a bit distracted at times, but when she prodded him, he didn't elaborate other than to say that it was the usual problems at the Bar. With Puck out of jail and taking over the management, Tasa thought Whistle's workload would lessen, but it hadn't slowed down. Puck was full of ideas and had Whistle working on a number of projects. The thieving of alcohol had trickled down to a random disappearing bottle here and there. Not that the brothers were any less bitter about it. Stealing from the club was a deep violation of trust, and it drove them to the brink that they couldn't catch their wily thief.

It was late when Tasa's stomach grumbled. Whistle suggested getting takeout, arguing that he didn't want her ass out of bed. After hours of luxuriating under the covers with him streaming TV shows, Tasa stretched out, thoroughly sated, as he got dressed to go out. The man was relentless when he wanted something. It was obvious how he'd reached stardom as a violinist at such a young age. He was dogged when it came to pursuing a goal. Now, his goal was her.

With a peck on the nose, he ordered her to remain in bed. She waited until she heard the front door close behind him before getting out. Tasa roamed around the apartment until she ended up in the second bedroom, where she had begun painting one of the walls with an accent color. In each room, she'd decided to paint one wall with a color that popped, in her attempt to leave her mark on the very walls of the apartment. She was dressed only in a pair of shorts— something she never wore while living in New York outside of running on the treadmill—and a T-shirt. The apartment had an old radiator system that heated the place like a sauna. The storm had lessened, but she could hear the *ping, ping* of icy rain hitting the windowpanes.

She congratulated herself for keeping her boundaries—mostly—in the face of the force of nature that was Whistle. It was an achievement that she hadn't broken down and kissed him after that one time when she lost her virginity. She was still fighting the good fight; if she maintained that boundary, then she could continue denying just how essential he was becoming to her.

Turning on her phone, she flipped through her catalog of music and clicked open Violetta's Act I aria from her favorite opera, *La Traviata*. The notes floated through the room as she opened a can of paint. Singing along, she raised and lowered her voice along with Callas, raising her arms, one hand holding a paintbrush. As she neared the window, she cracked it open and happened to look down in the small alleyway behind her building.

A burly man, in a massive overcoat and a hat shielding most of his face, stood in the shadow of the corner of the building across the way. Despite his size, she almost missed him because he was so still. But it was second nature for her to study her surroundings for potential threats. Even though she always had Nikki or another bodyguard trailing her, Alex had insisted on teaching her how to navigate their world safely. That included awareness of her environment and self-defense. As he always said, they were one and the same.

This guy was good. Only a high level of professional criminality or law enforcement allowed that level of skill. Before she could panic at the realization that she was being watched, a stark black shadow crept up behind the big guy. Unbeknownst to him, the shadow stretched longer over the concrete as the interloper edged closer and closer. Tasa almost wanted to shout out a warning, but pressed her lips closed.

In one symphonic move, the second, slimmer man wrapped his fingers around his burly opponent's throat and squeezed. The paintbrush dropped from her hand, splashing paint on the wooden floorboards.

There began a silent but deadly tussle.

Squinting her eyes, she strived to follow their trajectory in the darkness. The two men struggled, thrashing as they shifted in and out of the light cast from an overhead streetlamp.

Suddenly, a flash of metal gleamed high in the hand of the slim interloper before plunging down. Callas's voice hit a crescendo just as the knife sank into the burly man's throat.

The big man crumbled to the ground.

As if sensing her presence, the victor's face, twisted in an expression of triumph, turned up toward her window.

She gasped, hand shooting to the base of her throat.

"Whistle," she breathed out.

As if he'd heard her, his gaze locked on her. She knew her body was illuminated from the light streaming behind her. He broke their stare. Twisting his head right and left to take stock of his surroundings, he made a shooing motion with his hand.

She complied immediately, stepping back from the window. But not before her eyes recognized the slack face of Nikki, head on the blacktop, his throat gaped open, blood gushing down his gleaming white button-down shirt as his great overcoat lay open.

Pressing her fist to her mouth, Tasa whimpered.

Nikki had found her.

Fuck, fuck, fuck!

Alex was sure to be close behind. Hurrying to shut off the light, she returned to her position and spotted Whistle dragging Nikki's body around the corner. Her one-time friend and bodyguard's Italian loafers were the last thing she saw of him.

All that remained was a dark stain on the concrete.

Hands trembling, Tasa flew into her bedroom and wrenched open the closet. Yanking out her carry-on, she tossed it on the floor and struggled with the zipper. Throwing whatever she could get her hands on into it, she heard the lock of the front door disengage.

Dropping everything, she sprinted into the living room and skid to a halt as Whistle calmly closed the door behind him and locked it with deliberation.

Motioning for her to be quiet, he murmured into his cell phone, "Yeah, Hoodie. I got an issue. A body in the bed of the truck, under a tarp."

He nodded as he listened to whatever Hoodie replied. "Good, meet you in ten minutes."

Shutting his phone, he pocketed it and approached slowly, like he was afraid she'd startle and run. But she wouldn't. Far from it.

Rushing, she slammed into him, skimming light touches over his face, throat, and down his chest, looking for wounds. Thank goodness, there were none. Splatters of blood dripped down one of his cheeks, but she swiped it off and quickly realized it wasn't his.

She let out a little sob of relief.

Whistle shushed her, burying her face into the crook of

his shoulder.

"T-that was Nikki," she stuttered. "He's my bodyguard and a-a friend. A good soldier. Alex is coming for me."

"No, he's not," Whistle said.

Her eyes flew up to him. He tightened his arms around her.

"That was no friend of yours. He was going to keep you for himself," Whistle snarled. "I overhead him talking to a superior, maybe Alex. He lied through his fucking teeth. Said he hadn't found you, that he'd already left Poughkeepsie and was following your trail to Albany. He spewed that shit, all the while looking straight up at your window. Hell, with the light behind you, I could see you plain as day. He was up to something bad, the fucker." His eyes were alight with an unholy fury. Fury based on possession. "Was that bastard crushing on you or something?"

"I-I mean, sure, he checked me out, but Nikki took a blood oath to be a Lupu soldier. I was as off-limits to him as a blood sister. My brother trusted him with my life."

Whistle snorted. "You underestimate the effect you have on men, Tasa. No man in his right mind would pass up the opportunity to snatch you if he could."

She shuddered at that thought. Whether Whistle was right or not, she was under no illusions of Nikki's propensity for violence. If he really wanted her, and something as sacred as a blood oath didn't stop him, she'd have been at his mercy. And she knew for a fact that man had none. Was she sad for Nikki? Of course, she was. He'd been a solid presence in her life for many years. Until now, he'd been loyal to Alex and the family. She grieved the fact that he'd lost his mind because that's exactly what must have happened if he intended to kidnap her for himself.

"He already stopped by the Bar yesterday, threatening Puck about a situation having to do with his time in jail. I clocked him as mafia, but not Russian. He was so focused on Puck that I didn't put two and two together until I did my rounds of the building like I do every evening. I recognized him right away. He'd come to the Squad Bar under the guise of harassing Puck, but he'd been sniffing around for *you*."

Her fingers curled into his arms, nails biting through the cloth. "I have to go, Whistle. I have to run."

Tightening his hold on her, he bounced her in his arms. "No, you don't. It's the opposite. Alex thinks Poughkeepsie has been swept and that there's no trace of you. That bodyguard of yours did us a favor. You're safer here than you'd be crossing New York State, trying to escape. Who the fuck knows who's checking the different transport options and the highways."

"I'm ..." She swallowed hard. "I'm indebted to you." An act like that .... Her head wobbled as she attempted to shake off what she'd seen on the street below. Blood was a big deal in *mafie* society, especially with her family whose motto was "Live and Die by Blood." Blood was the element that bound her people together. She was doubly bound to Whistle now.

Despite what he'd overheard, Tasa had no idea what Nikki's true motivations had been. Willing to give him the benefit of the doubt, she allowed herself a moment to grieve his passing. To whisper a Romanian prayer for his soul and to say goodbye.

After that moment, she turned back to the man who was eyeing her possessively. He'd be hard-pressed to release her, and after killing Nikki, she couldn't do that to him. To be honest, she didn't want to run. Whistle had risked his life for her. The thought that he might have died down there, while she was helpless to save him, had Tasa seeking his mouth with her own.

She was done with boundaries.

This man hated to kill, but he'd done so for her. The barriers plummeted like curtains taken off their rods and left to drop to the ground. He had earned the right, he *deserved* to have all of her, and she'd never hold anything back from him again.

Their lips touched, skating over each other for a brief moment before quickly morphing into something desperate and greedy. Tasa's fingers stabbed into his hair, latching on and dragging him closer. She couldn't get enough of his taste, his scent winding around her like a fast-moving mist. Groaning into his mouth, she gave him everything. Showed him what he meant to her.

He was the one to break off, and she protested with a moan.

"I want you," she begged.

"You have me, babe, but I have to go and take care of the body."

She nodded even though her fingers trembled as she forced herself to let go of her death grip on his locks.

"You okay here alone, or you want me to bring you to the club?"

"I-I'm okay."

Pulling out his gun, he placed it in her hands. Her

fingers curled around the handle. "You know how to use one," he assumed correctly.

"Yeah."

"Go into the bedroom and stay there, gun within easy reach. I'll be back in two hours tops." His eyes delved deep into hers, delivering strength as he asserted, "You can do this."

"Yes," she replied in a touch stronger voice.

Releasing her, he dropped another quick kiss on her lips. "Had I known this is what it would take for you to kiss me, I would've killed a man a long time ago," he joked.

She huffed out a sound of disbelief.

Whistle opened the door, pausing to listen for anything out of the ordinary, before gesturing for her to close and lock the door behind him. Once he was gone, she barricaded herself in the bedroom, gun in hand, and waited for his return.

CHAPTER SEVENTEEN

I T WAS PAST midnight by the time Whistle texted Tasa, just before Hoodie dropped him off in front of the apartment building. He didn't want her to freak out when she heard him coming in and take a shot at him.

By the time he pushed the door open, she was there, gun dangling from her hand. Body tense and thrumming on high alert. Her hair was a wild, tangled halo around her as if she'd been raking her fingers through it for hours.

He could relate.

It'd been an exhausting three hours as he and Hoodie got rid of the body and any traces of the attack. Afterward, he stopped by Kingdom's house to alert him of what had happened. He decided that it was better to keep it to themselves for now. Whistle was good with that. The less people who knew, the better. He'd already involved Hoodie before speaking to Kingdom, which his president was not pleased about.

"Is it done?" were the first words out of Tasa's mouth. Whistle almost laughed. Her question was exactly what a mafia wifey would say to her man as he walked through the door after disposing of a dead body.

"Yeah," he answered with a sigh, weariness slowing

down his movements. Nikki was a big guy, but it was more than that. After spending a lazy day in bed with Tasa, Whistle had been caught off guard. If he'd stayed with his father and the Bratva, spies would have been a weekly, if not daily, occurrence.

"Good," she replied simply. Laying the gun on the counter, she finally came to him. First, she tugged off his jacket and cut. Then she led him to the couch, pushed him down, and proceeded to take off his boots. She saw that he was mentally drained and was doing everything in her power to comfort him. Whistle leaned back and patted his thigh. She immediately slipped onto his lap, twined her arms around his neck, and nuzzled into his throat.

He let out a long, depleted sigh and closed his eyes. It had been god-awful to trudge out in the dark pitch-black woods, far from the city, dig a grave, and bury a gutted man. By the cut of his suit, his shoes, and the fourteen-carat-gold chain bracelet on his wrists, Tasa's former bodyguard wasn't a regular mafioso thug. Alex would be off their scent for a while, but eventually, the trail would turn cold in Albany and he'd circle back around to Poughkeep-sie. How Whistle was going to keep Tasa safe and close to him in the long run, he had little idea.

At least there had been a breakthrough with the kissing. He wasn't far off earlier when he joked about killing a man for her kisses. It wasn't the kisses alone, although they were damn close to spectacular. It was the boundary toppled and subsequent intimacy that was the real prize.

Still nuzzling against him, she murmured, "I made some food if you're hungry. I figured you didn't get takeout, and I had to keep myself busy after an hour of sitting on the bed, gun in hand, waiting for you to return."

"Later," he grunted out. He'd eat after she stripped him of the memories of what he'd done. The memory of the heaviness of Nikki's dead muscles, heavier than any living being, were seared in his mind. There was something grating about carrying dead weight.

Then there was the annoyance of dealing with the blood. The metallic odor, edged in rot, clung in one's nostrils long after the body was disposed of. Or the sticky substance that was nearly impossible to get rid of for days if given the chance to dry underneath fingernails. His gaze flicked down to his own hand curled around Tasa's hip. He'd stopped at Hoodie's room in the clubhouse and cleaned off, scrubbing his skin raw until there wasn't a speck of dirt or blood left. It pissed him off to no end when Tasa had swiped drops of blood off his cheek earlier. He needed to drown in another scent, another type of weight, preferably the weight of this woman writhing beneath him.

"Undress," he commanded gruffly.

She lifted off him, and standing up, shrugged out of her shirt, immediately exposing her delectable tits. Her full upturned breasts swayed as she shimmied her tiny shorts down her long-toned legs. *Thank fuck for small mercies on this hellish day.* Her minuscule panties went next. He needed this. He'd earned it, dammit.

Straddling him, her mouth instantly latched onto his. She kissed him. Willingly. He opened and thrust his tongue inside without hesitation, lashing her with strong strokes. Squeezing a firm breast with one hand, he slid the other down to her pussy. He needed her primed, and he needed it now. His finger dragged through her folds, teasing her entrance and then moving up to toy with her clit. Their tongues dueled and fought, each seeking dominance. Soon, she was squirming on top of him, begging for more as she clawed at his shirt like its existence was a personal insult to her spoiled little princess ass. Those nicks and scratches drove him crazy.

Breaking contact, he pulled back a little. She was already ripping at the hem of his shirt, tugging it up his chest and bending over to lick and suck at his nipples. Gripping the back of his collar, he hauled it off and tossed it away.

"I want you so bad," she confided in a husky tone. Usually, it took a little more time to get Tasa's tight pussy ready for him, but her body was coiled taut with the same anxious energy that vibrated beneath his own skin. She was already slick, that much he knew from playing with her, but she wasn't calling the shots.

Not tonight.

Tonight, he'd killed a man after making an oath to himself that he'd never do so again unless it was his last resort. Unless it meant imminent death. That wasn't what had happened. Not that he regretted his decision because he'd made the most efficient choice. Nor could he afford anything less with Tasa's safety on the line.

But an oath broken was an oath broken. It left him unsettled for the simple fact that it brought him closer to resembling his father and brothers. Their poisonous words of reasoning and praise whispered in his ears. Lies to convince him he'd had no choice when he damn well knew that wasn't true. Those voices had to be eliminated, and Tasa was going to help him do that.

"We're going into the bedroom. I'm tying you up,

baby," he announced.

She nodded eagerly as if she understood his inner conflict, his need. Her eyes pleaded, communicating that she was desperate for relief as well, but hers manifested differently. She wanted to be on the receiving end of his control.

Standing, she sauntered toward the bedroom, hips swaying from side to side like the siren she was. Grabbing the gun, he was at her heels. She fell into bed, splaying her thighs to show off her dewy pussy for him. He loved that she was so comfortable with her body. Alone in the apartment with her, she routinely walked around half-naked, completely at ease. Placing the gun on the nightstand, he chucked off his jeans. His cock was standing proud, urging him toward where it wanted to be.

"Let me see you play with those gorgeous tits of yours, princess."

Moaning, she kneaded her heavy breasts. Looming above her, he toyed with her stiff little pearl for a while. She pressed her feet against the wooden edge of the bed and lifted her hips for him, silently pleading for more. Hey, he was all about satisfying his woman, so he slipped two fingers inside with ease. Christ, she was ripe.

Dropping to his knees, he went to town on her pussy, licking and sucking until she was imploring him to take her. Instead, he pulled away and yanked his belt from the loopholes of his jeans.

"Scoot up," he ordered.

So eager, she turned onto her belly, got to her knees, and crawled to the head of the bed, giving him the show of his fucking life. She swung her ass this way and that, tempting him to take her. Oh, he knew what she was doing, but it wasn't going to work.

"Hands up."

Turning onto her back gracefully, she lifted her hands above her head. He straddled her and lashed her hands to the headboard with his belt. He jerked back as her tongue flicked out and licked the tip of his cock. *Fuck.* Devilish vixen. Her eyes were glued to his dick. What he loved about Tasa, besides the fact that she was his, was that she was game for anything. Many women were. That's not what made her special. Tasa was the mixture of innocence and no-holds-barred sexiness. That combination fucked with his control. That along with the wonder and awe that glistened in her eyes. She watched him like a hungry tigress as if she couldn't get enough of him. He was the only man that put that hungry glint in her eyes. It went to his head, making him greedy for more of her attention. No, scratch that, for *all* of her attention.

"Behave," he growled.

She gave him an unrepentant grin. "This *is* me behaving."

He had to shut his eyes and take a deep breath to regain control because all he wanted to do was ram his cock into that slick heat of hers. He already knew how snug and wet it was for him, only him. Forever him.

His hands pressed her legs open, and he took a second to relish the moment his crown pushed into her. One inch, two, three. In and in he went until he filled her to the hilt. Burying his face, he nipped and snarled into her skin, scraping it with the bristles of his scruff. He'd intentionally decided to grow his beard so he could roughen up her skin.

Make it a nice rosy shade of red. That, along with the bruises and his teeth marks, killed off any qualms he had about marking her. The more he branded her with his mouth and cock, the better he'd feel.

She was pulsing tight as he began to move inside her. He lifted his head to better watch her tits bounce each time he thrust. Angling his hips, he hit that magic spot and rubbed his pubic bone against her clit. Turning her slightly, he landed swats on that sweet ass of hers with an intensity he'd never allowed himself to unleash before.

Instead of being the frightened, gorgeous girl that she was, she spurred him on, "Yes, Whistle! Harder!"

Well, fuck him.

"This how you want it, baby?" He slammed, rough and deep. "You want hard, huh?"

"God, yes," she cried out.

He pulled back and snapped his hips harshly, laying on another rapid-fire series of smacks. "How rough can you take it, Tasa? 'Cause I'm gonna fuck you till you forget your damn name."

Again, he withdrew to pummel inside her. She twisted beneath him, reflexively tugging at his belt but unable to get free, keening out his name on repeat as he rutted into her with abandon. He gave her everything as she bucked beneath him. His balls ached for release as the past and the present whirled around his head. Everything shot out of him at once: his hateful self-recriminations along with his come. Fucking her was like an exorcism, releasing those twisted feelings of frustration and helplessness. Frustration at breaking his oath. Powerlessness because he couldn't bind her soul to him as easily as he could her body.

Stiffening above her, he blanked out as he came. Plunging in one last time, he held still as he emptied himself. Tasa's head lulled to one side listlessly, mumbling incoherent words as she milked him dry. His lips drifted over hers reverently. He loved that he could do that now. Simply kiss her and have her spontaneously open her lips and kiss him back.

He felt absolved, cleansed, and ... complete.

With some difficulty, he managed to roll off her and went to undo the belt. Bringing her arms down slowly, he worked her hands gently as blood rushed back into the area.

Grinning up at him, she gushed, "That. Was. The. Best. For once, you didn't treat me like a princess. You didn't hold back. It was amazing."

His brows drew together. "I don't treat you like a princess."

She blew out a mocking sound with her lips. "Yeah, right."

A smirk inched up the side of his lips. "You've got complaints now? Funny, I don't hear you complaining when you're coming all over my cock. Don't worry, now that I know you like it rough, I'll never hold back again."

She pointed an index finger at him reproachfully. "See, you just admitted to holding back."

He fell back on her, enjoying the feel of her curves as they lined up perfectly. Reflecting on her accusation, he supposed that he tried to keep a tight rein on his control.

"Part of it was because you were a virgin. I wanted to ease you into it," he admitted.

She snorted in disgust.

"I didn't realize I was doing it," he elaborated. "You do

remind me of the precious, sheltered girls I knew back in Brooklyn. But now that I know just how nasty you are, I'll be sure to go full force on you."

Tasa's finger traced his nipple. Following the dip in the center of his chest, she brushed over the bumps of his six-pack.

"I thought you enjoyed sex with me, but after what you let loose tonight …," she trailed off with a disappointed shake of her head.

Placing a finger beneath her chin, he lifted it up, but she kept her eyes cast down.

"Hey," he said. Her eyes raised slowly to meet his. "I love fucking you. Every way imaginable. I didn't want to hurt or scare you. Okay, a part of me assumed you were delicate, but I love every single thing I do with you." His tone dipped low. "Hell, you turn me on sitting across the table, eating dinner. I've had a helluva lot more sex than you, but there was something special about going through the journey with you, introducing you to things, bit by bit. But now that I know how you like it, there's no turning back, babe. You opened the cage, and there's no reining in the monster you let loose."

That elicited a rueful chuckle from her. Her fingers twirled away at his skin, twitching his cock back to life. "When you say it that way, it doesn't sound so bad."

"Oh, baby, now that I've discovered your inner bad girl, I'll make sure to do everything in my power to treat her right."

A little pout pursed her lips as she fiddled with his nipple, scratching her nail against it in a way that was guaranteed to get her flat on her back again.

Reeling himself back, he demanded, "What are you thinking in that head of yours?"

She gave a little one-shouldered shrug. "I don't know. I guess I've been coddled my entire life, and this is the first time I felt like you handled me just right. Like a grown woman. But there's something else I want … a fantasy," she ended softly, watching him from underneath her eyelashes.

That sultry tone, coupled with the innocent shy look, punched the breath out of him. "What is it?"

He placed his hand over her finger to stop the distraction of her caress.

"I want to fight you." She glanced up for an instant, embarrassment and determination warring in her big brown eyes. Glancing back down, she went on, "And for you to take it from me." Her tongue darted out and licked her lips. Her upper teeth caught her bottom lip in their hold as the words quivered out. "By force."

Yup, he was hard again. Moving over her, he slipped his cock, still glossy from their orgasms, between the soaked folds of her pussy. "That's what you want?"

"Yes," she confirmed with a determined lift of her chin. Her eyes finally met his again.

"Oh, baby, had I known what a dirty girl you were, I would've stopped playing nice a long time ago. We'll need a safe word to play that rough, though."

"Suck," she answered promptly.

"Suck? You want your safe word to be *suck*?" he asked, his eyebrows lifting in surprise.

"If I can't go through with it, then I'll *suck* your cock."

Chuckling, he let his gaze languidly wander over her body. "You …" was all he got out. What had he done in his fucked-up life to deserve her, he'll never know. She kept him on his toes. She instinctively knew when to yield and when to hold strong. Then there was her wit and that little bite of sass she threw his way that made him hard as fuck. Now that she'd given him her taboo fantasy, he was hooked forever.

His hands went to her pillowy breasts topped with perky dusky-pink tips. Tweaking them, he positioned his now-rock-hard cock at her opening. "You do realize I'm a male in my twenties, right?"

She giggled. Outright fucking giggled. Everything she did dug into his balls. "I have the stamina of a stallion, and you have the audacity to talk to me like that? Pretty bold, girlie. Brace yourself for a hard fuck. After telling me that the word 'no' isn't in your vocab, from here on out, you're in for it."

He swung her legs up, lashed her ankles together in one hand, and laid them over his right shoulder. Rising to his knees, he lifted her up by her legs, giving her no choice but to take his stiff pike of a cock.

"Hands up," he demanded, and she swiftly followed his instruction. "You don't make a fucking move unless you want a spanking," he gritted out. Breaching her, he gave a thrust so hard that he bottomed out. She wiggled her hips to accommodate him, and then started moaning as he began to drill into her.

Fuck, this woman was going to be the death of him.

CHAPTER EIGHTEEN

EVER SINCE THE incident with Nikki, Whistle's stress over her safety began to try Tasa's patience. He was getting to be as bad as Alex. No, she didn't miss the irony behind that fact. While the man and his intentions may be different, the results were the same. Since they'd moved close to the Bar, she'd been deprived of her bus rides. Alright, fine she could accept that. But she wasn't even allowed to walk to work or dance practice alone.

Tasa was trying her best to maintain her composure, digging deep into her reserve of patience. After years of Alex, fantasies about escaping were her go-to mental safe space when she felt powerless. There were times, she had to talk herself off the ledge, reminding herself she wouldn't be any safer elsewhere and that she didn't want to leave Whistle.

Whistle had left to take care of "club business" with Puck and came home with scuffed knuckles and a bite mark. While she cleaned and dabbed his cuts with an antibiotic ointment, his cranky grumblings over the bite had her falling on her butt in a fit of giggles.

Thankfully, there was a party at the clubhouse that evening, and Tasa was looking forward to hanging out with the other women, dancing, and relaxing after the stress of the week. She'd gotten closer to the old ladies and Sammi over the past couple of months, and of course, she'd get to see Jazz.

The place was a madhouse. A loud, booming bass shook the floorboards beneath her feet as she stepped into the building packed wall-to-wall with people. Wrapping her in the cove of his body, Whistle maneuvered them to the bar where he got them beers. She was bouncing on the balls of her feet, raring to go, when Whistle got caught up in a loud conversation with one of the brothers.

Finally, she caught sight of Jazz's bobbing dark head. Squeezing Whistle's arm, she shouted near his ear, "I see Jazz. I'm going to go dance with her."

His eyes flickered over to her friend, skated critically over the crowd, and finally returned to her. Nodding his assent, he brought her in for a breathtaking kiss.

"Behave," he growled in her ear and gave her a little warning tap on her ass.

Slipping through the press of bodies, she made her way to Jazz and grabbed her arm.

"Hey!" greeted Jazz with a hug. She was wearing a skin-tight leather mini dress that barely covered her assets, but as always, she pulled it off with class. Throwing her arm around Tasa's shoulders, she dragged her over to the group she was dancing with. Tasa recognized one of them, Carrie, as a hanger-on who had been coming around for over a month. Jazz became insta-friends with whomever was around the clubhouse.

"I love your dress," exclaimed Carrie. Tasa grinned broadly as she fingered the black velvet bodycon minidress she was wearing. It had a high neck with a sliver of a cutout in the center that showed off the curves of her breasts. It even gave her enough support so she could go braless and dance. Thank the fashion gods for a sexy and practical dress like this one.

"Thanks, it's one of my favorites, and it's so comfortable to dance in," she returned over the sound of the music.

The group moved as one unit in the area that had been cleared for dancing, and Tasa began shaking her hips. She was joke-twerking beside Jazz when she suddenly felt a pair of male hands land on her hips.

Twisting around, she found herself plastered against a biker she didn't recognize. She was about to tell him to get off her when there was a fracas. Dancers parted to make way for Whistle, nostrils snorting with fury. He took her by the arm and whisked her behind him in an instant. Looming over the other man, he crossed his arms over his chest.

The only static human on the entire dance floor, he hollered out, "Mine."

The other biker raised his hands in surrender, turned himself to the nearest female body, and started grinding into her.

Behind Tasa, one of the girls gasped out, "So hot."

Narrowing her eyes at Whistle's broad back, her lips flatlined. She was less than pleased at his stance in front of gawking bystanders. Clenching her eyes shut, she took in a huge intake of breath. *Not in public. Remember, you're here to have a good time.*

She was not about to have her night ruined with an argument or, worse still, a scene. Sidling to his side, she warned, "If you don't want to ruin my night, you better stay here and dance with me."

Whistle's eyes lit up with a dangerous, sexy gleam. *He takes it as a challenge, damn him.* She backed up a step, then another, but bumped against another body.

Yanking her against him, he curled over her and said along the curve of her ear, "My pleasure, baby girl."

Heck, that melted every ounce of her residual anger. She slid her hands up his chest, beneath his leather cut, and dug her nails in, just the way he liked it. Growling, he grabbed handfuls of her ass and ground his erection into her. Their bodies melded together, and they moved in a sensual dance, clinging to each other. Tasa loved dancing, and the chance to dance with him, with the hard feel of his cock rubbing against her belly, was erotic and illicit. Then he lowered his head and started tonguing the exposed skin in the cutout of her dress.

Moaning, she gripped his head and brought his face closer. He nosed some of the fabric aside and made his way, by licking and sucking, closer and closer to her nipple. Her inner muscles clenched and released as her hips pulsed upward to scrape against his thick shaft. Good God. Whistle was nothing if not well hung. She soon lost touch with her surroundings, following the beat of the music and the flicker of their hips.

This was a perfect example of what being with Whistle was like—lost in their own world, even in a throng of people. Everything fell away until they were the only ones that existed. Whether they were alone in their apartment or dancing in a vortex of roiling bodies made no difference.

She stifled a cry as he latched onto one of her nipples

and sucked it to the roof of his mouth. Panting above him, her eyes lifted off the crown of his head and caught the face of one of the girls.

Jaw dropped open, tongue practically lagging out of her mouth, the other woman made no attempt to hide her interest.

The voyeur crashed her out of her reverie, and she jerked Whistle off her. His eyes blazed with lust and possession. He wasn't used to her pushing him away. In fact, this had to be the first time. His hands tightened around her waist, but whatever he saw on her face had his head snap to the side, where he caught the other woman staring.

Comprehension flitted across his face, and he crushed Tasa into him, cradling her face into his chest. Then he drove through the writhing bodies to the edge of the dance area.

Shielding her, he moved until he found an empty spot on one of the leather couches. He took the only seat, propped her on his lap, draping her legs over his, and nuzzled in the crevice of her breasts.

"I fucking love this spot. Had my eye on it since the moment you walked out of the bedroom, wearing this dress. Wanted to taste you. Right. Here." His tongue dipped in between her breasts pressed together. "I'm gonna fuck these beautiful babies when we get home." She shoved at his shoulders, but he shrugged with an unrepentant grin. "Just sayin'."

Tasa choked out a laugh. At this point, it was only a matter of time before she ended up back against the wall, riding him for gold. He already had one hand massaging her breast, and if she didn't step away from him, she'd soon find herself getting fucked somewhere in the clubhouse or leaving early. Her only chance of staying was to break away from his overpowering aura, if only for a few minutes.

"I have to go to the bathroom," she said.

His eyes were stark with need when he lifted his head from her chest. His hand slid down and cupped her pussy. "Fine, but no touching what's mine."

A surprised giggle slipped from her lips. "Oh, how am I going to achieve that, hmmm?" she uttered in his ear. She was going to the bathroom to cool off, and he was thinking, what? That she'd rub one off in a stall. How very male of him.

She scrambled off his lap but his arm tightened around her. Gripping her to his chest for a moment, he then released her with a low warning, "Come back quick."

Tasa edged around the ground floor before hitting a hallway with a bathroom. The one-person occupancy bathroom was clearly being used as a powder room, taken over by women vying for space at the mirror to fix their makeup.

Recognizing Carrie, Tasa squeezed in beside her. The other woman shuffled to the side to make room for Tasa, side-eyeing her as she fixed her mascara.

"Wow, if that's what being property is like, sign me up," she exclaimed.

Tasa blinked at the reflection of the woman in the mirror. "What?"

"Damn, that Whistle is as sexy hot as a man can get. I mean, you're so lucky you're his property. What more could you possibly want? It's not often a Squad brother restricts himself to *one* woman."

She cringed. The words hit her square in the chest. Of course, Jazz had told her what "property" meant in biker lingo. It was much like a wife for civilians, but with deeper implications. Having once been contracted to another man in an arranged marriage, however, Tasa had first-hand experience of what it really felt like to be property. While she rationally knew it wasn't the same, the word had a disturbingly familiar ring.

"I-I'm not his property," Tasa denied, the corners of her lips dipping low.

"Pfft, you don't have to play it off to me, girl." Carrie winked as she elbowed Tasa in the ribs. "It's hot as hell, the way he got all possessive and growly over you. You're a lucky bitch."

Tasa swallowed around the constriction of her throat. Clearing it, she smiled wanly at Carrie. It wasn't the woman's fault that she'd poked at a sore spot. The woman was genuinely rejoicing for her, and Tasa had seen her share of snarky, envious people to recognize an honest expression of goodwill.

Twisting the lipstick in her fingers, Carrie smeared on a fresh layer of deep red. "I mean, he's so badass. It was like a pissing match. *Gawd*, so hot."

A pit yawned open in her gut. The muscles of her throat screwed shut. Every word coming out of Carrie's mouth mocked how she felt toward Whistle. It wasn't even his physical beauty, although she knew that drove many women to him. He'd touched her with the depth and sensitivity of his soul, along with his passion, honesty, and integrity. Sure, she wasn't thrilled to be the object of a pissing match for a bunch of growly males, but Carrie's words sullied it, made her feel dirty, and not in a good way.

And the whole "property" business made her want to scream. She was already struggling with how much independence she'd conceded since being with him. Yes, her safety was a real concern, but that didn't detract from how much it chaffed.

Whirling around, she pushed through the mass of women jostling for space by the mirror and fled into the relatively empty hallway.

Rushing blindly, she slammed into a body.

A familiar voice said, "Whoa, hey, Tasa!"

Jazz.

Her hands wrapped around Tasa's tremoring shoulders, concerned eyes peering down at her.

"Hey, hey, what's up? Are you okay?" Jazz's eyes were narrowed, looking above her head at the bustling bathroom. "Did some bitch upset you? Just show me who it is, and I will kick that woman's ass."

Gripping Jazz's hands, Tasa shook her head violently. "No, no one disrespected me." Taking a deep breath, she focused on her friend's face. "Jazz, am I Whistle's property?"

Jazz's gaze snapped to hers. "What? Why do you ask that?"

"Carrie said something about me being Whistle's property. I don't want to be owned by anyone. Ever," she ended in a harsh whisper.

Jazz's arm gently swept around her shoulder and brought her in for a tight hug. "Sweetheart, don't pay any mind to what people say." She steered Tasa to a quieter corner at the end of the hallway. Away from people and noise, she held Tasa's gaze and said, "Let me ask you something, and be honest, okay?" Tasa gave a short nod. "Are you happy with him? I mean, does he genuinely make you happy?"

Tasa's gaze dropped and fixed on the floor as she chewed her bottom lip thoughtfully. It didn't take much time for the answer to be evident in her mind.

"Yes," she answered quietly.

"Then, that's all that matters. Look at me, girl." Tasa raised her head. "He's a good man. I've seen good men, and I've seen bad. I've had good men, and I've had bad. Let me tell you, straight up, he's one of the best. But the most important thing is how he makes you feel right here," she said as she touched Tasa's heart gently. "I've been around you two, and I see how he makes you feel. But I want to hear it from you."

Tasa made an audible gulp. "I-I … care for him. I do." She may have been fighting it, but confronted with a demand for the truth, it was undeniable.

"That's the only thing that matters. You've been coming around the clubhouse for a couple months, and the talk of "property" and "old lady" might sound intense, but it's not something you need to worry about. All of that is superficial, girl. What matters is how you and Whistle feel about each other, and I can tell you from experience, what you have is a rare thing, so don't take it for granted. I know your independence is important to you, but believe me, love is not something you want to throw away. That's a regret waiting to happen."

Her chest loosened the more Jazz spoke. Taking in a

deep breath, Tasa centered herself. Jazz was right. She shouldn't get her feathers ruffled over anything Carrie said. The only thing that mattered was what happened between her and Whistle. Tasa was no fool; she knew from first-hand experience that what they had was rare. Her parents had a loving relationship, but her father dominated their relationship. Alex was nowhere near close to settling down. The only woman she'd ever seen him show interest in was Nina, and he fought it like a rabid canine in a dogfight. Nicu and Luca, well, they were thoroughly uninterested in anything beyond hooking up. *Bunica*'s stories of her love affair with her grandfather, who she met when they were both married, was the closest she'd heard of true love.

As always, Jazz's levelheadedness pulled her off the ledge.

She squeezed her friend's hand and said, "You know I love you, right? You know that?"

Jazz's throaty laugh echoed out. "Of course, I know, bitch." Wrapping her arm around Tasa, she led her toward the exit, tutting, "Stop being silly. Now let's go find your man before he comes looking for you."

Jazz linked her arm in Tasa's and led her out of the hallway. She spotted Hoodie not far away, leaning against a wall, half-hidden in the shadows. His eyes were on Jazz. Glancing sideways at her friend, she saw Jazz's lack of awareness. She gave Hoodie a soft smile, but his eyes darted away. He ignored them as they passed him.

They wound their way through the crowds to Whistle, who was sitting in the same spot, neck craned, on the lookout for her. How could she not love that man? He might be arrogant and pushy, but he was devoted to her.

He was her rock. She wasn't about to let her past or irrational fears get the best of her. Giving Jazz a chin lift for a thank you, he swept his arm out, and she fell into his lap. His arm wrapped around her protectively, and Tasa nuzzled into his throat. Breathing in his delicious cedar musk, she was grounded once more.

CHAPTER NINETEEN

T ASA WAS IN the middle of a never-ending shift. At least, that's what it felt like. It was a hectic night of reverie, as if the denizens of the city had made a pact to go crazy at the same time. Plus, it was Mardi Gras. After the party at the clubhouse the night before, Tasa was thoroughly worn out. Whistle and she had stayed late and then went home and fucked like rabbits until they collapsed from exhaustion.

Leaning against the end of the bar, where she was taking a half-second break, a tweak of pain between her thighs reminded her of how well Whistle had used her up last night. Gazing down the long bar, Tasa observed a raucously drunk woman, blonde and skinny, with layers upon layers of Mardi Gras beads hanging from her neck. With a shriek of laughter, she threw her head back so sharply, Tasa feared she'd snap her neck. Squinting, she caught Whistle leaning over to pour the woman another drink just as she nabbed the collar of his shirt and yanked until his lips were inches away from hers.

Tasa stiffened, her spine snapping straight up.

Flapping her eyelashes, the woman angled her head to the side in such a flagrant manner that Tasa mentally gagged. Whatever she said to Whistle must've been mighty suggestive because, was it her imagination, or had his cheeks turned a little ruddy? Jesus, to make a biker blush was quite a feat.

As the woman continued to hit on Whistle, Tasa's hands balled into tight fists. Of course, Whistle was drop-dead gorgeous and attracted women like moths to a flame. Usually, they attempted *some* level of subtly. Even the woman at the grocery store the other day had pretended to use subtlety to get close to him and had backed away when Whistle put her in her place. And why wasn't he doing the same thing right now? The woman lasciviously licked her abnormally plumped red-smudged lips, and Tasa grimaced. *Good God, does she think that's* sexy?

That was her man she was gushing over. Tasa was about to move toward them when Gunner, the bartender, blocked her view.

"Hey," he called out, a hand over hers. Tasa's attention swung to him. "She's drunk," he tried to justify. "And Whistle's dealing with her. He got her an Uber home. Gonna take some time 'cause that bitch is seven sheets to the wind, yo."

Tasa ducked from side to side to get further glimpses of the hussy, but Gunner kept blocking her view.

Growling under her breath, she spit out, "Gunner, I'm a grown woman. I know he's trying to be diplomatic with a customer. I'm not going to flip out." *Lie, lie, lie, I'm so going to flip out.*

"Sure about that? 'Cause the look on your face is like you're about to go for her throat, and I can't have that. I need you on the floor." He pointed to one of her tables, where a customer had his hand stuck out straight to the

208

ceiling, waving the check holder in the air. *Dammit.* Tipping her head to the side, she caught sight of the woman fling her arms around Whistle and lay a slobbering kiss on his cheek with a smacking sound that could be heard from across the bar. *Gross.* Digging her nails into her hand so hard that she was sure to break skin, Tasa fumed.

"Go get me the check, Tasa," Gunner told her as he prodded her out from behind the bar.

Barely reining in her temper, Tasa expelled a harsh breath and stalked toward her table, smoothing her expression at the last possible moment before snatching the leather check holder from her customer's swaying, drunken hand.

Muttering a "be right back," she hustled back to the bar and took care of the bill without even bothering to check her tip. Returning to her table, she laid it on the surface with a sugary smile and began clearing away the dirty dishes.

Loaded down with a heavy tray, she hurried off into the kitchen. After disposing of the dishes, she swung the kitchen door open and caught sight of Whistle single-handedly boosting up the woman plastered against his side and maneuvering her through throngs of customers toward the exit. In a gap between moving bodies, she witnessed the woman's hand slip down and boldly squeeze Whistle's ass. Tasa's red cheeks flashed hotter. Her head about to explode, shattering her to smithereens like a detonated dirty bomb.

She was pissed at the floozy, but truthfully, her anger toward Whistle was building fast. Why was he letting himself get pawed by that barracuda? If it had been her getting groped by a drunk man, Whistle would've jumped in immediately. Yet here she was, expected to stand by the sidelines and put up with this? That's essentially how Gunner had told her to handle it. The double standard was way too much.

This was her childhood all over again. Nicu was able to do whatever he wanted while Tasa had to sit by, like a good girl, mutely bearing the inequities, as her brother traipsed around the city doing whatever he damn well pleased. Once again, her own needs were ignored while having to endure the unbearable. Her eyes stung with unshed tears.

The woman pressed her mouth against Whistle's neck. Tasa spun around and stormed back into the kitchen. She had to go check on her customers, but if she went out there, it could get ugly.

Another waitress entered the kitchen, and Tasa grabbed her by the arm. "Hey, Steph, can you hold down my tables for a few minutes. I can't go out there right now."

Steph gave her a sympathetic look. "Oh, yeah, with the way that chick's mauling Whistle. *Eww.* She's so nasty. Take your time, hon."

Oh, Steph was sweet. It was beyond generous of her to tell Tasa to "take her time." They both knew that was an impossibility, but hopefully, the worse would be over within the next few minutes, and Tasa could get back on the floor.

Moving out of the path of the busy entranceway, Tasa flattened herself against a wall and attempted to calm her ragged breathing. She counted: one, two, three, four … exhale … one, two, three, four … hold …. The instant she stopped, her lungs clogged up once again with churning anger. Even worse than Steph's pity and the embarrassment of some random lush hitting on Whistle in front of her coworkers was how bothered she was by the very fact that another woman was touching *her* man.

Because she wasn't just bothered by it, she was downright incensed. Again, she was brimming over with jealousy. She'd never experienced the visceral desire to tear another person from limb to limb before. While she thought she'd managed to keep her heart *un*attached, this showed, beyond the shadow of a doubt, that she more than simply cared for him. Whistle was hers, dammit. She was viciously, jealously possessive of him. She was … she sputtered in disbelief because she was … in … *fuck*. She heaved out a dejected breath. She was in *love* with him.

Plunging her face in her hands, she wanted to claw her eyes out. Despite her best efforts, she'd fallen for that handsome mafia bastard. Fallen. So. Hard. She was screwed. Screwed!

Tears leaked out of the side of her eyes, and that only fueled the boiling pit of rage in her gut. Rage at herself for allowing herself to slip and slide until she ended up here. Rage at him for exposing this fault line in her meticulous plan to live with him and be intimate with him without falling for him. He'd ruined her so that her heart felt like it was being ripped out of her chest with ugly, sharp claws.

This was what she fought so hard to avoid. The pitfalls of getting caught up in another person. And it was just her luck that, with this newly unearthed jealous nature of hers, she had fallen for one of the sexiest men alive. A man who had to do absolutely nothing for women, and men, to trip over themselves like fools in an attempt to get his attention.

She was setting herself up for a life of misery.

No, it had to stop. She couldn't fall in love. Okay, fine, that ship had sailed, but she had to leave before she got in so deep that she was stuck by his side for good. She could barely gather the strength to continue with her shift, fully knowing that there were more than a dozen customers out there, waiting for her. How was she going to deal with a lifetime of this? There was no way. She had to cut herself loose. Immediately.

Pushing off the wall, she dashed at her tears, wiped her nose, and shoved the door open into the bar. Using every bit of willpower she had, she avoided the entrance and focused on her job.

CHAPTER TWENTY

THINGS WERE BAD, Whistle could tell. One look at Tasa's face, and he knew he was fucked. Granted, he may have let that drunk chick get in a kiss or two to play off on Tasa's jealousy.

His woman was composed all the damn time when it came to him, and he'd foolishly let his bruised ego get in the way. For half a moment, he'd relished in the fury on her face; the narrow-eyed look she'd tossed their way, wanting to claw that woman's eyes out. He was ashamed to admit that it was a balm to his dumb-ass ego.

The night before, he'd heard how Tasa had reacted when Carrie called her his property. The panic he caught in her eyes when she'd come back from the bathroom at the clubhouse. He knew something was wrong, and it wasn't long before the grapevine that was the club came back with the incident that had occurred in the bathroom.

Of course, he had to fall in love with the most commitment-phobic woman who walked the surface of planet earth. Fuck his shitty luck. Of course, he'd spent the night fucking her possessively. He had an inkling of how sore he'd left her the following morning. Another sign that his basest instincts had taken over.

Like his father.

Fuck.

Her lack of willingness to surrender and admit she loved him was driving him fucking insane.

So he'd let that drunk-ass woman slobber over him, knowing Tasa was watching the entire time. Was he proud of himself? Fuck, *no*. Did it feel better than he'd admit to any living man? Fuck, *yeah*.

By the time their shift was over and they were back home, Tasa was dead on her feet. As tired as she was, though, she also looked like she was about to blow. And the second the apartment door closed behind his ass, she didn't disappoint.

Whirling around, she squared her shoulders and advanced on him. "What the hell happened earlier tonight, Whistle?"

He bit back a smirk. He couldn't stop from appreciating her; brown eyes turning into molten cauldrons of heat, the green glints sparking off like shards of emeralds. Her slim fingers curled into fists and her little nose twitched with irritation. Tendrils of hair had slipped out of her bun, leaving her wild tresses flying around her face. She looked like a hissing wet kitten.

Some men were turned off by a jealous woman. God knows that shit never interested him before. But for Tasa, it meant she was unraveling. And he wanted her to fall apart, to let go of her standards, to capitulate to what was between them.

Whistle took a steadying breath because he couldn't provoke her any further than he already had. She was at her breaking point, and he didn't want it to get out of hand.

"The woman?" he feigned.

"Yes, the woman!" she seethed, hands clenching and releasing at her sides as she thrust her face in his.

He slipped past her and hung up his jacket. "She was drunk. So drunk she didn't realize what she was doing. She didn't mean any harm by it."

"What if I let some strange man kiss me?"

He paused in the middle of placing the hanger back in the closet. "That would never happen," he replied, in a dangerous low voice. A jolt of rage shot through him. Just having another man touch her on the dance floor the other night had enraged him.

"Oh, is that so? Such misogyny," she mocked. "You wouldn't let that happen, is what you really mean. And yet, it's okay to let a woman slobber all over you like a bitch in heat."

"Jealousy isn't a good look on you," he retorted calmly. Bald. Faced. Lie. It was the hottest look ever. His cock was already pressing against the teeth of his zipper, begging to be freed and let loose on the woman he loved. "Why? You want a strange man slobbering on you? From experience, I can tell you it sucks, and if she weren't a paying customer, there'd be no way in hell I'd let a skank like her touch me."

Shutting her eyes, she pulled in a deep breath as if snatching at the last remnants of her patience.

"Are you a biker or what? Since when do you care whether someone's a paying customer or not? I've never heard such a lame excuse in my life. Do I not satisfy you that you'd prefer a woman like her groping you?"

His eyebrows slammed down over the bridge of his nose. Was she *insecure*? That angle had never occurred to him. The idea was ridiculous, but then again, this was Tasa's first relationship. These were new experiences for her. Perhaps he should've been more careful with her own ego. God knows his was suddenly a terribly volatile and tender thing.

"You can't be serious? Babe, you know I love watching you get possessive of me, but you have nothing to worry about—"

"Don't I?" she sneered. "When the man who says he loves me, says he wants to be with *me*, lets another woman grope him in public?"

She threw off her coat and slapped it down on the couch. With a huff, she plopped down and yanked her boots off one by one.

He took a place beside her and leaned to kiss her, murmuring, "Babe—"

"Don't."

Jumping up, she tugged him to raise him to his feet.

"Where are we going?"

"To the bathroom, so you can wash your face and brush your teeth," she growled, pulling at him.

He almost buckled over in laughter but held it in for her sake.

Following her into the bathroom, he folded his arms over his chest and watched as she took a washcloth, soaked it in scorching hot water, and doused it with facial cleanser before prying his hand open and slapping it in his palm. Barely suppressing a grin, he wiped his face and handed it back to her. Taking it, she thrust his toothbrush, layered with toothpaste, at him.

"Here."

"She didn't kiss me on the lips," he noted.

"Can't be too sure. God only knows what cooties she had. Ugh, you're so disgusting," she muttered under her breath, motioning at him impatiently to start brushing.

"What can I say? Women love me," he declared before pushing the toothbrush in between his lips.

"Don't remind me because taking advantage of it also makes you a pig," she grumbled. "That's a real down point to being with you. An ugly man, I could handle. A normal looking one, great. One that looks like you—" she swept her arm out to encompass him from head to toe, "—is a pain in my butt, I tell you." Rubbing her eyebrow, she blinked rapidly. "I don't consider myself an insecure person, but I didn't sign up for this. I had no idea I could feel or act this way, and I don't like it."

Spitting out, he rinsed and touched her cheek. "Hey, Tasa, hey. I'm sorry. I shouldn't have let it get out of hand. I'm used to being hit on by women. To tell you the truth, it didn't occur to me that you might get seriously upset. A little riled up, sure. A bit jealous, maybe, but … I fucking love you, woman."

"Don't say that …"

"Why the fuck not? That's how I fucking feel, and I'm not ashamed of it. You have nothing to worry about with me and another woman. That shit will *never* fucking happen."

Shaking her head, she cast it downward. "Maybe not now, but someday."

Whistle ground down on his back teeth. Did she not hear his declaration of love to her? Fuck, he'd created this situation by toying with her feelings, but he had to make her see. Capturing her chin, he raised it until she was forced to look him in the eye. "*Never* gonna happen."

"What about when I'm old? You're still going to look like this," she snapped, her hand flapping to take in the whole of him. "Instead of being a sexy hottie, you'll be an *older* sexy hottie, a *silver fox* hottie. With my luck, more women will flock to you."

"Fuck no," he shot back. "I've never felt this way toward a woman, Tasa. What I get from you, I'll never get from another. Sure, you're fine as hell, and I want to fuck you every second of every day, but my heart is in the mix, and just like my cock, it knows no bounds. It spares no fucking quarry. Already told you, you're *mine*. No other women will be mine. Not like you. And before you try to minimize how I feel, it has nothing to do with the fact that I popped your cherry."

He hooked his arm around her waist and pulled her into his body. Pressing a kiss against her temple, one on each of her eyelids, on the tip of her cute, pert little nose, and a gentle one on her lips, he intoned, "I'm fucking crazy about you. I'd live and die on my sword for you. Hell, I've already killed for you, and I'm not saying that so you owe me a damn thing. I'd do it again in a motherfucking heartbeat. And the way you felt tonight is proof that you care for me, too."

Tasa's fingers gripped his shirt, nails digging to the point where he felt the half-moons pressing through the cloth into his skin. Her face fell into his chest, and she mumbled, "I can't fall in love with you." She knocked her head. *Bump.* "I can't." *Bump.* "Can't." *Bump.* "Can't." By the end, she was sobbing, drenching his shirt in tears.

Fucking hell. His heart was about to break and shatter to pieces on the damn bathroom floor. This was supposed to push her into claiming him, not distancing herself. He hadn't meant to trigger a crisis of faith.

Fuck him and his luck.

He wrapped his arms around her, rocking her in place until her wracking sobs subsided into occasional sniffles. "Come on, baby girl. Let's get you to bed."

Nodding into his chest, she muttered miserably, "Give me a moment alone. I'll get ready and come out."

Covering her face with kisses, he pulled away with a quiet "okay" and gently closed the door behind him.

He passed a hand over his brow. If she left, it'd wreck him. A desperate sensation of helplessness settled in the center of his chest because there was no way he would use any of the weapons in his arsenal to force her to stay. That was what his father had done, leaving his mother a prisoner in the web of his so-called love. Growing up, he'd been separated from his father and brothers, never allowing for a connection to develop. Later, he emotionally stepped away from his mother's obsessive fever and drowned himself in the violin. His relationship with the Squad was the nearest he'd come to normal. Although he was both loyal and bound to them, Whistle remained, in his core, a loner. That's why he and Hoodie got along so well. Until now, he hadn't needed anyone to survive emotionally. Tasa was his person. She was essential, and his need for her was on a level he'd ever imagined possible. He needed her like he needed his next breath. Tonight, his patience had frayed, and he'd cracked, jeopardizing everything he'd painstakingly built with her.

But no matter how desperate he felt, no matter how powerful the roiling angst lodged in his chest, no way would he succumb to his father's ways and lock her up against her will. Whistle knew every plot out of the man's playbook, but he refused to transform into that monster. Even if it meant letting her go.

What was that idiotic saying? If you love someone, set them free. If they come back, they were yours; if they don't, they never were?

Fuck that saying. Fuck this goddamn ruined world of theirs because he knew in his gut that she was his. He also knew she was chewing on thoughts of leaving him.

And if she did? There wasn't a damn thing he could do about it.

CHAPTER TWENTY-ONE

JEALOUSY WAS AN awful thing. Like a viper, it slithered into one's heart, intent on killing the love that lay there. Tasa was disgusted with herself, with him, with that useless woman. She'd made him brush his teeth, but that didn't take away the vision branded in her mind. There was only one way to get rid of it.

Stalking into the bedroom, she tore off her clothes, prowled over to Whistle lying in bed, and attacked him. She took that woman's kiss, her touch, every memory of them, and tore it away.

Whistle devoured her mouth with a brutality that had her gasping for air. No, he didn't kiss her; he fucked her mouth with his. Her fingers gripped his arms, muscles flexing under her touch. She barely managed to keep herself from sliding off the bed and melting into a puddle on the floor.

God, she loved this man. Everything about him, from his expressive, stunning eyes to his demanding, relentless soul. That knowledge sifted through her, cementing her decision. As if he sensed her unspoken conclusion, he made it one of the most tender sessions of lovemaking they'd ever shared. He began by kissing every inch of her skin, throwing in a bite or two to mark her for good measure before turning her onto her belly.

Snagging her bra off the floor, he used it to lash her wrists and stretched it up to the headboard. The irony wasn't lost on her that he could only fulfill his fantasies of binding her to him while they were in bed.

Moving behind her, he propped her on her knees and then slid them out to their sides. With her wrists bound and elbows digging into the mattress, the bra stretched a taunt line up to the headboard. Back arched and knees spread wide, she was perfectly balanced but with little room to maneuver. He had her exactly where he wanted her, open to him and at his mercy. Biting into her bottom lip, she dropped her head and moaned low. Between her thighs, she could see a glimpse of him raised on his knees. Good grief, being this exposed, knowing he was staring down the swells of her rear to the folds of her pussy, had her growing slick with arousal.

His hands encompassed her ass cheeks, parting them wide. She shifted on her knees as cold air rushed over the newly exposed skin and her puckered back hole.

"Don't move," he growled, and she froze, the sound of her ragged pants the only thing in the room.

His fingers dug into her flesh.

"*Fuck*, look at that glorious cunt on display for me."

She heard—no, felt—him shift around until his face was so close that his exhalations tickled her lower lips. He didn't do anything. Just continued to stare and breathe on her. Her belly quivered with anticipation as she clenched and released her core, desperate, oh, so desperate for him to touch, lick, finger her. Hell, do *any*thing at this point.

"Whose wet little cunt is this, Tasa?"

"Yours," she rushed out. Jesus, she couldn't ever imagine another man's hands touching her.

"Damn straight, it is. This is *my* cunt, you hear, girl. *Mine*," he seethed, the hot breath from his mouth prickling her skin, causing goose bumps to break out on the outside of her thighs. She'd surely die if he didn't do something soon.

And thank God, he did.

"One more taste," he whispered so softly she almost didn't hear him. Then he went at her, eating her out like a starved man. His tongue was everywhere, stabbing inside her, flat against her clit, tracing and delving into every inch of her. He fucked her with his entire mouth, tongue and teeth and lips. After making her wait for so long, suspended in that vulnerable position, she reacted instantaneously to his assault. Grinding back, she smeared her juices into his face.

His finger slid in, twisting and turning until it hit that soft spot. Oh, he knew exactly when he'd found it because she jolted back into him. Wicked man that he was, he went deeper, crooking that naughty finger, and battered into her tender spot, sending her spiraling.

Head tossed back, she screamed. Her elbows rubbed themselves raw into the bedsheets as she thrust her entire body, not just her ass, back and forth as his tongue and fingers worked their magic. A great shudder coursed through every cell as she came, her climax whipping her back and forth and from side to side. No longer in control of her muscles, she spasmed and twitched as his mouth dragged her to oblivion.

Whistle's enchanted tongue stayed with her, easing up, little by little, as she slowly came down. Finally lifting his mouth off her, he pet her ass and caressed down her flanks.

She barely finished letting out a sigh of relief when he slid himself home in one hard thrust, adding a sharp crack to her ass. A loud wheeze gusted out of her. If she hadn't been so wet, his rough entrance would've hurt, but she was all smooth, relaxed muscles.

An open receptacle for him.

Building her up again with strong, possessive thrusts, he demonstrated once again how well he knew her body, her soul. The heartless bastard also made sure to give her a taste of his frustration, bringing her to the edge of her peak and yanking it out of reach in the nick of time. He played her like the virtuoso he was. Bound up and immobile, she clamped down on his shaft every time he pulled out, to push him to the breaking point, but that bastard held strong.

Fatigued and somewhat delirious, her head slumped down. Cheek pressed against her forearms, she watched him with one eye from a tight angle. His forehead was slick with perspiration, a notch toggling between his brows as his gaze zeroed in on her entrance with intense focus. Those eyes of his shifted from clear to dark as his thrusts got faster.

"Need … to … fuck you," he grunted out. She instinctually bucked back, hips grinding. Watching him struggle to keep control was so hot. "Need to fuck and teach this cock-teasing pussy who's boss. Dirty girl, look at you. Spread out with that tight pink cunt taking my cock. That's right. Take it, baby. I'm gonna use it till it hurts."

A series of smacks rained down on her as if to punish her for making him feel too much, too good. She moaned, pushing back to meet his thrusts until he lost his control.

She had the privilege of witnessing it from the moment

he began to unravel. His mouth went slack. Grunting harshly, he let go of the reins and rutted into her, taking without apology. One hand gripped her ass hard enough to leave bruises. The other hand clapped her cheek. His cock drilled into her, swelling larger and larger, and then she popped off again. Yanking at her bra until she heard a tear of fabric from what seemed like a far distance, she stiffened as she keened out a low whine. He came right behind her. She absorbed his brutal thrusts as his hips pounded against her ass and his balls slapped at her clit, *slip, slap, slip, slap*. Then she felt his cock pulsing his seed inside her.

They stayed like that for a long moment, panting in synchronicity with him planted inside her.

Afterward, as they lay quietly entwined in bed, she listened to his even, steady breathing. The rise and fall of the wall of heat at her front pricked her nipples to awareness again.

Inhaling deeply, she whispered, "Tomorrow."

She gulped. "I'm leaving."

His hand, fanned over her belly, stilled. Silence. His fingers dug in at five points across her abdomen.

At last, he released a pent-up breath and confirmed, "You sure?"

Tears sprung out of the corners of her eyes, unbidden. She squeezed them tightly, but they leaked out anyway. She buried her head in his chest to hide them.

"Yeah," she croaked out. "I've got to stand on my own two feet, go on my way, like I'd always planned."

"It's not spring yet," he asserted, an undercurrent of pain threading through his voice.

"I know," she rasped out. "But it's time. Are you going to stop me?"

"No, babe. You know I'm not." His arm looped around her waist, securing her closer to him. "But I don't want anything to happen to you, and you're safest here with me."

Safety had been Alex's excuse as well. She knew it wasn't fair to superimpose Alex over Whistle. They were different in too many ways, but security wasn't an argument that would win with her. Not when her heart was so *un*safe around him. "That's not enough to prevent me from leaving."

"I know," he replied plainly.

He was so strong. It was his own depth of conviction that gave her the strength to take up the task ahead, but she didn't want to think about it anymore. They still had this last night together. With his bicep as her pillow, she burrowed into his chest. His shaft twitched against her belly. There was no way they'd be able to keep their hands off each other, and she was grateful for it. She didn't want to think ahead, when the day would break over the horizon and douse the bedroom in light. Then reality would intrude and break into their bubble for the last time. In the comfort of his warmth, his love, she'd relish every moment she had with him.

THEY STOOD CHEST to chest, Whistle sitting on his bike, Tasa cradled between his splayed thighs. His arm hung loosely around her waist, his nose scenting her throat as he was wont to do.

Cupping the back of her head, he lifted his head and locked eyes with her. "Whether in Poughkeepsie or Canada or fucking Hawaii, you're mine. That's an irrevocable, undeniable fact, Tasa. When you want to acknowledge that truth, you'll come back."

God, she hoped that wasn't true. Tasa's gaze broke from his searing one and fixated on the bus. His words struck a lightning flash of harsh fear on top of the rising dread in her heart. She was already half-convinced but had to stubbornly, blindly cling to the mad hope that she could break free. She promised herself that she'd continue the journey. In her journal, she had a little atlas dotted with red marks of every place she intended to visit, starting with Montreal. It would've ended anyway. She was just saving them extra heartache by leaving now.

There was no denying that this was a thousand times more painful than when she left Port Authority, in midtown New York. Then she'd felt a mixture of delight, nerves, and the humming thrill of an unfolding adventure. She'd barely gotten a taste, and now, she felt like her heart was being put through a shredding machine. She hadn't even made it past an international border, for God's sake. Was she going to give up her life, not having managed to travel farther than a couple of hours away from her place of birth? Was she that weak that she couldn't withhold the sacred oath she'd made to herself?

Looking at Whistle's beautiful face, stark with hurt, she could only think of what a horrible person she was to put a man like him through this. She didn't deserve him. She was a curse for him. There was a line of women waiting for her to move out of the way, who would kill to take her place. Perhaps Jazz wasn't one of them anymore, but there were a slew of others. Like the bat signal, there was probably some valiant woman flashing a covert sign over the city, calling all females to converge on the clubhouse.

"I have to go," she said, her voice scratchy. Dammit, she was going to cry again. Clearing her throat, she swallowed around the lump lodged inside. A sick part of her was desperate for him to beg her to stay and break her will. At the same time, she prayed he didn't so she would go on as planned. Seriously, she was a hot mess.

Knowing she was close to breaking, he wouldn't tempt her. He wanted her to come to him of her own volition. Meanwhile, she wanted to stand on her own two feet and walk the surface of the earth like the globe-trotter she was. She had to hand it to him; the man was uncompromising in his self-knowledge. He knew his own worth, and he knew he was worth her whole heart.

He opened his arms for one last hug, and she took it, her body begging for her to stay. She clung to him, tears coursing down her cheeks. Fingers laced behind his neck, she pulled him in for one last kiss and then broke away, dragging her carry-on behind her.

She didn't look his way again, although she felt his searing eyes on her through the large windowpane of the bus station. She felt him when she got to the ticket counter, and she felt him when she waited in the line to board the bus. His gaze never wavered for an instant. Finally, as the bus pulled away, she allowed herself the weakness of searching for him across the windowpane. Through a blur of tears, she watched his face, expression bleak. He didn't break their stare until the bus swung around and their view was brutally cut off. She buried her face in her hands and bawled.

CHAPTER TWENTY-TWO

ASA WAS GONE. *Gone.* Christ, his heart was screeching, bellowing out like a wounded animal that had its leg chewed off. Whistle wanted to roar out in pain, pound his chest, and then—hunt her the fuck down. Hunt her down and drag her back to him by her hair. Yeah, he was a fucking animal, and any scraps of civilization had vanished with her.

But instead of doing what his heart and body were goading him to do, Whistle balled his hands into fists and let out another shuddering breath. One of many since he'd watched helpless, idling on the sidewalk, as the bus pulled away from the station with his woman inside it. The control it took to turn his bike around instead of following that damn bus was superhuman.

It'd been a month since she was gone, and he was doing no better now than he was on the first day. The night after she left, Hoodie brought him to a down-and-out bar, where he could brawl. It was the kind of place where no one called the police to break up a bare-knuckled fight happening in the back alley. He and another man, probably crazed with grief like himself, stripped off their tops and wrestled, punched, and kicked to their hearts' content. In the aftermath, Whistle stumbled to his feet smearing blood from his nose with the back of his hand while Hoodie helped stabilize him on his bike. By some miracle, he'd made it home without crashing. He twisted open a bottle of Vodka, and Hoodie was kind enough to stay and drink with him till they'd passed out.

Hoodie said something that was a blur at the time since they were both stinking drunk. "The problem is that she's bonded to you. Bonding pushes a person to want to stay and commit. Some people can bond, but not commit. She's not one of them, so she's busy fighting a war with herself. She's her worst enemy. Not you. Not the woman who hit on you."

"Then, why do I feel like I fought a war and lost."

"Your war is with Tasa's heart, and it's not a war you can win without her."

Whistle had no choice but to keep the apartment. It was where he'd been his happiest, even if memories assaulted him everywhere he turned. It was like being stuck in a medieval torture device, but he couldn't have let it go if he'd tried. Lucky for him, he didn't try. The only change he made was to move barbells and a weight set into the spare bedroom, where he worked out for hours on end. It was either that or fighting, and fighting was no longer a viable option. A brawl inevitably meant getting arrested and getting arrested meant going to jail. He couldn't afford to be trapped in county jail in case Tasa might need of him. What if something happened to her? No way he could afford to be behind bars.

Tasa might not have been in his life for long but fuck if that gave him any solace. He barely ate because the only food he had any appetite for were the dishes she prepared. He slept poorly; the little bit of shut-eye he managed to get was in their bed. It was the only place her scent lingered. Little by little, as it faded away, so did the rest of his sleep. It took about a month from the day she left before he finally conceded that he couldn't smell her in the pillows anymore. A blast of fury took him in a stranglehold. His entire life revolved around grappling with an undeniable craving that he couldn't satisfy. It was hell.

A few days after that day, there was a knock on the apartment door. Despite his insomnia, he'd managed to doze off on the couch when the rap of knuckles on the door jolted him awake. He grunted and turned on his side, ignoring it. He didn't give a fuck who it was because he knew who it wasn't. It wasn't Tasa. He'd made sure she kept her set of keys.

The knock came again. This time firm and hard.

Gripping his head, he sat up and shouted, "Coming," and then grumbled, "The fuck, man. This better be good."

Without bothering to check the peephole, he twisted the doorknob and threw the door open. His gaze landed on a refined-looking man in a dark cashmere coat, impatiently tapping his hat against his leg.

Raking the man from head to toe, Whistle snarled, "Who the fuck are you, and what do you want?"

With a sardonic raise of his eyebrows, the man replied succinctly, "I'm Alex."

Whistle's eyes narrowed. One look, and he already hated the fucking guy. This fucker was the reason for Tasa's obsession with independence. *He* was the reason his woman left.

"Answer my second question," Whistle ground out as he inspected him. He now spotted the resemblance. Her brother shared Tasa's facial structure, although his jaw was more angular. Their coloring was similar except that he sported green instead of Tasa's soulful, brown eyes outlined by thick lashes.

Alex gave him a long-suffering look. "I'm here to speak to you about my sister, Tasa Lupu." His hand flicked toward the door. "Would you mind inviting me inside? I'd rather not discuss my private affairs in a common hallway." His eyes took in the dusty tiled floor of the corridor with a critical eye and a curling lip. Whistle couldn't give two fucks what this guy thought of where he and Tasa had chosen to live. This had been their fucking oasis. Anyway, the *Lupul* may come off as a sophisticated, pin-striped museum curator, but he was a dirty gangster, just like Whistle.

Stepping back, he mockingly gestured for the *Lupul* to enter.

"Be my guest," he returned in a taunting tone.

Nodding, Tasa's brother passed Whistle and stopped in the center of the living room, looking about with a mild air of curiosity. Not disdain. Which Whistle supposed he should be grateful for if he could summon the desire to care, which he couldn't.

"Tasa never liked my mother's interior-decorating taste. I can see her hand in the choice of wall paint. She always had a good sense of color," he noted impassively.

This man was one cool mofo, Whistle would give him that.

Strolling around the room, the *Lupul* ended up by the

row of windows and cast a long look down to the street. Turning his face slightly, still refraining from making eye contact, he inquired in feigned disinterest, "So, is that where Nikki met his end?"

"Who?" Whistle replied haughtily.

"My man. I last made contact with him when he was in Poughkeepsie searching for my sister."

"How do you know he was in Poughkeepsie? Maybe he was someplace else?"

"Because I'm not fool enough to trust any of my men going off alone when it came to searching for my one and only *fucking* sister." Okay, clearly, Whistle had touched a sore point.

Alex continued, "His GPS tracker last placed his whereabouts ..." He gave a dismissive flick of his wrist. "Before he disappeared, that is."

"You trusted him too much," Whistle growled.

Alex Lupu turned his back to Whistle again, clasping his hands at the small of his back. "In what sense?"

"In the sense that the prick had no intention of returning Tasa to you once he got his filthy hands on her. His intention was to keep her for himself. To do whatever the fuck he wanted to her. You should be thanking me for getting rid of that dirty bastard, not challenging me," he gritted out between clenched teeth.

"I see .... So, as you see it, I should be thanking the man who took my sister's virginity for killing one of my most loyal soldiers." He sneered with a short bark of laughter.

"Her virginity was voluntarily given away. With much pleasure. I can attest to that. Can't say the same for a man who intended to take what wasn't his—and take it by force."

Her brother finally turned fully around. Sharp eyes locked on Whistle. "Oh, and you thought she was *yours?* Ha!"

"Damn straight, she's mine. She gave me her virginity with her free will, and the moment she did, you damn well better believe she became mine. Only mine," he snarled.

Alex's lip curled up contemptuously. He spread his arms wide as he demanded, "Where is she now, this Tasa of yours? If she's yours, then why isn't she here?"

"Motherfucker, if you have to ask, then you don't understand shit about her. It's not your goddamn business, so, no, I'm not going to defend my actions to you, but I can tell you that I don't keep women caged like prized birds. This shit is between Tasa and me," he finished harshly, slamming his closed fist over his chest. "And that's how it'll stay. Between. Us."

"You think I imprisoned her for the hell of it? For fucking fun?" he snarled, a fissure showing in his cool demeanor. "You clearly don't understand either, but I'll attempt to explain a pesky, little problem of mine. I have enemies. Powerful ones. Vicious ones. I've dug around a little about your family and your past. You're the *third* son. *Third.* Don't fucking judge me when you don't know what it's like to be *buried* in responsibilities. When my father died, I had an entire family to protect and provide for. Every Lupu is shackled with obligations, not just me. Not just Tasa."

"Not true," scoffed Whistle. "You drank the fucking Kool-Aid like every one of your kind, believing that there's only one way to live the life. You could've done things differently, but you consciously chose to follow in your father's footsteps. That's on you. Don't make it seem like what you did to Tasa was part of some twisted-ass family legacy."

"Fuck. You. You have no idea what it means, Nikoli, to have a father you love and respect demand an oath of you as he's *bleeding* out. Your father's a violent brute with no sophistication whatsoever. Do you know what my name "Alexandru" means? Protector of men. I take that seriously. I will *always* protect my blood, my people. Not only was I left with a grieving, inconsolable twelve-year-old girl when he died, but she was his favorite. Hell, deep down inside, she's my favorite."

He threw up his hands. "You've seen her. She's everyone's favorite. When she left and I thought she was taken, I would've scorched the earth if she hadn't texted her grandmother and best friend to let them know she was alive. I'd have hunted down every man, woman, and dog to find her."

Whistle could see the truth in her brother's pose and tone of voice. There was no doubt, and it came as no surprise to Whistle, that she meant quite a lot to him. Tasa turned heads wherever she went. She was a looker for sure, but it was more than that. There weren't many strong women who also carried an alluring hint of vulnerability around them that called out to the most hardened soul. Customers were constantly spilling their guts to Tasa or stopping by to leave her homemade goodies and gift cards for Starbucks. That didn't happen to any other employee at the Bar.

"And when she started to mature, I found myself with a real problem on my hands," the *Lupul* continued. "She was only thirteen, and I caught my soldiers' eyes straying in the middle of a conversation with *me*, their boss, the one who could end their life in a heartbeat, whenever she stepped foot inside the café. The lust in those grown men's eyes ..."

He shook his head. "Honestly, it disturbed me. I buckled down on her and became overly protective."

His fingers flicked disgustedly toward Whistle. "Clearly, my best efforts were wasted." His eyes landed on Whistle with unveiled disgust. "Now, I find that she's chosen a Russian, of all things, and a group of bikers riding with half-dressed women on the back of their bikes. It's my fault. I pushed her to this extreme. Worst of all, she tied my hands, and I'm powerless to kill you."

"Christ, Alexandru, I understand what I did when I took her virginity, and I'm ready to do right by her, but she doesn't want it."

He let out a derisive huff. "You think that's what's stopping me from ending you right here, right now?" A slow, malicious smile spread across his lips. "Oh, she hasn't told you, has she?" He made a tutting sound. "She's used you and hasn't even told you."

The blood went cold in his veins. Whistle's jaws clenched down so hard he was certain bones would snap under the pressure. "Tell me what?"

"You poor fool," he murmured with a derisive chuckle. "If you hadn't taken her virginity and I weren't left to deal with you, I'd almost feel sorry for you."

In a flash, he was in Alex's face, hand shooting out and gripping his throat. "What the fuck is it? What's wrong?"

Alex's eyes bore into him, hatred and pain burning into his. "She's pregnant, you fool. I can't kill you because your tainted Russian blood is flowing through my nephew or niece. *In her belly.*"

Alex swiped the hand at his throat, and Whistle stumbled back.

What?

"You lie," Whistle rasped out.

Alex made a disgusted noise at the back of his throat and spat on the floor. "Why would I lie about that? You think it's something I'm proud of? A Russian half breed in my clan's bloodline? From a father that's clearly insane. Yeah, and for the record. *I'm not a fucking liar.* Don't ever question my honor again."

Blindly, Whistle fell to his haunches, expelling harsh breaths. He clutched his head, searing with pain, and let it dip between his splayed knees. *Mother*fucker. Had she done it on purpose in a misguided attempt to keep Alex from killing him? Had she known she was pregnant when she left? Even if she didn't, how could she stay away from him *now*? Leaving was bad enough, but keeping his baby … a baby.

Baby, baby, baby.

His baby. He could barely wrap his mind around it. He could barely keep at bay the raging beast inside him that wanted out. To hunt her and the baby and drag them back here to the safety of his arms. His inner beast was circling in the cage of his ribs, snarling and snapping to be set free.

He shook his head. No, he refused to hunt her down. That's what men like Alex and his father would do, and there was no way he was following their twisted ways. Alex was inflicting as much damage as he could to create an irreparable rift between him and Tasa. Whistle knew in his gut that there was no way he was going to be separated from his kid. That wasn't fucking happening. Ever. Tasa may be stubborn, but she wasn't malicious or heartless. He just had to hold on *tight* and give her a little space to sort herself out.

Above his bowed head, he heard disembodied words directed toward him. "Are you going to finally do your duty and track her down? She needs protection more than ever now."

Shaking off the darkness at the edges of his vision, he gasped out, "No. Leave her alone."

"Leave her alone?" Alex jeered. "She could be in danger. Not only her, but your *child*."

"Give me her address. I know you've found her. I'll put men on her to make sure she's safe."

"You idiot, don't you think I've already put men on her? Christ, I thought you'd go get her. What in the fuck is wrong with you?" he stated incredulously. "The man imprisoned you and your mother for years in that gaudy monstrosity of a mansion. 'Homeschooling,' my ass. It was always about locking your mother away because she tried to leave him. After what your father did, I expected more from you. Turns out you're just a little Russian pussy."

Whistle shot to his feet, nose to nose with Alex, and slammed his chest against the other man's. It wasn't Alex's paltry insult that had pushed him to the edge. It was all about Tasa, his child, and their safety. "Fuck that. She's mine, and I will protect her. I swore to set her free, and I keep my fucking oaths. She's *my* woman, and that's *my* baby. I will fucking decimate you before letting you walk out of here without telling me where she is."

They stared each other down, menace shooting from their eyes like live sparks, but whatever Alex found in Whistle's made him eventually take a step back and break eye contact first. There was no doubt that was a rare occurrence for this man. It had nothing to do with Whistle and everything to do with Tasa. He was hedging his bets on Whistle, probably hoping that somehow Tasa might come back to him. For that to be true, it meant Alex was making a calculated move based on his belief that Tasa loved Whistle enough to return.

Thank fuck Alex broke first because Whistle didn't want to have to explain to Tasa that he'd killed her brother. Despite her exasperation, she was the kind of loyal that would love a heartless fucker like Alex till her dying day.

"Give me a paper and something to write with," Alex said.

Whistle stalked over to a drawer in the kitchen, rummaged around, and pulled out one of Tasa's stationary pads and a fountain pen. She had a thing about fancy stationery and pens. He returned to Alex, who made a disgruntled noise in the back of his throat at seeing her fountain pen. He may have his faults, and fuck knows the list was probably a mile long, but her brother cared as much as that soul-sucking bastard could.

As he scribbled an address on the pad, Whistle declared, "She got pregnant so you couldn't marry her off."

Alex's head snapped up, his eyes slitted thinly. "No, asshole, she got pregnant so I wouldn't kill you."

Surprisingly, that admission did something to his chest.

Loosened it and tightened it at the same time. It was a balm of sorts because if he knew one thing, it was that Tasa loved him. That was never the issue. She'd fallen for him as hard as he had for her. Their last argument had been proof of that. She wasn't ready to face how deep her feelings for him ran and the impact honoring her love for him would have on her life plans. Regardless of whatever her brother wanted, Whistle wasn't about to force her to return. He wouldn't be satisfied with a beautiful, caged animal the way Alex would. For the *Lupul*, if she was safe, he'd done his duty.

Whistle wanted so much more for her, and he prayed she'd find her way home to him on her own because he was barely holding on to his sanity. And that was before he'd learned he was having a kid.

A kid.

His kid.

Their kid.

Christ.

The thought was so overwhelming that he'd need time to process it. Fuck if he knew what to do if she didn't return voluntarily.

Handing the pad and pen to Whistle, Alex stated, "You didn't think for a moment that I'd leave her exposed, did you?" Shrugging, he went on with a nod to the pad, "I left my number. Tell me when your men arrive so I can order mine to stand down."

Stroking his upper lip, Whistle asked, "Have you seen her?"

"I have."

"How is she?"

"She's good. I'm taking care of everything. We came to an agreement of sorts, and she's living on her own for now. I've urged her to contact you in hopes that there can be an adequate resolution to this debacle."

"Why the fuck did you do that?" Whistle shot back. "That'll only make her stay away longer."

Sighing heavily, Alex pinched the bridge of his nose. "She's as stubborn as our father. Always has to take things to the bitter end. Gets obsessed with things. Once upon a time, it was the opera. Now, it's this so-called freedom of hers. Hopefully, the welfare of the child will rise above these piques of hers." His eyes returned to Whistle and gave him a steady look. "I believe it will. If nothing else, I hope I've taught her the meaning of the *familie*."

With a final nod, he sauntered out of the apartment like the entitled, arrogant bastard he was, leaving the door wide open behind him. Whistle waited until he heard Alex's footsteps fade away on the stairway before moving to shut the door.

Fuck, now came an excruciating wait.

CHAPTER TWENTY-THREE

"**I** FUCKED UP."

Alex's voice came through Tasa's cell phone. Now that he'd found her, she ditched her burner phone and took back the cell he brought with him when he tracked her down in Montreal. They'd been talking on the phone regularly since that first conversation at the little-furnished, one-bedroom apartment she'd rented, where they'd both laid their cards on the table.

It was the first time she realized how much her eldest brother loved her, how much he was willing to bend for her sake. If only he'd been more flexible from the start, she wouldn't be moping in a depressive state in below-freezing April temperatures in Canada. Or working a small barista job that didn't have half the camaraderie she'd found at the Squad Bar. She missed the Bar, she missed the Squad members, she missed Jazz, but mostly, she just plain missed Whistle. Somehow, she'd thought it'd be much easier than it was to pick up the pieces and forge ahead. Independence had never felt so lonely and … empty.

Despite Alex's unwarranted suspicions, she hadn't gotten pregnant on purpose. Still, she was grateful that it saved Whistle's life. She'd severely underestimated Alex's fury. His loyalty and love for her led him to lay the blame entirely on Whistle. Just when Tasa had talked him off the ledge about losing her virginity and becoming pregnant, Alex's fury spiked red-hot again when he learned that Whistle let her go.

Alex was trying, and Tasa had to remind herself that he was stressed out about her being pregnant and living alone. It was going to take baby steps for changes to manifest in such a stubborn, domineering *şef*.

Tasa's brows gathered as she stared at him through the screen of her phone. "E-excuse me?"

"You heard me. I'm formally apologizing because I'm painfully aware that I fucked up. When Tata died, I took over as your father. Never having had a child of my own, and never having had the chance to rebel myself, I came down hard on you. Since I was buried in a rubble of responsibilities, I assumed your life was easy. I thought I could impose any restrictions on you because there was no way my baby sister had it as hard as me.

"I was the man of the house, and you were my responsibility. But, Tasa, I was young. I was stressed out. Especially in the early years, I lived every day in petrifying horror of fucking up. His last words to me were 'Take care of the family, of your brothers, but especially of Tasa. She's a baby, and I won't be there to see her grow into a woman, Alex. You have to take my place and make sure you do right by her.'"

Tasa's throat closed up, thankfully stifling the cry that was clawing its way up her vocal cords. It wasn't just his apology but the acknowledgment of what he'd put her through that had her knees buckling. She dropped down on the sofa. Unlike her apartment with Whistle, there was the bare minimum of furniture, scattered haphazardly across the place.

Swallowing down her tears, she murmured, "Thank you. You don't know what that means to me, Alex."

"I don't suppose you'd forget about the workshop and consider coming home?" he asked gruffly.

He was relentless.

Tasa was barely showing, but the workshop was in a month, and she feared she'd have a baby bump by then. She'd made an appointment with Madame Pierrette and explained her situation. Thankfully, *la grande dame* was thrilled and insisted that as long as she had a healthy pregnancy (and signed a bunch of waivers), Tasa could dance while pregnant. Nowhere but in *avant-guarde* art would they be *delighted* to have a pregnant woman prancing around the stage. Madame Pierrette was already working on modifications to suit her needs, but Tasa was no longer so sure what she wanted anymore.

"No," she said through a teary smile.

"And the Russian? Have you spoken to him?"

Her smile widened. He still had trouble calling Whistle by his name.

"I can't. If I do, I'll break."

He let out an exasperated sigh. "It's not breaking, Tasa, and he—" Alex cleared his throat. "He cares about you. Would want to know about your pregnancy. It is his right."

Tasa fixed her gaze outside the window on the neat, little alleyway outside. "I know … I-I just need time alone. To think."

"He's not the type to give up, you know." He paused a

beat, then let out a long sigh. "I paid him a visit," he confessed.

Tasa's spine snapped straight. "Is he okay? Did you hurt him?"

"No," he growled. "Christ, I'm not a complete monster. He is, and will always be, the father of your child. My niece or nephew."

There was a feminine voice murmuring comforting, almost cooing sounds, on the other end of the phone. Tasa couldn't see who it was, but since when did Alex have women around? She could count on one hand the times she'd caught sight of him with another woman. He was usually so very discrete. And never in the house. It was past ten o'clock in the evening. Was this mystery woman at *home* with her brother?

Tasa's forehead furrowed. "Who's that?"

The phone camera flew up to the ceiling, and there was a rustling noise as if there was a physical tussle for the phone.

Then Alex came back on, his tone beleaguered. "It's Nina."

"Nina? As in *Nina*, Nina?"

Her best friend and her brother? That seemed the only plausible explanation for her presence in his apartment at this time of the night. Whoa, what a breakthrough!

Nina was nothing like Tasa. She didn't have ambitions of a career, to the great dismay of her mother. Between only wanting a family of her own and her gentle personality, she was a perfect fit for her domineering brother. Despite teasing Nina and dropping hints that Tasa would approve of their union, her bestie refused to admit to wanting Alex.

Tasa understood her deep reservation. Alex, with his commitment to Romanian customs, was the epitome of risk for someone as cautious as Nina. As the *Lupul*, he was expected to marry a good Romanian girl, and a *mafie* princess, at that. Alex didn't simply meet expectations; he far exceeded them. The fact that they were together was close to miraculous. Another sign of the changes in her brother. Tasa couldn't help but feel a twinge of pride that perhaps her big escape had had something to do with this unraveling of his rigidity. Before now, he would've never put his own desires, not even his greatest happiness, ahead of his duty.

"Fuck—"

There was more rustling and a rash of hushed words spoken between the two of them that she couldn't make heads or tails of.

Then a breathless Nina got on the phone. "Hey, Tasa, yes, it's me, and yes, I know what you're thinking."

"I very much doubt that," replied Tasa with a laugh.

"We … how shall we put it? We were working together to track you down, and … one thing led to another," she rushed out.

Tasa let out a little shriek. "Oh my God, oh my God! I'm ecstatic; I mean *ecstatic*. We'll be sisters for real." Then she pulled back, her eyebrows knitting together. Wait a minute, this was Alex they were talking about. "Are you sure, Nina? I mean he can be so overbearing."

"Don't try to talk her out of anything," griped Alex. "This is exactly why I didn't want you talking to her."

"Me!" Tasa reared back, offended.

"It's not exactly what you think," Nina interjected.

"Wrong, it's exactly what you think," touted Alex.

Tasa's head was spinning. Shoving Alex out of the screen, Nina said, "Go back to him, Tasa. I know you must love him if you gave him your virginity—"

"Can we not bring that up ever again?" interjected Alex.

"We must," she insisted. "Tasa, you went on about how you didn't care, but the truth is that you remained a virgin until him. You wanted it to be with someone you love."

Alex groaned in the background, gripping his head, muttering, "*Please, let this stop.*"

"And now you're going to have a baby," Nina forged on. "What's holding you back?"

"I had exactly one relationship, with a man whose level of gorgeousness borders on obscene. Half the city's been on the back of his bike. Who knows if he's even thinking of me," she muttered. Her fingers wrapped around her knee and dug in.

"No worries there," scoffed Alex. "You're driving him insane. He's nowhere close to giving up on you, Tasa. He's as crazy as his father. Don't underestimate him. You want to continue with your independent life, then go ahead, but don't put it on him. That wouldn't be fair. And, for the love of God, do not put me in the position of defending him. I hate that man."

"You'd rather I be with him than alone," countered Tasa as she gazed at the white wall facing her. Unlike her apartment with Whistle, all the walls here were white. Her heart squeezed. She couldn't seem to garner the enthusiasm to decorate the place like she had when she was building a home with Whistle. *Home.* No, this place didn't feel like home.

"I'd rather you were here, in the city, with me to take care of you. That's always been my intention. Other than that, you know I'll cover every expense and take care of you and the baby because you are a Lupu, and I love you."

Nudging Alex out of the frame, Nina added, "You don't seem happy. I can tell, so don't try to deny it. If you were happy, that'd be one thing. From what Alex told me after the visit, Whistle's deeply in love with you. He's concerned about you, but he's unwilling to break his oath to you. Don't let the distance drive a wedge between the two of you, Tasa. Tell me you're happier without him, and I'll drop this discussion immediately."

Tasa picked at the fluff of her sweater and swallowed around her tightening throat. Dammit, yes, okay, she missed Whistle. She missed his arrogant, bossy ways. She missed waking up to him curled around her protectively in the morning. In fact, she hasn't had a good night's rest since leaving him. A small whimper almost fled from her lips, but she stamped it down in time.

"I'm not hearing anything," Nina said. "I have my answer. Go back to him, Tasa. For you and your child. But especially for you. You deserve happiness. Okay, so that happiness happens to be some place different than you first intended. So, it doesn't fit what you had plotted out in your head. Don't act like Alex and get fixated on how things should be instead of going with the flow of life."

"Hey," threw in Alex.

Undaunted, Nina continued, "Suck it up and stop making you and the man you love miserable for no other reason than he doesn't fit into your grand plans. Follow your heart. If you want to travel, I'm sure he'll go out of his way to make it happen, and then you'll get to share those memories with him in a life you build alongside him."

"Let me think about it ..." Tasa replied in a small voice.

"You do that," her friend said in a firmer tone than she'd ever heard from Nina. Maybe she was getting practice sticking up for herself with Alex.

"I miss you," she confided.

"I miss you, too. As soon as we can, Alex and I will visit. Wherever you happen to be."

"Thanks," she whispered. "I love you, Nina."

"Ditto. Now, go think your head off and make the right decision, Tasa," she confirmed before ending the call.

CHAPTER TWENTY-FOUR

WHISTLE COULD SWEAR he heard her voice. He was scrounging for the last of whatever was in the fridge when the hairs on the back of his neck pricked up. The hairs went *flick*, straight up to their ends. He heard it again, a tinkle of a laugh in the hallway. Like the sound of an angel. His heart pounded in his chest. Edging closer to the front door, Whistle pressed his ear to the wood and heard the murmurs of their elderly next-door neighbor.

Unable to stop himself, he swung the door open and blinked.

Tasa.

She was back. It'd been ninety-one days. He'd counted.

His blood ran hot, cold, hot again, and then rushed south to his cock.

Her thick sable hair cascaded over her shoulders, and fuck if he didn't want to wrap it in his fist and drag her through the door and straight into the bedroom. She wore a pale-coral sundress that accentuated her shape and fell to mid-thigh, showing off her long, toned legs. He did his best not to focus on her belly, but what he saw so far was the kind of lush that had his cock up and at attention.

"Well, it's good to see you back, dearie," Maddie said as

she laid a trembling hand on the stairway and gripped it tightly. Tossing her head toward Whistle, she added, "This one has been as quiet as a church mouse since you've been gone. Not one woman has graced his doorstep, and I should know. I'm home almost all the time, and I'm a light sleeper. Smallest noise can wake me up."

"Umm … okay, well, thanks, Maddie. Good to see you, as well," replied Tasa.

Eyes fixed on his woman standing a foot away from him, Whistle shrugged. He wasn't aware he had such a fan in his elderly neighbor, but he'd take it.

Unable to take his eyes off her for fear that she'd vanish like a mirage, he stepped into the apartment, clenching the door hard enough he was surprised it didn't splinter in his hand. The instant she crossed the threshold, he slammed the door shut, corralled her against it, and slapped a hand beside her head. She jumped slightly, but not of fear. Not his vixen. Her deep, rich-brown eyes were dilated already, and again, he was sure it was his imagination, but did her rack look fuller than before? Hell, yeah. Full and lush.

His eyes raked her from top to bottom, and one of his hands settled on her hip. Squeezed that ripe flesh of hers. Christ, she was more gorgeous than he remembered. And this was coming from a man who had spent his days fantasizing about her and his nights dreaming of her. Her cheeks were flushed, and her big eyes sparkled.

She opened her mouth to speak, but after being deprived of her for months, there was no way in hell the following minutes were going to be spent talking.

Pressing a finger over her lips, he warned, "Don't."

He replaced his finger with his lips, plunging his

tongue inside her warm, wet mouth just as he wanted to do with his dick. She moaned around it, and he slanted his head, going in for deeper access. Her arms came around his neck, pulling him down as she raised on her tiptoes. Good, she wanted … no, needed this as much as him. He pressed closer, rubbing his hardening cock against her belly, and her hips twitched in response.

"Christ, that feels good. You have no fucking idea how many times I've dreamed of holding you since you left." He thrust his face in the crook of her neck and tasted her with open-mouthed kisses. *Fucking delicious.* He couldn't wait to dip into her cunt and reacquaint himself with the taste of her honey.

"No more dreaming."

Knotting his hand in her satiny tresses, he gave it a rough tug. His eyes bore into hers. "Did you come back to stay?" His heart battered against his chest bone as he waited for her response.

She nodded as much as his grip allowed.

"The words, Tasa. I wanna hear them."

"I came back for good."

With a tight nod, he released her hair, slipped his hands under her skirt, and took handfuls of her tight ass.

"I need you, Tasa," he rumbled out. Lifting her, he felt her shudder as her legs swept around and her ankles met at the small of his back. *Thump.* The sound of her purse dropping on the wooden floorboards. Unable to stop, he walked her to the bedroom, kicking the door open.

Throwing her on the bed, he fell on her, barely re-straining himself from tearing off her clothes. His hand immediately grasped one breast while the other zeroed in on her pussy. Gushing wet.

Primed. For him.

Before he fucked her, he was going to remind her of all the reasons she should stay with him, starting with his tongue. He ripped her panties off. Gripping her knees, he pushed her legs wide, spreading her open to him. Her pretty pink cunt glistened with drops of moisture. And the scent of her arousal coming off her made him dizzy.

He planted his chest to the mattress and took his first long lick. Christ, he'd missed this. He hadn't fucked since she left, not even his hand. He wasn't wasting a drop of his come. It was hers, and he saved it for her. He licked up and down continually, then switched from side to side before latching onto her little clit. First came gasps, then came his name, then his name in raw screams.

Focused and in the zone, he followed her movements, not letting her wiggle away when it got to be too much. He continued his full-frontal assault until her muscles seized and spasmed around his tongue. She jerked above him, thighs clamping on either side of his head. His thick beard scraped her sensitive skin red.

When he finally lifted his head, her blazing eyes were fixed on him. "I want you inside me."

Didn't need to be told twice. He was already delirious with her scent, and the tip of his cock was leaking. But it was more that. It was about Tasa. Staring down at her, tousled hair spread across the bed like a dark halo, heaving tits, rounded belly, and swollen pussy. Here was a vision of his life. His future.

Yanking off his shirt and then shucking off the rest of his clothes, he blanketed her and pressed into her slick heat.

He scooped up her legs, cradling them in the crook of his elbows and reveled in the feel of her tight muscles wrapping around his shaft, devouring him. It was fucking bliss. He drove into her until her thighs quivered. Each time he drew out, his gaze swept down to watch his cock glistening with her arousal. Fuck, that was a beautiful sight. One he hadn't been sure he'd ever see again. It humbled him. He'd never take her for granted.

"Look at that beautiful sight. Your sticky, hot cunt spread open around my cock."

Her pussy gushed, coating him down to his balls. She white-knuckled the sheets, twisting them in her fingers as her head knocked from side to side. He stroked himself in short, hard thrusts as her inner walls torqued his shaft as if choking it for all it was worth. The small of his back spasmed. He was about to blow any second.

"Look at me," he grunted out. Her eyes urgently found his and stayed. Mouth stretched open to the extreme, she puffed out a strangled sound, and her lithe body jerked and flopped around as she came a second time.

Now. Now, he could let go. Not a moment too soon because she started milking him and he lost it. Balls slapping her ass, he pounded that glistening wet slit of hers, claiming her pussy.

"Mine, mine, mine," he chanted as he slammed inside her and let his climax overtake him.

It took a good many moments for his soul to find its way back into his body. When he regained consciousness, he found himself face planted in the mattress, Tasa's soft curves crushed beneath him.

"Fuck, fuck," he groaned as soon as he realized he'd

collapsed on top of her. His cock twitched inside her, but he pulled out, causing her to hiss. Maybe he should've been gentle instead of mauling her like an animal, but he wasn't above being smug about how hard she'd come. He admired her flushed skin. Rolling off her, he turned back to face her and found a pair of eyes narrowed on him.

"Don't smirk like that."

His little smirk broke into a wide grin. "Sorry, not sorry?"

She leaned over and sunk her teeth into the crook of his neck. "Bastard. You can't help gloating, can you?"

Feeling the teeth marks she tattooed on his skin, he retorted, "Apparently, someone needs to leave their brand."

She pressed her lips together to hold back a smile but burst out in a peal of giggles. Christ, he'd missed that sound. Yearned for it.

Her fingernails scratched the beard he'd started growing when she left. It was longer than ever. He couldn't bother to shave after she left.

"This is new. You look downright menacing," she murmured.

Her eyes abruptly turned soft, sad. It pulled at his chest.

"I thought I could go on as if I'd never met you. We may not have been together for that long, but you definitely left your mark. I missed simple things like walking home together, or cooking for you, having simple conversations about our day. Then I tried to use my jealousy to convince myself that you'd moved on. That another woman was already warming your bed. Alex upended that theory when he told me he saw you. He made it clear that you were here, waiting. I tried to force myself to stop thinking about you, but I couldn't. God, I've been such an idiot. I love you, Whistle, but I-I'm not sure you'll want me after what I have to tell—"

His fingertip stopped her next words. He heaved out a deep sigh of relief. The gaping hole he'd carried around in his chest when she left was filled to the brim by her words. Words he didn't dare hope for.

"I want you. I already know about the pregnancy. Alex told me. His way of trying to manipulate me to go after you."

She shook her head. "That man. He's so predictable in everything he does. Only one thought in his head. Family and security. I should've guessed he'd use it to try to get you to come for me." She turned fully toward him, putting her hands together and tucking them under her cheek. "But you didn't, even after knowing I was carrying your child," she finished with a touch of awe.

"I told you I'd stand by your decision, no matter what."

Her hand came up and cupped his cheek. "You're not mad? About me leaving? The pregnancy? Everything?"

His hands came over her belly, gliding over every inch as if trying to understand the swell beneath his touch. "Do I wish I was with you every second since you found out? Hell, yeah. But I didn't want you to come back because you felt you had no choice. That would've torn me up. I don't think I could've survived that. My mother stayed with my father for us, and I couldn't relive that again."

"You're not going to ask me if that's why I've come back?"

A half-smirk graced his lips. "I know you better than

that, Tasa. If you came, it's because you want to be with me. No other reason." His smile dropped off. "Now that you've come back, I need to know if you're here for good. I don't have the strength to live through you leaving me again." His eyes shot away from her. "Especially with a baby."

Her fingers entangled with his. She lifted his hand to her lips and promised, "I'm here. I'm yours. I came back knowing what it meant, Whistle. I came back for forever."

His eyes squeezed shut for a moment. They popped open and burned into hers. "Thank Christ." Touching her cheek lightly, he asked, "How did it happen? I know I've got some major super sperm, but you were on the pill."

Tasa nodded. She often took her pill in front of him after brushing her teeth at night. "I skipped a few days." She licked her lips and cleared her throat, her eyes darting away before returning to him. "Might have been more than a few days. It was when we moved. I guess with the excitement of the move, I got out of the habit. When I realized it, I doubled up, thinking it would fix the situation. Honestly, I was freaked out and didn't have the guts to check exactly how many days I missed."

Keeping his eyes steady on her, his caress light, he asked gently, "Why didn't you tell me?"

"I was scared," she blurted out. "Scared and in denial. Apparently, that's one of my coping mechanisms. Who knew?" she quipped. "I was in denial that I was pregnant. I was in denial of how much I missed you and that I wasn't happy. 'Not happy' is an understatement. I was downright depressed, but I still fought it up until the day after the workshop ended. I was sitting on my lone couch in my empty apartment, looking at my blank white walls, and my hand brushed up against this new tautness on my belly that I'd never noticed before, and I couldn't deny it anymore. There was no future for me there."

His fingertip languidly followed the horizontal line of her cheekbone across to her temple and down her face to her throat. "What about Madame Pierrette?"

"I was accepted into her dance company, but …"

"But …?" he prodded.

"I didn't want to stay. Alex would've paid for an au pair to help me with the baby, but it's *our* baby. When my belly was starting to change, that broke me. I wanted to be back with you to share it."

His hand fell on the slight curve of her growing stomach. "And what a fucking gorgeous belly it is. I can't wait till you're fat with our kid."

"See want I mean? I'd already been to ultrasounds without you. Was I really going to take childbirth classes alone and go into labor alone and raise our child alone? Especially when all I wanted was to be here, coddled in your arms as I am now, in our bed. In our home." Her chin trembled. "Like I said, I broke."

"Baby," he choked out, bringing her head into his chest. Her guilt was tearing at his heart, like a mangled flag twisting in the wind.

"I'm sorry, Whistle. I'm a stubborn idiot, and I put us both through so much. I took three months away from us. Took the first trimester of my pregnancy, *our* pregnancy, away from you," she said, tears moistening his skin. "I knew you'd want to be there with me, but I was living day to day, still processing that I was pregnant."

Her face turned up, eyes blinking. "How did you know I would come back? I didn't even know yet."

Whistle gave a gruff laugh. "I had no fucking clue, but I held on to two things. I knew you loved me, and I knew you'd never hurt the baby. Believe me, Tasa, my heart bled for you. You'd just gotten out from under your brother, and now, you had to toe the line and follow rules set out by yet another man. When I escaped and became part of the club, I acted out. I tested the brothers. Shit, you were a helluva lot more mature and put together than I was."

"That was it? You knew I loved you, and I wouldn't hurt the baby?"

He chuckled, tracing lazy circles around the curve of her hip. "Babe, you're loyal to your core, and when you love, you love deeply. No matter what Alex did to you, you stuck up for him every time I'd criticize him." A soft snuffling snort came through his nostrils. "I knew you loved me a fuck load more than that bastard. I just had to hold strong and wait you out."

Her fingers tripped down his torso and curved around his shaft, which began to harden at the contact of her slim fingers. "Oh, you knew I loved you, huh? Maybe I just loved your cock."

"I *know* you loved my cock. That was my secret weapon." He pushed his hips up, thrusting into her grip. "This thing. It's like a fucking beacon. All I had to do was point this fucker north and wiggle it around—" he rolled his hips in demonstration, "—and you woulda heard the call of the wild and circled back around. For another taste."

"Mmm," she murmured as she shimmied down the bed. "Speaking of taste …"

EPILOGUE

ASA STIRRED AS she woke. Whistle's arm was loped over her waist. It tightened and pulled her deeper into his chest. His body spooned hers, their legs intertwined. Waking like this was still a surprise, even after a year and a half. The heat at her back was solid. Comforting. Secure. She loved that. Although she'd only spent three months alone, they had traumatized her a little. Shuddering at the memory, she was grateful each and every time she woke up to the rise and fall of his chest at her back, knowing that everything was right in her world. She was where she belonged.

Glancing over her shoulder, she watched the movement of his closed eyelids. He was as handsome as ever. Painfully so. Turning into his chest, she traced the perfectly straight line of his strong, bold nose, dipped down to the indentation on top of his generous lips, coasted over his mouth, and ended at the almost imperceptible cleft of his chin. Then her finger glided up his strong angular jaw to the jut of his cheekbone.

His eyelids fluttered open, and a twin set of translucent blue orbs focused on her. One side of his lips ticked up in a lopsided grin. He was happy. Another thing she was grateful for. All it took was waking up in the morning beside her, and the pure, unadulterated joy that settled on his face had her belly turning to warm goo. She didn't have to be a special way; she didn't have to equal his gorgeous looks or even his bighearted soul. The only thing she had to do was be there and love him back. One would think it should've been this easy from the start. The long road to that point, well, she didn't know if it had been worth putting them both through hell. But in the end, it brought them to this place, with a growing baby kicking between them.

A second one, that is. The first was still, thankfully, asleep in his crib. It was only a matter of time. Another revelation since being back had been that she loved motherhood.

"I felt that," he murmured, his voice gritty.

"That was good morning to you, Daddy."

He made a low growl in the back of his throat. Another thing they'd learned together was how much Whistle liked when she called him Daddy in bed. "That so? You speak baby now?"

She smirked and made a tsking sound. "Sure, I do. It's my secret talent. You have your secret weapon—" she stared meaningfully at his cock, "—and I have mine." She dropped a kiss on his lips. "Duh, I'm a woman of many talents."

His hand landed on her ass and brought her closer until she knew he felt the next kick from the spasm of his abdomen in response.

"Mmm … don't I know it."

His hand pushed up her nightie to smooth a little slap

on her ass. She wiggled it in response and sidled closer to him when a squawk came through the baby monitor on the nightstand. "Sounds like someone's waking up," she mused. "He'll be hungry."

He groaned and whispered, "If you keep quiet, he won't hear you. He'll hang out for a while before making a fuss."

"Good luck with that hypothesis."

"Hey, sue me if I want to fuck my wife before starting the day. It puts me in a good mood, and that's beneficial to everyone, especially those good-for-nothing prospects."

She gave a little snort. "If I recall correctly, you were one of the worst prospects in the Squad. Sammi was telling me stories the other night, during our Moms' Night Out."

"Yeah, fucking ironic that Cutter handed that job over to me. Turns out, there's a method to their madness. I was too young and dumb to know it and thought they were doing it just to be pains in the ass."

"Humph, yet why do I suspect your experience no longer makes you sympathetic toward those poor guys."

"Damn right, it doesn't. My newfound sympathy is for the brothers who had to put up with my ass."

Whaa, came through the walls. His hand came down on her ass, a little harder this time as he grunted out, "Told you to keep it down. Now, Roman's definitely awake. Gonna have to teach you a lesson about how to keep quiet tonight, wifey. A very *hard* lesson for a very *bad* girl."

She beamed up at him. Ever since they got married, in the Romanian church in Manhattan, which had been quite a sight, what with bikers mingling with *mafie*, he was all about calling her wife or wifey. Turns out he loved stopping perfect strangers on the street to tell them that she was his wife. Tasa didn't mind. Whistle had earned the right to shout it from the rooftops. Through patience and tenacity and faith, he'd won the war with her heart, and he now owned every inch of it.

Wiggling her ass against his hand, she pushed herself into him and pressed her lips against his. He wrapped his hand around her head and curled his tongue inside for a long, breathtaking kiss before she pulled away to bring Roman into bed with them. Whistle might have good-naturedly groused about not getting to have sex, but he treasured the time they spent together before he left for the clubhouse or the Squad Bar.

Tasa changed Roman and put him in a new onesie before bringing him into their room to give Whistle a few extra moments of shut-eye. The instant Roman caught sight of his father, his bright crystalline eyes widened, and he grabbed at the air with a little screech of delight.

She lounged in bed as their son crawled on top of Whistle's bare chest and laid his head briefly against his father's, his slightly lighter locks mingling with Whistle's pitch-black ones. Roman was the spitting image of his father.

Speaking of fathers …

"Igor called me yesterday. He's stopping by later to take Roman out. A *dedushka* outing, he called it."

"What the hell happened to him?" Whistle reflected with a stupefied shake of his head.

"Roman is what happened to him," retorted Tasa.

Ever since Igor found out about his first grandson, he was a changed man. At least when it came to Roman, although the result had thawed his relationship with his son. Whistle's entire Russian family had been at the wedding, with Tasa in a wedding dress that did absolutely nothing to hide her protruding belly. She wasn't going to assume Igor was rehabilitated in other parts of his life, but he was always solicitous toward her and acquiesced to Whistle's long list of rules before being allowed entry into their lives.

Another unexpected development was Whistle's reunion with his mother. She convinced Igor to allow her to move nearby. Her life was them, and Tasa didn't know what she would've done without the older woman's guidance when Roman was first born. With her help, Tasa finally learned how to make a honey cake, based on Whistle's grandfather's recipe, and was enjoying integrating Russian customs into their lives. In truth, Whistle and Tasa would not have considered getting pregnant again so soon if his mother didn't spend part of every day helping Tasa with the baby. Igor made it up almost every weekend from Brooklyn, insisting on having "special *dedushka* time" with his grandson.

Whistle was propped up on his elbow, leaning over Roman and blowing raspberries into the crook of his neck, leading to a burst of giggles.

Tasa ruffled her son's hair and grazed the back of her hand over Whistle's cheek. He grabbed her wrist and gently bit one of her knuckles, eyes lingering on the dip of the T-shirt that she'd thrown on before getting Roman.

"Tonight," he warned. "Your ass is mine."

She planted a kiss on his lips before stretching out against the pillows in a provocative pose to tease him as she watched her man play with her son.

For once, she listened to her mother's advice and gave herself the time and space to enjoy her husband and new family. She'd eventually return to her plans of traveling with her brood or dancing or who knows what. Perhaps they'd buy an organic-apple farm in the outskirts of the city, as she had once joked to Nina. The sky was the limit with the man she loved by her side. Because if she was sure of one thing in her life, it was him, his love for her, and his willingness to do anything to make her happy.

THE END.

PLEASE REVIEW THIS BOOK!

If you enjoyed this book, please leave a review on the platform where you bought your book, Goodreads, BookBub or all three! I Every little bit helps for a new series from a self-published author, and your opinion counts to me!

Lend it, **recommend** it to a friend, spread the word, **tweet**, or **post** about it on your favorite social media platform!

MORE BY MONIQUE MOREAU

Fans of sizzling hot alpha bikers and the sassy, strong women who can tame them will love Monique Moreau's steamy new series.

THE DEMON SQUAD MC SERIES

HER HIDDEN VALENTINE, A SQUAD NOVELLA

There's a thief in the Demon Squad clubhouse.

Someone has been stealing from the Squad Bar and the brothers can't catch the wily culprit.

Club brother Hoodie knows why.

Because the thief is one of their own.

Having survived a childhood of betrayal, Hoodie learned early on that the worst treacheries always come from within. But even he was shocked when he discovered it's *her*. Jazz—the sexy, vivacious biker chick who Hoodie secretly craved for years. A gorgeous, vibrant woman like Jazz would never be interested in a scarred beast like Hoodie. Since she was crushing on his best friend, he chose to stay in the shadows. But he was out now.

After getting over the disappointment of unrequited love, Jazz focused her energy on paying her father's mounting medical bills. Stealing from the club nearly broke her heart, but she was the only thing standing between her father and death's doorstep.

When Hoodie discovers that Jazz is the thief, he makes

a bold move to save her. But as Jazz begins to realize that her prince charming was hiding in plain sight in the form of the brooding, silent Hoodie, she's convinced that a noble soul like his could never trust a woman who betrayed the club.

As Valentine's Day approaches, will Cupid have an arrow left over in his satchel for a mismatched love like theirs?

KINGDOM'S REIGN (BOOK I)
CUTTER'S CLAIM (BOOK II)
LOKI'S LUCK (BOOK III)
STANTON'S SINS (BOOK IV)
PUCK'S PROPERTY (BOOK V)

Join Monique's Mailing list to receive goodies and release information:

www.subscribepage.com/moniquemoreau

I have a Facebook group just for readers:
Possessive Alpha Reads

Like my Facebook Page:
facebook.com/moniqueauthor

Follow me on Instagram:
instagram.com/monique.moreau.books

Follow me on BookBub:
bit.ly/3gNvrsU

Learn all about my books:
moniquemoreau.com

ACKNOWLEDGMENTS

Thank you to my family for your support and patience each time I say, "Hold that thought!" while I pound out one more sentence. Thank you Alison Aimes for your encouragement, for being a fantastic and supportive beta reader, a mentor, and an all-around incredible person. Thank you Joy Daniels for brainstorming with me. A shout out to Monica Bogza of the Trusted Accomplice for editing. Veronica Adams from L. Woods PR for holding my hand through the process of birthing this latest book to the world! To all the blogger and booklovers who help spread the word and finally, but not least, to every single one of you who've picked up this book and given it a chance. Thank you!